Praise for the Work of Annie England Noblin

St. Francis Society for Wayward Pets

"Feel-good fiction at its finest. Annie England Noblin has crafted an utterly entertaining tale of unexpected chances and small-town secrets, and it's as sweet and comforting as a hand-knit sweater and a warm puppy in your lap."

—Susan Wiggs, *New York Times* bestselling author

"Noblin's masterful touch hits the sweet spot of humor and tragedy in this heartfelt book about the truest meaning of family, friends, abandoned dogs, and love."

—Jacqueline Sheehan, *New York Times* bestselling author of *Lost & Found* and *The Tiger in the House*

"Lively and heartfelt, the characters—both human and four-legged—in Annie England Noblin's *St. Francis Society for Wayward Pets* come alive."

—Lori Wilde, *New York Times* bestselling author

"Dogs, yarn, family secrets, a touch of romance, and a sisterhood of strong and caring women. *St. Francis Society for Wayward Pets* is as easy to love as a newborn puppy and just as irresistible."

—Marie Bostwick, *New York Times* bestselling author of *Just in Time*

"Fans of Noblin's canine-themed tales will beg for more!"

—*Library Journal*

Sit! Stay! Speak!

"Readers of Debbie Macomber will enjoy Noblin's first novel. It's an enjoyable story full of laughter, tears, and just plain fun."

—*Library Journal*

"Will delight fans of Mary Kay Andrews and contemporary women's fiction."

—*Booklist*

St. Francis Society for Wayward Pets

Also by Annie England Noblin

The Sisters Hemingway
Pupcakes
Just Fine with Caroline
Sit! Stay! Speak!

St. Francis Society for Wayward Pets

A Novel

Annie England Noblin

𝔀𝔪

WILLIAM MORROW

An Imprint of HarperCollins*Publishers*

P.S.™ is a trademark of HarperCollins Publishers.

ST. FRANCIS SOCIETY FOR WAYWARD PETS. Copyright © 2020 by Annie England Noblin. All rights reserved. Printed in the United States of America. No part of this book may be used or reproduced in any manner whatsoever without written permission except in the case of brief quotations embodied in critical articles and reviews. For information, address HarperCollins Publishers, 195 Broadway, New York, NY 10007.

HarperCollins books may be purchased for educational, business, or sales promotional use. For information, please email the Special Markets Department at SPsales@harpercollins.com.

FIRST EDITION

Designed by Diahann Sturge

Dog images throughout © Erik Lam/Shutterstock, Inc.
Cat images throughout © 5 second Studio/Shutterstock, Inc.

Library of Congress Cataloging-in-Publication Data has been applied for.

ISBN 978-0-06-274831-7
ISBN 978-0-06-298129-5 (hardcover library edition)

20 21 22 23 24 LSC 10 9 8 7 6 5 4

For my father and for his boy, Finn

St. Francis Society for Wayward Pets

PROLOGUE

ANNABELLE WATCHED THE LITTLE GIRL IN THE FRONT yard, smiled at the clumsy way she bent down to tie the laces of her yellow Batman high-tops. She was tall for her age, ten years old, and her dark hair fell unkempt around her face. On the front porch, a woman stood holding a plastic tray full of hot dogs. She too smiled at the girl as she placed the tray on a brightly painted picnic table.

"Mae, honey, go inside and brush your hair before the party starts," the woman said.

The girl turned her back to the street and to Annabelle, but she could hear the girl say, "These earrings are making my ears itchy."

"For goodness' sakes," the woman replied. She brushed the girl's hair away from her face. "I told you that you have to clean them every day. How long have you been wearing these cheap things?"

The girl's shoulders heaved up and down in that way only a child's can when they have an answer that won't be good enough for their mother. "They match my shoes" was all she said.

"It's nice you want to match your brother's party theme," the woman continued, clicking her tongue against her teeth and working the earrings out of Mae's ears, causing Mae to wince. "But was it really necessary to dress in yellow and black from head to toe?"

Again, Mae shrugged.

"Go on inside," the woman said. "Hurry it up, or we'll all be having cake and ice cream without you."

Mae ran past the woman and up the front steps of the house, lingering just long enough to stick her tongue out at the woman's back before disappearing inside. Unable to stop herself, Annabelle let out a laugh, and the woman in the front yard paused to scan the car-lined street.

Annabelle slid farther down into the driver's seat of her Volkswagen Beetle as the woman surveyed the neighborhood. She hadn't meant to loiter there, not really. She hadn't meant to drive down the cozy tree-lined Seattle street or park just far enough away to escape being noticed. No, all she'd meant to do was visit the yarn warehouse on the south side of town and pick up her order. All she'd meant to do was follow the rules of the document she'd signed—no contact, and certainly not any borderline stalking—and return home.

It was as if she'd willed herself there, as if her hands had a mind of their own, straying from the ten-and-two position to make more left turns than she should have made, to park on a street she should have forgotten. If anyone asked her how she got there, she'd have to tell them she honestly didn't know. She really hadn't known that there would be a birthday party in the front yard. She'd just wanted a look, just a small glimpse, before heading home.

Of course, she'd been to this lovely house on the quiet cul-de-sac before. If Annabelle closed her eyes, she could remember every single detail of the way the house had looked over a decade ago, a sprawling executive ranch without the freshly painted front porch or new vinyl siding. She remembered thinking, when she'd been welcomed inside, that it looked like the kind of place a kid could play hide-and-seek in for hours and not run out of hiding spots. The owners, June and Michael Stephens, welcomed her with open arms and her favorite meal—chili dogs. At the time, it had been the only thing she'd wanted to eat for several months. That night, she'd eaten four.

After dinner, June showed Annabelle the rest of the house, showed her the clean bathrooms and the sunny laundry room and the finished basement that had one of those large-screen projection television sets. This was the kind of house Annabelle saw on television sitcoms. It was the kind of house that hosted family gatherings at Thanksgiving and Christmas. It was the kind of house, Annabelle thought, where a person could feel safe. It was a far cry from the house she'd grown up in, with its dingy carpet and flaking wood paneling. In fact, it was a far cry from everything she'd ever known. Most important, it was a far cry from the *people* she'd known.

June left for last the room where she hoped her daughter would one day sleep. As Annabelle wandered around the room, fingering the ballerina lamp and the pink-and-white gingham curtains, she could feel June's eyes on her. She wasn't looking at her the way some of the women did—with jealousy or pity or, worse, disgust. No, June was looking at her with what Annabelle could only describe as something akin to longing. Once in a while, June would reach down and touch her own belly, as if there was an ache—a hunger—that she couldn't cure with a chili dog.

As Annabelle put on her coat to leave, she knew that she was supposed to say how nice it was to meet them and that she'd have someone from the Catholic Charities home where she was staying call the Stephenses to follow up. Instead, she put on her mittens, red wool that she'd knit herself, and took June Stephens by the hand.

"I choose you," Annabelle said to her. "I choose you to adopt my baby."

CHAPTER 1

THERE'S THIS LINE FROM *BRIDGET JONES'S DIARY* BY Helen Fielding that goes something like, "Oh God, what's wrong with me? Why does nothing ever work out?"

That's all I could think the moment I saw a grainy video of my boyfriend, Mariners left fielder Derek Mitchell, sucking the face off another woman in a dodgy nightclub playing on Channel 33 Action News at 6 o'clock for all of the greater Seattle metro area to see.

I don't know where the quote from *Bridget Jones's Diary* came from. I hadn't read the book in nearly twenty years—not since the summer before my freshman year in college when I was on a mission to lose half my body weight and also my virginity. Neither worked out, and I have to admit that I blamed Ms. Fielding just a little bit for writing a book in which I imagined myself, Maeve Stephens, the actual heroine, not-so-patiently waiting for her Mark Darcy.

"Oh my *God*," my coworker Alyssa said, hovering over me to press the refresh button on the computer. "Is that . . . ?"

"Derek?" I finished. "Yep."

"Who's the . . ."

"Whore?"

"I was going to say 'skinny bitch,' but I guess 'whore' will work."

I pushed myself away from my computer, disgusted. I had no way of knowing if the woman Derek was with was a whore *or* a bitch, and I felt guilty that calling her both of those things made me feel better. But it did, and I made a mental note to self-deprecate for betraying feminism the next time I saw my friends. I thought about calling him, but he was likely getting plenty of calls already. Instead, I stood up and continued cleaning out my desk. An hour before the video, I'd found out that the newspaper I worked for as a sportswriter, the *Seattle Lantern*, was bankrupt. They weren't *going* bankrupt. They weren't *facing* bankruptcy. They were *already* bankrupt, and we found out at 4:55 p.m. that we had the evening to clear our desks. Tomorrow, the paper and our jobs would cease to exist.

This was total bullshit. I was thirty-six years old, out of a job, and had just been publicly humiliated. The only thing I could do was hope that my parents hadn't seen the video. When I heard my phone ring in my pocket as I was walking toward my car, carrying a box full of the last two years of my life, I knew it was my mother.

I set the box down in the parking lot and answered. "Hi, Mom."

"Darling, are you okay? Your father and I just saw. Your aunt Jolee called us. We went to the YouTube and found it."

Oh great. YouTube. "I saw it."

"I never liked him," my mother continued. "Didn't I tell you I didn't like him?"

"No."

"Yes, I did."

"Mom," I said. "You told me last week that you hoped we got engaged and had adorable, baseball-playing babies."

"Softball would have been okay too," she said, sniffing into the receiver.

"I'll call you when I get home," I replied. I just didn't have the energy to tell her about the paper closing. She and my father would insist I come over, and all I really wanted to do was spend the next millennium curled up in my bed with my laptop and every season of *The Office* on Netflix.

"Okay," my mother said. "Be careful."

I hung up the phone and bent down to pick up my box. When I straightened, there was a man standing in front of me. He was wearing a dingy Mariners cap (of course) and a grim expression. "Give me all your money," he said.

"Oh, you've got to be kidding me," I replied. "Are you seriously robbing me right now?"

The man, who was also holding a small switchblade in one of his hands, was taken aback. "Ah, well, yes?"

"Great." I dropped the box back onto the pavement. It bounced once and then toppled over on its side, spilling paper clips and flash drives out onto the man's feet. "My day is complete now," I said, pulling my purse from one of my shoulders and handing it to him. "I just lost my job an hour ago, and my boyfriend was caught making out with someone who was most definitely not me. They played it on the news. You see it?"

The man's eyes widened as he took the purse from my outstretched hand. "You're Derek Mitchell's girlfriend?"

"I *was* Derek Mitchell's girlfriend," I replied. "He doesn't know it yet, but we're so over."

The man brought the switchblade up to his scruffy chin and scratched. "You're that sportswriter, huh?"

"I *was* that sportswriter."

"You know," he said, riffling through my purse and pulling out all the cash I had inside my wallet, a whopping $32.11. "I thought you'd be prettier in person."

Everybody's a critic.

"Are you kidding me?" I asked.

"Are you kidding *me*?" He held up the money. "This is all you got?"

I shrugged. "You can take the credit cards, but you won't get very far. Most of them are at their limit."

The man threw my purse on the ground, disgusted. "I ain't stupid. I just want the cash."

"Well, that's all I've got," I said. I looked down at his knife and briefly thought about running. I could probably get away from him, but in this neighborhood, in the dark, I wouldn't get very far. "Can I go now?"

He took a step back from me, his ratty Chuck Taylors scraping the blacktop. "Close your eyes and count to a hundred. I'll be watchin' you. Then get into your car and drive away. Don't call the cops."

"I won't," I said. I closed my eyes and listened for him to leave, hoping he would take my word for it about my credit cards. It was a mostly true statement, but I did have one card that belonged to my mother. He could have gotten to Guatemala on that one.

"Count!" he yelled from a distance.

"I was counting in my head!" I yelled back. "Fifteen . . . sixteen . . . seventeen . . ."

"Don't forget to break up with Derek!" he continued. "Me and my buddies all think you're bad luck!"

I rent a 640-square-foot loft on the sixth floor in the Crossroads district of Seattle. It's small, which makes it easy to keep clean, and I never have to worry about people asking to stay with me. My parents, who live in the suburbs, don't understand my need to live inside the heart of the city, and neither does my younger brother, Eli. My parents have always enjoyed their roomy ranch-style house, and in the summertime, we took trips to national parks and went camping and kayaking. I loved it growing up, but now I leave nature to them and to my brother, and I stay in the city as much as possible.

When I moved into this apartment five years ago, my mother got me one of those herb gardens for my window ledge. I tried to keep it alive, but I kept forgetting to water it. The thing died within a week. I'm not exactly the best at keeping anything other than myself alive, and sometimes even that's a struggle. The thought of actually having to be responsible for another life scares the shit out of me, so I keep my interaction with animals limited to trips to the zoo with my niece, Rowan, and my nephew, Theo.

The minute I was inside my apartment and had locked the door, I went to my wine rack and picked out a bottle. Tonight I wasn't even going to bother with a glass. I'd ignored no fewer than twelve phone calls on my way home and twice as many texts. Everyone, it seemed, had seen the news video. Honestly, the things that are considered news nowadays when legitimate newspapers like the *Lantern* can't even stay in business are infuriating. How was my love life a story?

Of course I knew the answer.

Derek was somewhat of a celebrity, and a newly minted one at that. We'd started dating last baseball season when he was brought up from the minors. I'd been sent out to do a story on him, and we went out for drinks afterward. Two pitchers of Bud Light later, and I was back at his place. It was the first time I'd *ever* dated the subject of one of my stories, but I thought Derek was worth it. He was funny and sexy, and he never bought me anything like an herb garden.

It wasn't long before Mariners fans started to notice him—mainly for his ability to play, but the way he looked in that uniform sure didn't hurt him any. I enjoyed being his girlfriend. We got invited places I never could have gotten invited to on my own. I got inside stories about athletes I never could have gotten on my own. I got box seats I never could have gotten on my own. I admit, our relationship was probably a little superficial, but we had fun together.

Now baseball season was over, and it seemed like he was having an awful lot of fun with someone else.

Halfway into my bottle of wine, my phone rang again. Figuring it was my mother, poised to scold me for not calling, I picked it up. When I saw that it was Derek, I considered going out onto my balcony and throwing my phone into the bushes.

"Hello?"

"Maeve, hi."

"What do you want, Derek?" I asked. I took another swig of wine.

He sighed. "So you've seen it, then?"

"Everybody's seen it."

"I'm sorry, Mae," he said. I could just picture him running one of his hands through his thick chestnut-colored hair. God, I loved his hair. "I swear I didn't know anyone saw us."

"That's what you're sorry about?" I asked, setting the bottle down and standing up. "You're sorry you got caught?"

"I've been meaning to tell you."

I closed my eyes and willed myself not to press the end call button. "So it wasn't just a onetime thing with some random girl you met at a club?" I asked, verbalizing the silent hope I'd been cultivating since the drive home.

"Her name is Genevieve," Derek replied. "We met during spring training."

"I don't want to know her name!" I said. "I was with you during spring training, remember? When would you have met her?"

"She's a sportswriter too," he said. "In Florida."

"Oh my God." Suddenly I had a flash of memory. I'd seen her before. She was the one Alyssa and I made fun of because her press pass kept getting stuck in her cleavage whenever she bent over, and she bent over a lot. She'd interviewed Derek. Twice. "It's been going on that long?" I asked.

"She's moving here," he said. "She's already got a job at the *Post*."

"That's fantastic," I said, biting at each syllable. "That's just fantastic, Derek. Because I just lost my job today."

"What happened?"

"The *Lantern* is bankrupt," I replied. I was squeezing my phone so hard that my fingers were starting to cramp. "We all lost our jobs, but I'm so thrilled to hear that the woman you've been cheating on me with for almost our entire relationship has managed to procure a sportswriting job in *my* city."

"It's my city too."

"It was my city first," I spat. "You're just some Midwestern shit kicker from Kansas."

"I have never in my life kicked any shit."

I sighed. "Goodbye, Derek."

"Don't be like that, Mae," Derek wheedled. "I want us to end on good terms. I want us to be friends."

"Well, maybe you should have thought about that before you cheated on me," I replied. "You're a pathetic excuse for a man. I hope you know that."

"Fine," he said. "Be a bitch. Have a nice life."

"And your dick is tiny!" I screamed into the phone, even though he'd already hung up. It really wasn't tiny. It was like everything else about Derek—just enough above average for people to notice.

I set my phone down on the coffee table and walked into the bedroom. I was almost glad that I didn't have to go to work tomorrow. I wouldn't have to acknowledge that I'd been publicly humiliated. I couldn't imagine getting another job and being forced to cover a story about Derek.

I stood in front of the full-length mirror in my bedroom, yet another present from my mother I hadn't wanted. I didn't like to look at myself from top to bottom. The woman, Genevieve, was curvy in all the right places. And I was . . . I was curvy in no places.

As long as I could remember, I'd been one of the boys. I was tall "for a girl" at five ten. I had long legs, my favorite feature. I had thick, stick-straight brown hair and eyes that were the same color. I got lots of compliments on my matching hair and eyes. But everything else about me just sort of hung there. I was gangly, even at thirty-six, and clumsy. I couldn't walk in a pair of heels if my life depended on it. I was jeans and T-shirts and light beer on a Sunday afternoon before the big game. If Derek had wanted a woman like Genevieve, he should have said so from the beginning. I would have understood. I wanted to be a woman like Genevieve.

I threw a dirty towel over the mirror and climbed into bed without bothering to take off my clothes. Maybe I'd wake up in the morning and realize that this whole day had been a dream. More than likely, though, I'd wake up still jobless, still boy-friendless, and still $32.11 poorer.

Maybe the bum in the greasy Mariners hat was right.

Maybe I was bad luck.

I shook those thoughts from my head. If I wanted to feel better, I needed to stop drinking and go for a run. It was too late and too dark to go for a real run in the park like I preferred. The gym in the building would have to do. It smelled like sweat and protein powder, and the two meatheads who shared the apartment below me seemed to be permanent fixtures. Still—it was better than nothing. I'd been running since I was about fifteen and needed a way to deal with what my mother called "complicated female emotions." Right now I was having lots of complicated female emotions. I pulled a clean pair of Nike leggings from the clothing pile on my bedroom floor and the least wrinkled tank top I could find. I was pulling my hair into a ponytail when I heard a rapid knocking on my front door. It sounded like a tiny jackhammer, and I knew at once that it was my best friend, Holly.

She stood in the doorway, all five feet, one inches of her, looking me up and down and shaking her head. "Your pants are on backward," she said, brushing past me. "They'll evict you if you drunk exercise and puke in the trash can again."

"I'm going to get evicted anyway," I said, closing the door behind her.

"I heard about the *Lantern*," Holly said, sitting down on my couch. "I'm sorry."

"Thanks," I replied. "So it really doesn't matter where I puke. Either way, I'm puking and I'm evicted."

Holly laughed. "You can always come work for me over at *Bitch Rant*."

I sighed and plopped down beside her. "Nobody gets paid at *Bitch Rant*."

"True," Holly admitted. "But your mom would hate it."

"There's an upside to everything," I said.

Holly had been my best friend since our first semester in college, when we'd been paired up as partners in our biology lab. She was a whiz in science and math and managed to drag me through the class, kicking and screaming. Now Holly worked as a geneticist in the lab at one of the local hospitals. In her spare time, she ran an underground feminist magazine called *Bitch Rant*. She lived with her wife and twin daughters in a gorgeous house in an affluent Seattle neighborhood that made my parents' sprawling ranch in the suburbs look like a dooms-day bunker.

"Well, you know you're always welcome to come and stay with me and Christine and the girls," Holly said. "We've got plenty of room."

"I love you," I said to Holly, picking up a half-empty bottle of wine and taking a swig. "But we tried living together once, remember? It did not work out well."

"Surely you've learned to take your dishes to the sink," Holly replied. And then, glancing around my chaotic living room, added, "Okay, you're right. That's a bad idea."

"Speaking of your house," I said. "Why aren't you at home right now? Didn't you promise Christine you'd be home in time for dinner on weeknights?"

Holly touched my hand and gave me a look so sympathetic that I nearly burst into tears. "Christine saw the video," she said. "She told me to stay as long as you needed me to stay."

"In that case," I said, kicking off my running shoes. "Let's order a pizza. I'm starving."

Holly grinned. "You order, I'll pay."

I reached for my phone and replied, "As if I'd ever argue."

Chapter 2

TWO WEEKS AFTER I LOST MY JOB, AND AFTER ATTEMPTing to pay my rent with a maxed-out credit card, I moved back in with my mom and dad. My parents owned a sprawling house in a suburb of Seattle—a bedroom community. They'd had the house built in the late 1970s, several years before I was born, and it was my mother's pride and joy. She liked to talk about how it had been, for a time, the only house on the street—right at the end of the cul-de-sac, and she believed that every house built after it was built to model hers. During the summers, when most of my friends were taking family vacations to the beach, my parents were "working on the house." One summer they remodeled the kitchen. The next they ripped up all the old shag carpeting and installed hardwood floors. The summer I was ten and Eli was six, my parents remodeled the den, and we got a big-screen television set and beanbags to sit on for when we played Nintendo. My very favorite summer, however, was the summer I turned sixteen.

I'd been begging my mother for two things—my own phone line and to paint my bedroom. I'd long outgrown the pale pink walls and ballerina decorations, and despite my spectacular fail at my one and only ballet recital nearly a decade before, my mother was hesitant to give up on the dream that I would one day morph from the sullen teenager who wore too much eyeliner and listened to the Smiths into the frilly, lace-wearing daughter she'd apparently always wanted.

This fact had become something of a feud between the two of us—a fight that carried over into every single conversation we had for months. One weekend, after I'd flounced off in a huff to a friend's house, I returned home that Sunday to find my bedroom completely bare—even the ceiling fan was gone.

My mother stood in the doorway of my bedroom and held up a finger. "Before you say anything," she said, "why don't you follow me downstairs."

Reluctantly I followed her downstairs. Two brand-new walls now partitioned off what had once been a large, open room. There was new vinyl flooring, and I audibly gasped when my mother led me into the room on the left.

"Your father and I have been working on it for a few weeks," she said. "I knew you'd never come down here and see it before we finished, since you absolutely refuse to do any laundry."

I glanced around the room. My bed and dresser were there, and so were the posters I'd hung in my closet, because my mother wouldn't let me hang them on my walls. There was the television set that had been in my parents' room and one of those clear phones I'd been asking for since Christmas.

I dropped my overnight bag and gave my mother a hug. "I can't believe this," I said.

"This doesn't make you any less grounded for storming out of the house the other night," my mother replied. "The television and the phone will both be turned on in two weeks. You'll just have to stare at the ceiling until then."

I hugged her even tighter. "Thanks, Mom."

I now found myself back in my old bedroom staring at a faded picture of Morrissey and a useless clear plastic phone. My parents left me alone for a few days, allowing me the space I needed to wander around the house in an oversized T-shirt and stare aimlessly into the refrigerator.

After a week of this, however, my mother was over it. She started waking me up for breakfast and demanding I shower. She started sending me emails full of links for job openings.

One morning she swanned into my room at ten a.m. and said, "Today is lunch with the girls. You can go with us!"

I groaned.

The "girls" she was referring to were her two best friends, Carol and Melissa. The two of them and my mother were retired public schoolteachers. They both had daughters a few years older than me, and those daughters were both wildly successful. One of them was a lawyer like her father, and the other one, Kate, was married to a dentist who also happened to be my brother, Eli. In my mother's world, being married to someone successful also equated with personal success. Eli was successful because he was a dentist, and Kate was successful because she was married to him. I didn't want to go to lunch with them and spend the entire time explaining why I was thirty-six and back at home with my parents.

"You can take a couple of hours out of your day to go to lunch," my mother replied. "It'll be fun! And maybe they know someone who could give you a job."

"Doing what?"

My mother shrugged. "I don't know, but beggars can't be choosers."

"Am I at beggar status?" I asked. "Besides," I continued, "I was thinking about, I don't know, maybe going to graduate school."

"For what?" my mother asked. "Your one degree in English literature wasn't enough? You know English literature majors are only qualified for one thing—door greeters at Walmart."

"That's not true," I protested. "I could also clean off greasy countertops at McDonald's."

My mother sighed. "Oh, Maeve." That was her favorite expression—*Oh, Maeve*. She'd been saying it since I was old enough to talk. "Do you really want to go back to school?"

"I don't know," I admitted. "Maybe."

"Well," she said. "I guess it beats nothing at all."

My mother looked around my bedroom. "Look at this as a new start," she said finally. "Your options are limitless."

"I feel like my options are completely limited," I muttered.

My mother ignored me and walked to the closet, examining its contents. Finally she pulled out a pair of gray knit slacks and an aqua blazer—both items she'd given me and that I never wore—and said, "This will do, I suppose."

"For what?"

"For lunch," my mother replied, sighing deeply, a sign she was through asking me and was now telling me what I was going to do. "I'll iron these pants, and you can wear one of my shirts under the blazer."

I rolled over in bed and pressed my face into my pillow.

"And for God's sake, take a shower and wash your hair," she said on her way out of the room.

Two hours later, I was squeaky-clean and sitting beside my mother at her usual lunch spot. My sister-in-law, Kate, and her mother walked toward us, mirror images of each other in their tailored suits, shiny chestnut hair, and perfect posture. My mother gave me a look that told me to sit up straight, and I slumped down in my chair and scratched at my leg through the wool trousers. I was pretty sure they were giving me a rash.

My mother stood up and gave them both an air-kiss on each cheek. "Carol and Meredith are running a bit late," she said to them. "They said to go ahead and order when we're ready."

Kate sat down beside me and said, "I heard you were coming today, but I didn't believe it."

"Well, I for one am thrilled," Kate's mother, whose name

was Melissa, added. "Your mother says you've just been moping around the house for the last couple of weeks. It's good for you to get outside and get some fresh air."

"Yes," I replied. "It's way more fun to be depressed in the sunshine."

"She's joking," my mother said quickly, waving the waiter over to our table.

The waiter scurried over, and the other women proceeded to order white wine or some variation of it, and when it got to be my turn, I said hopefully, "What do you have on tap?"

Beside me, my mother cleared her throat, and I sighed and said, "I'll just have white wine."

"Any preference?" the waiter asked. There was a slight twitch playing at his mouth, as if he might want to smile but knew better.

I gritted my teeth. "Whatever you recommend."

He nodded and turned to leave just as Carol and her daughter Meredith rushed toward us. They gave him their drink orders (more white wine), and then filled the remaining places at the table.

Carol was a small woman with a pinched face and a mop of dark hair. She and my mother had been friends since high school, and I didn't have many memories from childhood that didn't involve Carol and Meredith in some way. I liked Meredith. We'd never been the kind of bosom buddies that my mother and Carol would have liked, but we had a mutual respect for each other. We'd been roommates for a semester in college before Meredith joined a prelaw dormitory, and she'd helped me out once when a creditor threatened to sue me. Meredith didn't look a thing like Carol. She looked more like her father, who'd been an offensive lineman for the Seattle Seahawks before a knee injury ended his career. Meredith was nearly six one, and as a lawyer, I figured she was a pretty intimidating force in the courtroom.

Meredith looked up from her phone and over at me. "What are you doing here?" she asked. "You never come to lunch."

Carol shot her a look. "We discussed this on the way over, Mer, remember?"

Meredith shrugged and looked back down at her phone. "You said a lot on the way over."

I stifled a giggle and looked down at the menu. I knew from experience that from the lunch menu my mother would order a dainty salad with a vinaigrette dressing on the side. I also knew that she would be starving before we got home, which meant that dinner in the evening would likely consist of pork chops or some other savory dish. I decided to humor my mother by ordering a salad as well. I'd have ranch dressing, though. With God as my witness, I wouldn't allow that to be taken from me.

There was sporadic conversation while we waited for our food—the kind of discussion that is polite but not too intrusive. I wondered if my mother had pulled each of her friends aside before meeting and asked them not to ask me any questions about my job or my love life. If she had, I was grateful. I smiled at her from across the table, and she gave me a little wink.

I was just going in for my second bite of ranch-covered hap-
piness when Meredith looked over at me and said, "So, Mae,
how is the job search going?"

I put the fork into my mouth and chewed as slowly as I
could, while the entire table watched me. "Well," I said finally.
"There's not a lot out there for a journalist these days, except for
a little bit of freelance work."

"Your mother says you're thinking about graduate school,"
Meredith said. "What would you go for?"

I shrugged. "I don't know," I replied. "I've always really liked
the idea of marketing, but since my degree is in English literature, I'd probably have to go back and take some undergraduate
courses before I could apply for any program like that."

"Sounds expensive," Kate's mother said.

"Nothing's been decided yet," my mother replied, shooting
Kate's mother an annoyed glance.

"Eli can always train you at the clinic to be a hygienist," Kate
said. "We never can keep anybody, it seems."

I bit at the insides of my mouth to keep from telling Kate
that the reason they couldn't keep any help was because she
was the office manager and completely unbearable to work for.
I knew firsthand what that was like, having played receptionist
for them when the clinic first opened several years ago. Instead
I said, "I don't think I'd be very good at that. You know teeth
freak me out."

"Beggars can't be choosers," Kate's mother interjected.

"I'm not begging anyone for anything," I said. Why did

people keep suggesting that term applied to me? I mean, sure, I'd lost my job and my apartment and my boyfriend, but that didn't mean I was desperate, did it? I certainly didn't feel desperate. What I felt, at the moment, was annoyed. "Besides," I continued, "Holly offered me a job writing for her magazine."

My mother almost choked on her salad. She shot me a warning glance from across the table, which I chose to ignore.

"Holly who?" Meredith asked. "Oh, *Holly*. I remember her. She has a magazine?"

"*Bitch Rant*," I said, not looking at my mother.

"*Bitch Rant*?" everyone at the table said in unison.

"It's a feminist magazine," I replied, and then I gulped down the rest of my wine. "It's very well respected in some circles."

"In *some circles*, I'm sure," Kate's mother said.

Kate's mother wasn't looking at me. She was staring over at my mother with such a look of pity that I was almost ashamed for mentioning *Bitch Rant*.

Just as I opened my mouth to smooth things over, my phone began to ring. I pulled it out of my purse and stared down at the screen. I didn't recognize the number. I sent the caller to voice mail and put the phone facedown on the table.

"Aren't you going to answer it?" my mother asked. "It could be about a job."

I rolled my eyes. She and I both knew that nobody was calling me about a job. She also knew I wasn't in the habit of answering numbers I didn't know. And random numbers flashing across the screen almost always meant one thing—debt collectors.

My phone started to ring again, and we all stared at it. When it began to ring for a third time, I snatched it up off the table and hurried out into the lobby to answer it, annoyed that whoever it was wouldn't leave me alone.

"Hello?" I said impatiently into the phone. "It's rude to call someone over and over, even if I probably do owe you money. I lost my job, though, so good luck squeezing anything out of me."

There was silence on the other end, and I felt triumphant that I'd likely scared off whoever it was. Then, after a few seconds, there came a timid, "Hello? Is this Maeve Stephens?"

I sighed. "This is she."

The person on the other end cleared her throat and continued, "My name is Alice, and I'm, well, I know your birth mother, Annabelle."

I pulled the phone away from my ear and stared at it. Surely I hadn't heard that right. I hadn't heard from my birth mother, well, ever, and I certainly hadn't ever gotten a random phone call from someone claiming to know her.

"Uh, yes?" I said, putting the phone back up to my ear. "How can I help you?"

There was a pause, and then, "I'm sorry to call you like this. I, uh, I got your number from the website of the newspaper where you work . . ."

"Used to work," I said automatically.

"I'm so sorry to tell you this, really I am, but Annabelle died two days ago," the woman named Alice said, her words coming out in such a rush that I had to ask her to repeat herself.

"I'm sorry," I said finally, because I didn't know what else to say. "How did she—I mean, she wasn't very old."

"She drowned," Alice replied, her voice cracking. "She was out on the lake in her little johnboat fishing, and she must've slipped and hit her head. She went overboard, and, well . . ."

I hadn't known Annabelle had a boat. Of course, I hadn't known Annabelle. In fact, everything I knew about her could fit on one hand—she was my birth mother; she was from Timber Creek, Washington; and now I knew she had a friend named Alice and apparently a johnboat, whatever that was.

"There will be a funeral, of course, here in Timber Creek," Alice went on. "I thought you might want to know."

"Thanks," I said, swallowing. That ranch dressing was really starting to stick in my throat. "I appreciate the call."

"The funeral is on Sunday," she said. "At the Timber Creek Disciples of Christ. Two o'clock."

I peered around the entryway of the restaurant. I could see my mother sitting at the table, smiling up at the waiter as he re-filled her glass of wine. Her blond hair was parted neatly down the middle and styled into a sleek bob. Her blue eyes, sparkling now, I knew would cloud over when I told her the news. She'd set her thin lips into a hard line, which caused them to nearly disappear. Sometimes I forgot, despite our obvious physical differences, that we were not related by blood. I forgot that she and my father had adopted me, a squalling, dark-eyed infant with a head full of even darker hair, at a few days old. I forgot there was another woman who'd given birth to me, a birth mother, she'd been called, living her life for the last thirty-six years like nothing ever happened—like I never happened.

"Are you there?" Alice asked, when I failed to say anything else.

I pressed the fingertips of my free hand into one of my eyelids. I just wanted this conversation to be over. "I'm sorry," I said, already pulling the phone away from my ear. "But I don't think I can make it."

CHAPTER 3

I FOUND OUT I WAS ADOPTED WHEN I WAS SIX. ONE OF MY cousins, a scabby-kneed tomboy named Jamie, told me on the Fourth of July during our family barbecue. She asked me if I ever wondered why I was so tall and dark when my mom and dad were both short and light. I said no. Of course I hadn't. I was six. It hadn't yet occurred to me that I should look like my parents.

"It's cuz you're adopted," she said, confident in her ten-year-old superiority. "My mom said you have another mom some-where else. That's why you look different."

I didn't believe her. She had a tendency to lie, especially when she was angry with me, like she had been at that moment. I wouldn't let her play with my Polly Pocket. The last time I'd let her near any of my toys, she'd flushed them down the toilet and then blamed me for it. "I don't believe you," I said.

"It's true," she replied.

"Then why don't I live with that mom?" I wanted to know.

Jamie shrugged, already bored with the conversation. "She didn't want you, I guess."

I wondered about this Other Mother.

Who was she?

Where was she?

Why didn't she want me?

Most of all, I wondered if this Other Mother would show up at my house one day and want me back. Would my parents have to give me back to her? What would my life be like then?

I got myself so worked up that my mother found me sobbing underneath my Strawberry Shortcake comforter.

"What's wrong, pumpkin?" she asked, pulling the comforter back so that she could see my face. "Why are you crying?"

I pulled away from her and drew my knees up to my chest. "Jamie says I'm dadopted."

"She says you're what?"

"Dadopted!"

That was when my mother picked me up and took me into the living room, well past my bedtime, and sat me down on my father's lap. "I am your mommy, and Daddy is your daddy," my mother said. She said it carefully, slowly, pronouncing every syllable. She wasn't smiling.

"So I'm not dadopted?" I asked.

"It's called *adopted*, sweetheart," my father said. "And yes, Mommy and I adopted you."

"But all it means is that you came to us differently than Jamie came to her mommy. It doesn't mean we love you less. It doesn't mean we aren't your parents," my mother replied. "It just means that we got to pick you out, especially for us."

"Oh," I said, chewing over this new information. "Do I have another mommy somewhere? Like Jamie said? Another mommy who doesn't want me?"

My father shifted me on his lap and stole a glance at my mother. "*We* want you," he said. "You're our best girl."

I grinned at him then, because it was always something he said to me, and I was forever telling him that I already knew I was his best girl. I was his *only girl*, after all. He let me ride on his back to the bedroom, and he pulled out the top drawer of his dresser, the one that held socks and silver dollars. He handed me a picture of a girl I'd never seen before. She looked young. She looked like she could be my sister.

"This is your birth mother," he said. "Her name is Annabelle."

I stared down at the picture. The girl wasn't smiling, but she looked like maybe she wanted to. Her hair was dark and straight and parted down the middle. She had large green eyes and a wide mouth. Her nose was slightly turned up at the end. "She looks like me," I said.

My father nodded. "She does. She's very pretty. This is an old picture, taken a year before you were born. She's older now, but she probably still looks like you."

"Why did she give me to you?" I asked.

My father sat down next to me on the bed and rested his hands on his knees the way he sometimes did when he was thinking about what he wanted to say. "Mommy and I couldn't have a baby," he said. "Annabelle loved you very much, but she couldn't take care of you. She was very young, and she didn't have a mommy or daddy of her own to help her. So she asked us to take care of you and to love you and to be your parents."

"Why didn't you just adopt her?" I asked. "Then we both could have been yours."

"That isn't the way it works, sweetheart," my father said. "I wish it was, but it's not."

My parents let me sleep with them in their bed that night, right in the middle between them, the way I liked it. Neither one of them complained when I accidentally kicked them or got up three times to go to the bathroom. I didn't ask any more questions.

The next morning, I heard my mother on the phone with her sister Brenda, Jamie's mother, and she was crying. Jamie didn't come to our house much after that, and my mother seemed more than a little pleased when, ten years later, Jamie got arrested for check forgery at the local CVS.

The next year, my mother and father became foster parents through a Catholic charity in Seattle, and Eli came to live with us. At first I thought my parents becoming foster parents meant that we'd have a baby in the house. I'd already envisioned myself walking the new baby up and down the cul-de-sac in the stroller I'd gotten for my Baby Alive for my seventh birthday. I'd planned to dress the baby up and pretend to be her mother.

Then one night after dinner, a nun showed up with Eli. He didn't have anything with him except a Catholic Charities logo coat and a trash bag. He was small, even for three years old, with sandy-blond hair and these bright blue eyes that looked entirely too big for his body. I hid behind my father when he answered the door.

Eli's mother had turned over temporary guardianship to the Sisters of the Sacred Cross. They ran what was, for all practical purposes, an orphanage. Most of the children, however, went to private foster homes. Eli, with his sweet disposition and desire to be loved, was a perfect fit for my parents, who were first-time foster parents, and despite my initial reservations, Eli and I grew close during the first six months he lived with us. He was smart and easygoing, despite the fact that I overheard one of the nuns telling my parents that he'd likely spent the majority of his time alone in an apartment taking care of his infant sister while his mother went to work all day. Sometimes he cried at night because he missed his mother and sister, and I'd sneak down the hallway to his bedroom, crawl into bed with him, and sing him silly songs my Nana and Pop taught me on vacation.

Just when I was beginning to believe that Eli would be with us forever, the Sisters of the Sacred Cross came to get him one afternoon while I was at school. When I got home, his room was empty. My parents explained to me that Eli's mom had taken him back.

I'd been mad at Eli, because it hurt my feelings that he didn't want to stay with us. Later, I was jealous because Eli had a birth mother who loved him and wanted him back. I wondered what made Eli so special that his birth mother couldn't live without him. I figured it was probably because he never snuck sticky fruit into his bed at bedtime and never argued when it was time to wash his hair.

Two months later, Eli came back. All my parents would tell me was that something "bad" had happened while Eli was living with his mother, and that this time they hoped he would get to stay forever. I knew I should feel bad that something happened, but I was so excited to have him back. But he was different when he came back with the nun this time. His eyes were hollow. He didn't smile. He didn't even talk. When I tried to play with him, he'd sit on the floor and stare off into space. My parents never left him alone, and he went to see a special doctor three times a week in the city. My mother took a leave of absence from the high school where she worked so she could stay home with him.

Eli's mother never asked for him back again after that, and my parents adopted him the next year. I found out later that his mother and sister had been murdered and that he'd likely seen it happen. I was never jealous of Eli after that. I never got angry when he got better grades than me in school or finished first in a track meet. I never felt slighted when my parents bragged about him for being a dentist and living in an exclusive neighborhood. Everything he had was hard earned, and for many years, until the summer I was sixteen, I happily kept my own mother tucked away in my father's sock drawer.

Now, however, my own birth mother was dead, and I wasn't sure how I was supposed to be feeling or even what I should say about it. I'd managed to come up with a story about an interview for a job, so that I didn't have to tell anyone at the lunch table what was really going on, but my mother saw it written all over my face and demanded that I tell her on the way home.

The minute we walked through the door, she started cooking dinner, nearly three hours too early. She couldn't help it. It's what my mother did when she was stressed—she cooked, usually something smothered in gravy. This time it was pork chops.

"Do you think I should go to the funeral?" I asked her. All I really wanted to do was go down to my room and call Holly, but I couldn't leave my mother alone like this. If I didn't watch her, she'd go to the grocery store for more food we didn't need.

My mother didn't answer, busying herself with the pork chops.

"Mom?"

"I can't tell you what to do," she said finally.

I rolled my eyes. "You've been telling me what to do for my whole life. You're suddenly stopping now?"

My mother flipped a butterflied pork chop onto its back and looked over at me. "I don't have any experience in this department," she said. "I didn't even go to my own parents' funerals, you know that."

"I'd go to your funeral," I said. "*You're* my mother."

She smiled at that. "I am your mother," she replied. "I will always be your mother, but I didn't give you life." My mother paused, and then pointed her spatula at me. "However, I do give myself credit for *keeping* you alive for the last thirty-six years. That's no small feat."

"That's true," I agreed. "It's been a constant battle, pretty much since I tried to eat those mushrooms in the backyard when I was four."

"Don't remind me," my mother groaned. "I'm fairly certain poison control knew me by name that summer."

We both looked up when the door opened, and my father came rushing through, still wearing his golfing glove and his visor askew on top of his bald head. Now that he was retired, he spent most of his free time on the golf course. My brother and I joked that golfing was the one thing he loved more than the two of us. Well, golf and his grandchildren, Eli's two kids—Rowan and Theo.

I knew that my mother must have called him when we got home during that five minutes I was in the bathroom. Otherwise, he wouldn't have come in before five o'clock, and he certainly wouldn't have come home still wearing his golfing gear. My mother allowed nothing golf related at our house, and all golf talk and golf wear was relegated to the clubhouse at the club.

My mother shot him a look when she saw him, and my father immediately pulled off his visor and glove. "I'm sorry," he said, focusing his eyes on me. "I forgot."

"Really, Dad," I said, standing up to give him a hug. "You didn't have to come all the way home. I'm fine. It's fine. Really, it is."

He held me out at arm's length and eyed me suspiciously. "I came right home when your mother called," he said.

I sighed and sat back down. "I don't know why you're making such a big fuss over it," I continued. "I'm *fine*. It's not like I ever knew her anyway."

My father and I had always shared a special bond. It wasn't more important than my relationship with my mother, but it *was* true that I got along better with my father than I did with my mother. I chalked it up to personality, but I also knew it had at least a little bit to do with not knowing who my birth father was.

I'd wondered about my birth father, sure. I'd wanted to know who he was and where he'd come from and what he looked like. But my parents couldn't tell me any of those things, and so his existence was merely an abstract thought—a passing curiosity I had once in a while when my mind wandered—unlike the reality of knowing not only who my birth mother was, but also that she didn't want me.

"It's okay if you're not fine," my father said, forcing me out of my thoughts.

I realized that staring off into the distance at the slightly dingy spot on the wallpaper above my father's head probably didn't do much to convince them that I was all right.

"I swear, I'm fine," I said again. "Really. I just need some time to digest the information, that's all."

My parents shared a look with each other. They knew, just as well as I did, that I'd once tried to make contact with Annabelle. The summer I was sixteen, I'd sent her a series of letters in secret, only to be found out when every single letter came back to our house, unopened, "return to sender" scrawled in black ink across each one. I'd admitted to them, my face flushed and tearstained, that I'd found Annabelle's address on some adoption paperwork in their bedroom. I don't know what I'd expected, really. I guess at the core of it all, I'd hoped for some kind of affirmation. I'd had fantasies of keeping up a correspondence until I was eighteen, when she'd want to meet, and I would finally, at long last, stare into the face of someone who looked like me—who was part of me.

Instead what I got was dismissal. My birth mother couldn't even be bothered to read my letters. They weren't very long, and I'd been so nice in them, never once writing that I was angry or hurt about being adopted. I'd used the prettiest Sanrio stationery with scented envelopes. But in the end it hadn't mattered. I burned the letters in our backyard fire pit. I begged my parents not to mention it again, even after they suggested the address they'd had was old and that my birth mother might not even live there anymore. I knew they were just saying that to be nice—to keep me from the heartbreak that had already happened.

And I hadn't for nearly two decades.

Now I was folded into a kitchen chair and my parents were exchanging worried looks and I felt sixteen all over again and all I wanted to do was pretend like none of this was happening.

My father glanced at the stove, where the pork chops were starting to burn. "The, uh . . ." He motioned to my mother. "The, uh, pork chops."

My mother's eyes widened and she sprinted to the stove. Flames licked the edges of the pan, and instinctively my mother reached in to grab the handle.

"June, no!" my father yelled, but it was too late. My mother's arm up to her elbow was engulfed in flames, and my father covered her up with a wet dishrag just as the pan of pork chops came crashing down onto the kitchen floor.

We all three stood there for a few seconds, letting the shock wash over us. My mother's arm was still outstretched, the dishrag hanging limply over what we all knew was scorched skin underneath.

After what felt like forever, I found my voice and managed to croak out, "Are you okay?"

My mother's eyes were wide, but she made no attempt to move until my father pulled away the dishrag, and we all gasped.

"I think we need to go to the ER," he said.

"I'm fine," my mother insisted, but even she didn't sound convinced. "I'll just run it under some cold water."

My father was already putting on his jacket. "I'll pull the car around out front. Mae, wait with your mother."

I nodded obediently, found her shoes and purse, and then led her outside. We waited silently until my father appeared with the car, and I couldn't shake the feeling, as I slid into the back seat and my father sped off down our quiet cul-de-sac, that what had just happened was entirely my fault.

CHAPTER 4

IT WAS A SLOW NIGHT FOR SEATTLE MEMORIAL HOSPITAL, and the ER was surprisingly empty minus an elderly woman in a wheelchair covered by a hospital blanket and a man in an expensive-looking suit who walked brusquely, if not painfully, up to the receptionist and whispered something that caused the woman behind the desk to blush, and they ushered him back without even taking his information.

"What do you want to bet he's got something stuffed up his rear end?" my father whispered to me. He named a really famous male celebrity.

"Him?" I asked. "That was never confirmed, you know."

"Stop it, you two," my mother said, giving us a look of disapproval. She'd since regained her composure and had been insisting for the last twenty minutes that she didn't need to be in the ER and lamenting her spoiled pork chops.

"It happens more than you'd think," my father said knowingly. "One of my buddies at the club has a son who's an ER doctor. People shove all kinds of things up there."

My mother was about to respond when her name was called by the triage nurse.

"I'll wait here," I said as my parents stood up, and the triage nurse gave me a grateful smile. I figured she'd had enough for the afternoon already, what with Mr. Suit waddling in and everything.

After they'd disappeared behind the double doors, I stood up and stretched, raising my arms high above my head. It felt so good to stretch. What I really wanted to do was go running, something I hadn't been doing much of since I moved back in with my parents. I'd been too depressed, even though running was pretty much the only thing I'd ever found that could help me clear my head. There was something about the pounding of my feet on the pavement, the sharp and almost desperate intake of air into my lungs, and the exhausted satisfaction that came with running that helped calm whatever problem happened to be coiling around like snakes in my brain.

I briefly considered running up and down the halls of the hospital but decided that was probably a terrible idea and settled instead for a stomach-churning cup of coffee and a chair at the farthest corner of the ER waiting room. I watched two families come in and sit down—one with a coughing, feverish-looking baby and the other with a small boy with a long cut down one of his skinny legs. As they were led back, and my entertainment lapsed, I looked down and checked my phone.

I'd called Eli while we were on the way to the hospital, and he'd been in the middle of a root canal. I told the receptionist not to interrupt him. Still, I knew he'd come by as soon as he could. It was just four o'clock in the afternoon, but it felt like midnight, especially in the windowless emergency waiting room, and I was suddenly very tired.

Just as I was drifting off to sleep, my father came out from behind the double doors and said, "It's not nearly as bad as it looks. The doctor is going to wrap it up and prescribe a cream."

He collapsed in a chair next to me.

"Where is she?" I asked.

"They're finishing up. I just came out to tell you and to call Eli," my father replied.

"I already called Eli," I reminded him.

"Oh, that's right."

I sat up to face him. "How is Mom?"

"She's all right," my father said. And then, as if suddenly remembering the reason for the entire debacle, he asked, "Are you okay, kiddo?"

"I'm fine," I replied, trying to sound more confident than I felt. "Just tired."

My father leaned back in the chair and smiled at me. "You know, we brought you home from this hospital, your mother and I," he said. "Nearly thirty-seven years ago."

"I know," I said. I'd heard the story at least a dozen times

over the years—about how long and skinny I was, about how I
had a full head of dark hair. "Please don't tell the entire waiting
room about how I pooped on your shirt in the elevator, because
you'd put my diaper on backward."

My father grinned. "That's my favorite story."

I couldn't help returning his grin.

"Your mother was so afraid that Annabelle might change
her mind," my father said. "She had some time, you know, to
change her mind after you were born, even though the paperwork was all set; nothing was certain until we had you."

I sat up. This was a part of the story I hadn't heard before.
"You really thought she might change her mind?" I asked. "Annabelle, I mean?"

My father nodded. "Your mother did," he said. "But I was
confident Annabelle wouldn't. That child—and she was seventeen, mind you, but she was still just a child to look at her—was
determined."

"What do you mean?"

"She loved you, you know," my father replied, his voice quieter than it had been before. "I know you don't believe it, but
it's true."

I felt my eyes well up, even though I did my best to hide it.
"Then why . . ."

"Shhh," my father said, the way he used to when I was little and had a scraped knee from falling out of my treehouse.
"There's no sense in that kind of talk."

"It doesn't even matter now," I said finally, rubbing furiously at my eyes.

"So it was Alice who called you, then?" my father asked.

"Yes," I said, somewhat surprised. "You know her?"

"She picked Annabelle up from the hospital," he replied. "And Annabelle spoke of her often during her visits with us before you were born. They were incredibly close and, I think, all the other one had in the world."

I tried to think about how I'd feel if I lost Holly but couldn't bear to imagine it. It was too awful. "Alice must be pretty upset," I said, realizing as I said it that *upset* was probably a gigantic understatement.

"I know you don't see it this way," my father continued. "But it was nice of her to call you. I'm sure it wasn't easy."

"I'm sure it wasn't," I agreed.

I thought about the way I'd spoken to her, the clipped tone I'd used, especially as I told her I wouldn't be making it to the funeral.

"You wouldn't be betraying us to go," my father said, nudging me gently out of my thoughts. "To the funeral, I mean. Your mother and I, we'd go with you if you'd like."

I took my dad's hand and squeezed it. "No," I said. "That's okay. I think Mom has had enough excitement for this week. I'll ask Holly."

"So you're going?"

Before I could answer, my brother burst into the waiting

room, still wearing his scrubs. He glanced from me to our father. "Is Mom okay?" he asked.

"She's fine," Dad replied. "Just a second-degree burn, nothing too major. She ought to be out anytime now."

Eli sat down next to me and sighed. "I had five people ask me for directions around the hospital, and one nurse tried to force me into a surgery," he said, shaking his head. "I guess I should have changed out of my scrubs before I came in."

"I wish you were a real doctor," I grumbled. "Then I could come and see you instead of having to pay out of pocket for someone to tell me my knee hurts because I need to lose fifteen pounds."

"You don't need to lose fifteen pounds," Eli replied. "And I'm hurt that you don't consider me a real doctor. What is it that you think I do all day?"

"Punish children for eating sugar?"

Eli shrugged. "Fair."

We stood up when my mother pushed her way through the double doors and out into the waiting room. She stuck her bandaged arm out to us triumphantly, like a prize she'd won, and then said, "Come on, you three. Let's go get something to eat. I'm starving."

"Where do you want to go?" my father asked her, taking her by her other arm and guiding her out of the waiting room.

Turning around to wink at me first, she said, "Anything, anything at all, but pork chops."

ANNABELLE

April 1984

ANNABELLE WATCHED THE YELLOW SCHOOL BUS DISAP-pear down the street, its red taillights fading into the early morning fog.

"Is it gone?" came a voice from beneath Annabelle. "Answer me! It smells like shit in here."

Annabelle jumped down from the table on which she'd been standing. "You're the one who suggested we hide in this nasty shed," she retorted, dusting off her jeans. "I said we should just ride the bus to school and then ditch, remember?"

"Too risky," Alice replied, shaking her head. She pulled a pack of Virginia Slims Lights out of her back pocket and offered one to Annabelle. "Besides," she said, pausing to light their cigarettes, "my brother won't go anywhere near that school, and we'd have to walk forever before he'd pick us up."

Annabelle didn't even know why Alice was worried about being caught ditching school. They'd been doing it nearly every day this year, their senior year, and she doubted the teachers or anybody else even missed them. In fact, she figured Mr. Morrow, the principal, was probably relieved. Alice, with her blond curls and fierce hazel eyes, was a force to be reckoned with and had a bit of a reputation despite her short stature (she was just five foot one). She'd been born with her left leg shorter than the right, and she'd always worn a special shoe. When they'd been much younger, in elementary school, Alice had also had to use a special walker to get around, and Annabelle knew that her best friend had had to learn to be tough early in life.

Annabelle, for her part, was much milder in comparison, both in personality and appearance. She was tall and lanky with straight brown hair and even features. She had a quiet nature and let Alice do most of the talking, which often got them into trouble, and being a loyal friend, Annabelle never let Alice fight her battles alone. *Yes*, Annabelle mused. *Principal Morrow is probably plenty relieved we've been skipping class.*

"There's Billy!" Alice said, peering around the side of the shed's door. "Come on."

Annabelle grabbed her backpack and slung it over one shoulder. She'd packed a change of clothes and her toothbrush. She hoped they'd stay at Billy's that night instead of going back to their house—well, Alice's house, where Annabelle had been living for the last three years since her parents died in a car accident. If they were lucky, Alice's father would be drunk before he even got home for dinner and would forget about the two teenagers altogether.

Billy rolled down his window when he saw them, a thick cloud of cigarette smoke escaping through the crack. "Hurry up," he said. "You're gonna make me late for work."

Both girls sidled into the back seat, huddling close together for warmth. It was still cold in Washington. Annabelle often fantasized about moving to Florida or California—someplace where it stayed warm year-round instead of freezing most of the time. As she considered this, Billy turned around from the front seat and gave her a wink. Annabelle felt her face grow hot, and she was relieved, not for the first time, that her dark skin kept her secrets instead of flushing bright pink the way Alice's did when she got angry or embarrassed.

"The house is a mess," Billy said, lurching the old LeBaron forward. "You could pick up a little while you're there, Al."

From the back seat, Alice rolled her eyes. "I'm not Mom," she said. "Do your own housekeeping?"

"I ain't the Ritz-Carlton either, so if you want to keep staying at my place, you better start helping out," Billy replied. His tone was jovial, but both girls knew he meant business. He'd been letting them hang out nearly every day for the last two months at his tiny shotgun house a few blocks from the factory where he worked.

"Fine," Alice replied. "But I'm not washing your underwear."

Again, Annabelle felt her face go hot. She'd known Billy all her life, as he was Alice's big brother—nearly five years older than they were. He'd spent most of his life in trouble, either with his father or with the law. He'd spent a year in prison on drug charges just after he turned eighteen, and to his credit, he'd remained free and clean since his release. Billy said having his sister and her "little friend" there to stay at his place kept him from being lonely and slipping back into his old bad habits.

Annabelle couldn't admit to Alice how much she liked Billy—how good-looking she thought he was. With his dark curls and full lips, Annabelle certainly wasn't the only girl in Timber Creek to have had a crush on Billy Monroe. Billy had plenty of offers, and he knew it. There was, of course, the added bonus that no young woman's parents wanted their daughters dating a young man like Billy, and so this made him all the more appealing to the daughters of upstanding citizens.

Years later, when Annabelle and Alice were in their early twenties and sharing an apartment together, Alice would bring home an album called *Appetite for Destruction* by a band called Guns N' Roses, and Annabelle wouldn't be able to stop herself from thinking about how much that sexy guitarist, Slash, reminded her of Billy. Now, though, from the back seat of the car, Annabelle tried to keep her gaze from falling admiringly on the back of Billy's neck.

Billy pulled into the driveway of his house and said, "The key is in the usual place. Don't go crazy."

"Shut up," Alice replied, pushing open the door and hopping out. "Don't tell Dad where we are if you see him at the plant today, okay?"

"Like I'd tell that old bastard anything," Billy snorted. He looked over and caught Annabelle's eye as she scooted out of the back seat and held her gaze for just a little longer than was polite, before peeling out of the gravel driveway, spraying the girls with rocks and dust.

"He's such an idiot," Alice said, patting at her jeans.

"I don't know," Annabelle replied absently.

Alice grabbed Annabelle's arm. "Oh, not you too," she groaned. "I won't be able to take it if my best friend falls in love with my stupid brother. He's too old for you anyway."

"I know," Annabelle said. "Besides, I'm not falling in love with him. I just don't think he's as stupid as you do."

"That's because he's not your brother."

"Probably."

Alice reached into her pocket and pulled out a wadded-up twenty-dollar bill and waved it in her friend's face. "Look what I lifted off Janet Galloway in the break room yesterday."

"You didn't," Annabelle replied. She shook her head. "You're going to get caught one of these days, you know."

Alice's mother worked at the grocery store part-time during the day when the girls were supposed to be in school. Once in a while, they'd go to visit her after three o'clock, and Alice regularly helped herself to whatever her sticky fingers could carry.

"Nah," Alice said, grinning. "Janet's purse was too heavy

anyway. She just had that rotator cuff surgery, you know. I'm just helping her out."

"Klepto."

"Would you rather not walk down to the gas station for Doritos and Pepsi?" Alice asked, knowing that Annabelle could never resist a bag of Doritos. "Fine. I'll buy Tab and Corn Nuts instead."

"You will not," Annabelle said, snatching the money out of Alice's hand and running down the street.

"Give it back!" Alice yelled, limping after Annabelle. "That's not fair!"

"Promise to buy Doritos?"

Alice sighed. "I promise. Now give it back."

Annabelle handed over the money and the two walked, arm in arm, down the street, a full day of MTV, cigarettes, and caffeine in their immediate and satisfied future.

CHAPTER 5

A RE YOU SURE YOU DON'T WANT ME TO GO WITH YOU TO the funeral?" my mother was asking, two days later, as I threw clothes into my overnight bag. "I hate for you to go alone."

I stopped packing, holding in the sigh that was threatening to escape from my mouth. "I told you, Mom," I said. "Holly is going with me."

My mother ignored this, as she'd always disapproved of Holly. It wasn't because, as people sometimes assumed, Holly was married to another woman. No, it was because Holly once accidentally insulted her new living room carpet one Thanksgiving home from college. "Well," my mother continued, "just make sure that whatever you wear to the funeral in the morning isn't wrinkled. I don't want them thinking you were raised by lunatics."

"Wearing wrinkled jeans doesn't make a person a lunatic," I replied, still unable to look at her. I felt guilty for even going, and she knew it.

"You aren't going to wear jeans, are you?" she asked, and I imagined that she was clutching her chest behind me. "Maeve, you can't be serious."

"Mom," I said, releasing the sigh and turning to look at her. "Of course I'm not serious. I have a black dress hanging up in the closet, and I'll even wear pantyhose if it'll make you happy."

"And a slip?"

"Nobody's worn a slip since 1992."

"June! Maeve!" my father called from the living room. "Eli is here with the kids!"

I grinned and hurried into the living room, where my brother, my five-year-old niece, Rowan, and my six-month-old nephew, Theo, were watching my father pretend to remove his thumb from his hand.

"That's not real," Rowan said, rolling her eyes. She looked so much like my brother had when he'd come to live with us all those years ago that it sometimes made my breath catch in my throat.

"Of course it's real, Ro," Eli replied. "Papa wouldn't lie to you."

I looked down at Rowan, winked, and then extended my arms to take Theo. "Show Daddy and Papa what I taught you," I said.

Obediently, Rowan made a fist and placed her thumb in between her index and middle fingers. She moved the other hand up to her fist and proceeded to show everyone how to make her own thumb disappear. "See?" she said, triumphant. "Aunt Mae taught me how to do it."

"Aren't you two clever?" my father replied.

"As a matter of fact, we are," I said. I scrunched up my face and crossed my eyes in an effort to make Theo laugh. Instead, his brow furrowed, and he began to cry.

"Why do you always do that?" Eli asked, taking Theo back from me. "He cries every single time."

"He got his sense of humor from his mother," I muttered.

Ignoring my comment, Eli said, "So you're off to Timber Creek?"

I nodded. "I guess so."

"Are you nervous?"

"Not nervous," I said. "More . . . apprehensive. I don't know what to expect."

"I get that," Eli replied. "I'm sorry you never got the chance to meet her."

"I guess it's probably better this way," I said. I crossed my arms over my chest and shrugged in an effort to appear nonchalant. But Eli knew me better than anyone else on earth, and I knew he wasn't buying it.

"Going will be good for you," he said. "It will give you some closure."

"I wasn't aware I needed closure," I replied.

"Trust me," Eli said. "You're going to want it."

I didn't argue with him. Instead, I looked down at Rowan, who was pulling on the hem of my shirt. "Where are you going, Aunt Mae?" she asked.

"I'm going out of town for a few days," I said, offering her my brightest smile. "I won't be gone for too long, I promise."

"Will you be back for my birthday?"

I laughed. "Of course. Your birthday isn't until June third."

"Daddy says you lost your job," Rowan continued. "I told him you could come and live with us. You can sleep in my room!"

I shot a look at my brother, who responded by giving me a sheepish smile. "Well, that's very sweet of you, Ro," I said. "But I don't think that's a very good idea."

Rowan nodded solemnly. "That's what Mommy said," she replied. "She said you should find a real job first."

"Rowan!" Eli exclaimed, his face turning roughly the shade of a boiled lobster. "What have Mommy and I told you about repeating our conversations?"

Rowan shrugged and skipped off to find my mother. I leveled another look at Eli and said, "Please tell Kate not to worry." I made a fist and wiggled my thumb at him from in between my fingers. "If unemployment doesn't work out for me, I can always become a magician. You can hire me for Rowan's next birthday."

I drove to Holly's house and sent her a text to let her know I was out front. It was nearly eleven a.m., but she'd warned me that the twins were in the midst of a sleep regression cycle, whatever that meant, and that sometimes they didn't even go to bed until four o'clock in the morning. This meant that both the twins and Holly's wife might still be asleep when we left for Timber Creek and that if we woke them up, I might not even live to regret it.

Holly opened the front door a few minutes later and an ocean of screaming and crying spilled out with her. She heaved a great sigh of relief when she slid into the passenger's seat, and I handed her a cup of coffee.

"Oh, thank baby Jesus," she said, breathing in the scent of the coffee through the plastic lid.

"What's going on in there?" I asked.

"You don't even want to know," Holly replied. "Drive fast before Christine changes her mind about letting me go."

"Your kids ought to be on a birth control commercial or something," I said. "I'm pretty sure their high-pitched shrieks would be enough for anybody to beg for the pill."

"I wish I had the energy to defend them," Holly said, closing her eyes. "Does it make me a bad person if I'd rather go to a funeral than be at home with two sleep-deprived toddlers?"

"After what I just heard, I think I'd almost rather be the one in the casket," I replied. "But seriously, thanks for coming with me. I really appreciate it."

"Well, I couldn't let you go alone . . . or with your parents."

"And I appreciate that."

Holly smiled over at me. "So, how big is this town . . . what's it called? Timber Falls?"

"No," I said with a laugh. "Timber *Creek*. My birth mother was born and raised there, I guess."

"And she never left?"

I shrugged and turned onto the interstate, yielding to a huge semitrailer with a "Honk If You Love Jesus" bumper sticker on the back. "I guess not."

"That's sad," Holly replied.

"You've never left Seattle," I reminded her. "I guess neither of us has, not to live anywhere else."

"I spent the summer in Boston after college," Holly replied thoughtfully. "That's where I met Christine."

"That was for an internship," I said. "And you came back."

"I guess you're right," Holly replied. "I guess it just seems worse when you never leave a small town as compared to a big city."

"Seems kind of judgmental to me," I teased.

"You haven't even begun to see judgmental," Holly replied. "Did you tell Alice or whatever her name is that you're coming to the funeral?"

I shook my head. "No," I said. "I found the funeral information online."

"Don't you think she'll want to know you're coming?"

"I don't know," I said. "I just . . . I wish I didn't have to do this."

"I know," Holly said. She reached out and patted my arm. "I wish you didn't have to do it either."

"It's the right thing to do, though, right?" I asked, hopeful she'd tell me I didn't have to go to this funeral and that I could turn my car around and drive right back home.

Instead, Holly nodded her head. "It's the right thing to do."

We drove the rest of the way in relative silence, listening to music and stopping once to grab snacks from a roadside convenience store. Holly looked around with some interest as we exited off the interstate and into the little town of Timber Creek.

"This isn't as bad as I thought it would be," she said as we drove down a shop-lined street. "It's kind of cute."

"What did you expect?" I asked. "Barefoot hillbillies?"

"Maybe a little," Holly replied, sounding slightly disappointed.

I rolled my eyes. "I don't know how Christine puts up with you all day."

I pulled into the parking lot of the hotel where we'd rented a room for the night. It was on the east side of town, farther out than I would have liked and sitting among what appeared to be a giant pasture of cows.

"Maybe we spoke too soon," Holly whispered.

"Be quiet."

Together we lugged in our suitcases, and I presented my ID and credit card to the bored-looking clerk. He rammed the card into the chip reader and then turned his watery eyes on me.

"Ma'am, this card doesn't appear to be working. Do you have another one you'd like me to try?"

"Uhhhh . . ." I said, trailing off in the hopes that he'd just forget about payment and let us stay in the room for free. When he did not, I continued, "Let me check."

I made a big production of rummaging around in my purse before Holly sighed and handed over her platinum Visa card. "Here," she said to him. "Just run mine."

"Thank you," I said under my breath.

"Well, it wasn't like that dude was going to accept the hairy Tic Tacs in the bottom of that gross purse of yours," Holly replied once we'd boarded the elevator. "So I figured it was pay up or sleep in the car."

I looked at her sheepishly. "I'm just flat broke right now, you know?"

"I *do* know," Holly said. "Don't worry about it."

"I'll pay you back."

"No, you won't."

"I'll buy you dinner, then," I said. "I at least have enough for that."

Holly's face brightened. "Oh, let's go find something quaint and local."

"You sound like such a hipster right now," I said, rolling my eyes.

We got into the room and flung ourselves down on one of

the beds in an exhausted heap. I don't think either of us could remember the last time we did so much driving, and neither one of us was particularly good at it.

Holly scrolled listlessly through her phone. "There doesn't seem to be anything that great that I can find," she said. "Maybe we should just get back in the car and drive around until we find someplace that looks good."

"That's fine," I replied, rolling myself off the bed.

"I'm going to shower," Holly said. She looked me up and down and made a face that told me under no circumstances was I dressed appropriately.

"What?"

"You might want to consider changing," she replied. "And brushing your hair too."

"Gee, thanks."

"You can borrow my flat iron. It's in my bag," she called over her shoulder as she disappeared into the bathroom.

I sighed and sat back down on the bed. I had two missed calls from my father, so I called him back. He answered on the first ring.

"Maeve! Are you safe in Timber Creek?" he asked.

"Yes," I replied. "I sent Mom a text. I guess she forgot to tell you."

"Sounds about right," he replied. "She's at her bridge club meeting anyway."

"I'm sure she can't wait to tell everyone about her near-death experience with the pork chops," I said dryly.

My father ignored this and replied, "How was the drive? Is the hotel nice?"

"It was fine, and the hotel is fine," I said.

"You sound tired."

"I am," I admitted.

"And maybe a little nervous about the funeral tomorrow?" he asked.

I nodded into the phone, even though my father couldn't see me, feeling as though I might start to cry. I felt homesick. This was ridiculous. I wasn't a kid at sleepaway camp for the first time. I'd been in Timber Creek all of an hour, and I was a thirty-six-year-old adult, for Christ's sake.

"Mae?"

"Hmm? Oh, I'm fine. Yeah, nervous. I feel weird about this whole thing. I didn't even know her, Dad, and she made it pretty clear she had no interest in knowing me."

"Don't say that, kiddo," he replied.

I smiled just a little then, because I loved it when my father called me *kiddo*. "You know just as well as I do," I began, "that she made it clear. You don't have to pretend she didn't."

"There is nothing easy about this situation," my father replied. "I wish I could make it go away for you, but I can't."

"I know," I said.

"I think you're doing a good thing," he continued. "Try to relax tonight with Holly, and then we'll see you tomorrow evening."

"Relax with Holly?" I asked. "Are we even talking about the same person?"

"I did say 'try,'" my father replied. "Call me tomorrow?"

"I will," I said. "Love you, Dad."

"Love you too, kiddo."

I put the phone on the nightstand between the two queen-sized beds and plugged my charger into the lamp. I'd always wondered why regular lamps didn't come with a plug-in—it seemed like there would be a market for that in homes and not just hotel rooms. I hit my head nearly every morning bending over to unplug my charger from the wall. Then again, maybe everyone else wasn't as clumsy as I was, and there was probably some sort of hotel catalog that only hotel owners were allowed to get and buy from . . .

"What are you doing?"

I looked up to see Holly standing in the doorway of the bathroom, wrapped in a towel, staring at me.

"Oh," I said, looking back down at the lamp. "Just charging my phone."

She raised an eyebrow. "You haven't even plugged it in."

I fumbled with my phone, and Holly came to sit down next to me. Her wet hair dripped down onto my jeans, and I playfully pushed her away from me. "You're dripping on me," I said.

"Oh, sorry." She scooted away. "Listen, you know, I didn't mean what I said before. You *don't* have to do this if you don't want to. We can check out of the hotel room right now, drive back to Seattle, and nobody will know any better."

I shook my head. "No, you were right. I do need to do this.

I'm sorry for being such a downer. Let's get dressed and go find a place to eat."

After a quick chat with the desk clerk and Holly's very firm insistence that she needed a beer, the clerk suggested we head downtown to a bar called Three Sheets. We giggled for a minute over the name and then checked our makeup in the mirror before going inside.

The bar was jam-packed, but we managed to squeeze ourselves onto two rickety and suspiciously damp bar stools.

"It's like 1980 came in here to die," Holly whispered to me, and then, because I couldn't hear her, yelled, "IT'S LIKE 1980 CAME IN HERE TO DIE."

She was right. From my perch at the bar, I surveyed the room. The decor was quaint, if not a little dated. All the tables boasted plaid tablecloths. The walls were wood paneled and there was at least one elk or deer head on each of them. There were pool tables in the back, and somewhere there was a jukebox playing Bruce Springsteen's greatest hits.

An overworked barmaid appeared behind the bar and handed us laminated menus without looking at us and said, "What can I get ya to drink?"

"What do you have on tap?" I asked.

The barmaid rolled her eyes to the back of her head and said, "Uh, ya know, the usual stuff."

"Like?"

When she rolled her eyes again, I said hastily, "Just give me whatever light beer you have on tap."

"Great," she replied. "And for your friend?"

Holly leveled her with a stare she usually reserved for her twins. "What do you have on tap?"

The barmaid heaved a sigh and began to recite the list, including some local microbrews. Holly gave her choice, and after I'd changed my order to match hers, we gave her our food order. She rolled her eyes once again when Holly requested her bun be gluten free.

"We don't have that shit here," she said. "I can give ya a hamburger patty with no bun or you can take the gluten."

I was surprised when she didn't finish that sentence with *and shove it up your ass.*

"Fine," Holly said. "I'll just take the burger on the regular bun."

All around us, people were laughing and drinking and eating. Waitresses came out with plates of food, and nothing on any of them looked short of amazing. Most of the people there were in groups of at least four, with a few couples taking up some of the smaller tables in the middle of the room. In the corner at the back of the bar was a man sitting alone. He had shaggy dark hair and a beard. His eyes were every bit as dark as his hair. Tattoos spilled out down one arm past the sleeve of his red flannel shirt. But what stood out the most was the man's sheer size. He looked like some kind of lost lumberjack.

He poured himself a glass of beer from the nearly empty pitcher sitting on the table. He was getting plenty of attention from more than one waitress, and I could understand why. He stood out not only because of his size but because he was devastatingly beautiful. There were plenty of good-looking men in Seattle. Every bar was full of eligible men doing their best to impress a potential mate, but for the life of me, I couldn't think of a single one I'd ever seen that compared to him. I couldn't tear my eyes away.

Every once in a while, he'd look up from his beer and scan the room. The third time he looked up, he caught me staring at him. He held my gaze for a few seconds before I thought to be embarrassed and focused my attention elsewhere.

"Who is that?" Holly asked, taking a drink of her beer that had been put in front of her and cutting her eyes toward the man at the back of the room. "He looks familiar."

"He does?" I asked. "Not to me."

"Are you sure?" Holly squinted her eyes and peered at him, her thick eyelashes nearly touching from top to bottom. "Oh my God," she said, burying her head in her shoulder. "He caught me staring."

"He caught me too," I admitted. "He doesn't look very friendly. Let's try not to make an enemy on the very first night."

"I'm going to go to the bathroom," Holly said, jumping up from the stool. "Hopefully I won't get herpes from the toilet seat."

"You don't get herpes from a toilet seat," I said to her. "You're a scientist. You know that."

"I know that this place looks like the bathroom is probably

disgusting," Holly muttered. "But I drank that beer too fast, and now I have to pee."

"Don't hover!" I yelled after her, and a couple of people stared at me with odd expressions on their faces before turning back to their conversations.

The door at the front of the bar swung open, letting in a rush of cold evening air, and in marched a woman in a tube top and what could only be described as pants designed to look like each of the woman's long, thin legs were snakes shedding their skin.

She stopped as the door closed, crossing her arms over her chest and glancing around the room. After a few moments, her eyes settled on someone behind me. She brushed past me, focused intently on the table right smack-dab in the middle of the room, where a man was leaning into a dark-haired woman wearing giant hoop earrings. Without either the man or the other woman noticing, the woman in the tube top grabbed a full pitcher of beer from the table next to them and proceeded to pour it over the head of the woman wearing hoop earrings.

Hoop Earrings stood up, gasping and sputtering. For a few tense seconds as the women faced each other, I thought I was going to witness a fistfight. Instead, Hoop Earrings let out a shriek and stormed off, prompting Tube Top to call after her, "I told you to back off, Leeann!"

"You bitch!" the man at the table hissed, standing up. "You fucking bitch!"

Tube Top turned to match his glare and said, "You better go pay your tab, Ronnie. Before Leeann's hair freezes outside and it starts to break off in little clumps."

Ronnie seemed torn between continuing his tirade against Tube Top and chasing after Leeann. Leveling another glare at Tube Top, he chased after Leann, calling her name over and over as he ran.

Tube Top turned to the couple she'd stolen the beer from, smiled, and said, "I sure am sorry about that. Let me get you two another pitcher."

She ambled up to the bar and stood next to where I was sitting. She nodded her head at the barmaid and pointed to the table where the couple was sitting. The barmaid sighed, rolled her eyes, and nodded.

I looked around for Holly, but when I found no sight of her, I tried to concentrate on the plate of food that had just been delivered to me. I was starving. I picked up a sweet potato fry and stuck it into my mouth and tried not to moan with pleasure.

Tube Top turned around to face me. Her sparkly eye shadow glinted from the bar lights. "Hey," she said. "Do I know you?"

I tried to chew and shake my head at the same time. "No," I replied, swallowing. "I don't think so."

She furrowed her drawn-on eyebrows. "I swear, I know you from somewhere."

"I don't know how," I said. "I've never been here in my life before today."

"You sure?"

"Pretty sure." I picked up my burger and took a bite. I wished she'd just leave me alone and let me eat in peace.

"I've got it!" Tube Top said, slamming her hand down onto the countertop. "You look like this woman who used to come into the gas station where I work. Oh, what was her name? She had all these cats. . . . What was her name? . . . What was her name?"

I set my burger down. "Annabelle?" I asked.

"Yes! That's her! How did you know?"

"She was my mother."

Tube Top pulled her head back, eyeing me. "Annabelle didn't have any kids," she said.

"She was my birth mother," I replied. "I was adopted as an infant."

"Oh shit," Tube Top replied. "I'm sorry. I didn't know that."

"I don't think most people did," I said. "It's fine. She died and that's why I'm here."

"I read her obituary in the paper, and it didn't mention you," she replied. "I have to work tomorrow, or I'd go to her funeral."

I stuffed another fry into my mouth, because I wasn't sure how to respond. They were quite possibly the best fries I'd ever eaten, but I'd lost my appetite.

"I'm Charlene, by the way," she said. She stuck out her hand.

"Oh, it's nice to meet you," I replied. "I'm Maeve."

"That's a weird name."

"Most people call me Mae," I said.

"I don't really have any room to talk," Charlene, formerly Tube Top, replied. "My middle name is Lucretia."

"Family name?" I asked.

Charlene nodded. "It was my grandmother's."

"Maeve was my grandmother's," I said. "On my dad's side. My middle name is Eileen. That was my grandmother on my mother's side."

"When you say your mother and father," Charlene said, "you mean the people who adopted you?"

"Yes," I replied. "I don't refer to them as my adoptive parents. They're just my parents."

"Of course," Charlene replied. "I'm being rude, aren't I? I've been told I don't have a filter."

"I've been told the same thing once or twice," I said. "Don't worry. It's really okay."

"I bet the ladies of St. Francis can't wait to get their hands on you," Charlene said, eyeing me.

"What?" I held a french fry in midair and stared at her. "Who are the ladies of St. Francis?"

Charlene let out a throaty laugh and replied, "Girl, you really don't know anything, do you?"

I was about to reply with a question about whether these ladies of St. Francis were some kind of convent or a cult or something when the man I'd heard referred to as Ronnie came hurrying back into the bar, snaking his way around the tables toward Charlene. I braced myself for what was surely about to take place.

"Hey, doll," Ronnie said, embracing Charlene. "Thanks for tonight. It was your best ever."

"You're welcome," Charlene replied, giving him a sly wink.

He pulled back and pressed a crisp hundred-dollar bill into the palm of Charlene's hand. "Same time next month?"

Charlene smiled. "You got it."

"I better get back out to Leeann," Ronnie said. "She was all over me in the car. I don't even know if we'll make it home."

Charlene watched him go and then placed the folded-up bill into her bra. When she looked over at me, I realized I'd forgotten to chew, the chunk of hamburger stuck in my cheek, like a chipmunk preparing for winter hibernation.

"I gotta tell ya, I wasn't sure if I could pull that one off tonight," Charlene said, shaking her head. "I was afraid Leeann would deck me for real this time."

I chewed up the mass of burger and washed it down with several gulps of beer. "What . . . just happened?" I asked.

"Oh, that's right," Charlene replied. "I forgot you're new in town."

I wondered how being new in town could possibly be an excuse for not comprehending what I'd just witnessed. "You pour beer over unsuspecting women's heads for money on a regular basis?"

"That's Ronnie and Leeann Parrish. They've been paying me a hundred dollars every month for the last four years to pretend like Ronnie is my husband, and I've just caught him cheating on me with Leeann," Charlene said. "Gets Leeann real hot, and it gets me another deposit into my dream vacation account. Saved up almost five grand. This time next year, I'll be sittin' on a beach somewhere with a drink in my hand while the rest of these suckers bundle up for winter."

"I don't even know how to respond to that," I said. "But good for you, I guess."

"Rich people are a bunch of weirdos," Charlene continued. "Leeann and Ronnie live up there in that fancy gated community. He's some sort of big-time real estate developer, and she's the principal at the only private school in town. They come down here to Three Sheets, because they don't think anybody will recognize them." Charlene leaned in closer to me, her voice just above a whisper. "It's the worst kept secret in town. Even if us working-class folks were too stupid to know who they were, their damn handyman is sittin' over there in the back, drinkin' five-dollar pitchers." She rolled her eyes.

I followed Charlene's gaze over to the man who'd caught me staring at him when I first entered the bar. "Yeah, I noticed him earlier," I said. "What's his deal?"

Charlene let out a snort. "What, you don't realize it when you're in the presence of greatness?"

"A great handyman?" I asked. I knitted my eyebrows together. "What are you talking about?" I asked.

"Girl, that's Abel Abbott," Charlene replied.

"Who?"

Now it was Charlene's turn to stare at me. "Abel . . . Abbott," she said, this time more slowly. "You know, *the* Abel Abbott."

I could feel my face light up with recognition. "Abel the Adventurer?"

Charlene nodded with satisfaction. "That's him, all right. Of course, I don't know if you could call him much of an adventurer anymore. He hasn't gone on an adventure or written about a damn adventure in years," she said. "Where's he gonna go on an adventure in Timber Creek?"

"So . . . he's not a handyman?"

Charlene laughed. It was a loud, infectious laugh. "I ain't got the time it takes to explain that mess to you," she said. "Suffice it to say that he hung up that adventure thing and picked up a hammer years ago. Now he likes to pretend he's just normal folk like the rest of us, but he owns damn near half the town."

I tried not to look over at him, but I couldn't help myself. I couldn't believe someone like Abel Abbott was living in Timber Creek. Granted, I didn't know much about him. Most of my knowledge came from the back covers of books sitting on my father's and brother's bookshelves. He was a modern-day mountain man, which I guessed wasn't far off from my original assessment of a lost lumberjack. He'd written several manly, outdoorsy-type books that men in cities read to make themselves feel like they were climbing Mount Everest. He wrote how-to books for would-be outdoorsmen, despite the fact that his core audience had probably never even been camping. Several years ago, while my brother was still in dental school, he'd all but skipped an important exam to go to a reading and book signing when Abel Abbott was at a Seattle Barnes & Noble.

Eli kept the signed book in his office, and it was one of the first things anybody saw when walking in for a consultation.

"He lives here?" I asked. "Like, right here in Timber Creek?"

Charlene nodded and pointed to Holly's untouched burger. "You gonna eat that?"

"I am," came a voice from behind us, and we both turned to see Holly standing there, her hands on her hips. "Sorry I got caught up," she said. "Christine couldn't get the girls to sleep, and so I had to sing to them."

Charlene looked Holly up and down, and I thought for a moment she was going to eat Holly's food anyway. Instead she jumped down off the stool and gave us both a nod, then disappeared into hazy smoke and noise.

"What did I miss?" Holly asked, staring after Charlene. "Seriously, did time stop in this town?"

"I'm not even sure I can explain it," I said.

In the corner, Abel Abbott stood up. He didn't even look in our direction as he paid his tab, despite the fact that Charlene had kept on talking about him loud enough for him to hear. It seemed as if every woman in the bar swiveled her head around to watch him go.

"Oh my God," Holly said, poking me in the side. "I know who that is! I know who that is!"

"Shhhhh," I hissed at her.

"It's Abel Abbottttttt," she continued, ignoring me. "Mae, it's Abel Abbott!"

For a moment his eyes rested on me as he moved past us, a

mix of amusement and surprise settling on what I assumed was normally his very serious face.

"He heard you," I said to Holly as soon as he was gone.

Holly shrugged and picked up her burger, taking a giant bite. "Well," she said, once she was done chewing. "This sure has been an interesting night."

I found myself wondering what kind of a town harbors famous writers, secret societies named after saints, and people so rich that they'd pay someone for foreplay, and how, exactly, I'd managed to land myself right smack-dab in the big middle of it.

ANNABELLE

April 1984

A NNABELLE WATCHED ALICE SLEEPING. SHE'D FALLEN
asleep sitting up, slumped near a family-sized bag of Doritos and several empty cans of Tab. It amazed Annabelle the way
her friend could fall asleep nearly anywhere, in any position.
She'd once fallen asleep in gym class using a basketball as a pillow.

Annabelle had never been that way, and she envied it. In
fact, she'd had trouble going to sleep at night for the last three
years since her parents died. She was sure anyone else would
say it was trauma from losing her parents, and they were right,
but it was partly because she missed her bedroom with her little
twin-sized bed. Like most people in their neighborhood, her
parents hadn't had much by way of money, but what they did
have, they spent trying to keep their only child happy and com-

fortable. Losing her parents had been the hardest thing Annabelle had ever had to endure, and she often thought that if she could just go back to that cozy bedroom, everything would be better somehow.

Knowing that her old house, her old bedroom, were right across the street from the ramshackle, dingy, cramped quarters where she lived now with Alice and her family made that thought nearly impossible to bear.

"Anna?"

Annabelle turned from her thoughts to see Billy standing behind her, a beer in each hand. "Hey," she said, standing up, making sure not to disturb Alice, who was quietly snoring.

"You, uh, want a beer?" Billy asked. He held one out to her.

Annabelle shrugged. She didn't really like to drink, but it sounded better than anything else. "Sure," she said.

"I rented a VCR after work," Billy said, motioning her over to the worn-out love seat. He'd gotten it secondhand from a woman at the factory, and the arms were duct-taped, but it was comfortable. "Have you seen *Trading Places* yet?"

"No," Annabelle said. She sat down beside Billy, suddenly very aware of how close they were. "What's it about?"

"It's about these two guys who trade lives with each other," Billy replied. "One of them is rich and the other one is poor. It's got Dan Aykroyd and Eddie Murphy in it."

"Sounds good," Annabelle said.

"There's leftover pizza in the fridge too," Billy replied. "Sorry, I don't really keep much in the house."

"It's fine," Annabelle said. "I'm not that hungry. We've been eating junk all day." She popped the top on the can of beer. "Alice didn't think you'd be home at all tonight. Are you sure it's okay for us to stay?"

"I don't mind," Billy said, turning to look at her. His dark eyes locked with hers. "I don't mind the company."

"She thought maybe you had a date."

"No, that's over."

When he didn't elaborate, Annabelle turned her attention to the television set, which was, she noticed, entirely too nice for the rest of the house.

"I didn't steal it, if that's what you're thinking," Billy said.

"I wasn't thinking that," Annabelle said, even though she had, in fact, been thinking that a little bit.

"I'm a drug addict, not a thief," Billy replied, a half smile forming on his face.

"Don't drug addicts turn into thieves sometimes?" Annabelle asked.

"Sometimes," Billy admitted. "But I don't use anymore."

"I know."

"People still talk about it, though, don't they?" Billy asked.

"Not to me or Alice," Annabelle said honestly. "Alice would punch anyone in the face who talks bad about you, even though she says she hates you."

"The girl I was dating?" Billy asked. "Lorna Ferrar—do you know her?"

"A little bit," Annabelle replied. "Her dad's the manager of the grocery store where your mom works, right?"

Billy nodded. "He hates me."

"Is that why you aren't dating her anymore?"

"She didn't really like me," Billy said. "She liked making her daddy mad."

Annabelle rolled her eyes. "She's a bitch anyway."

Billy laughed. "I couldn't have said it better myself."

From the couch, Alice let out a snore so loud she nearly woke herself up, and Billy and Annabelle had to stifle their laughter.

"She snores like a freight train," Annabelle whispered.

"She's always been that way," Billy replied. "Mom used to come into the bedroom and hold her nose until she woke up."

"She still does that," Annabelle said, grinning.

"What about you?" Billy asked. "Mom and Pop treating you okay?"

"I don't hate it," Annabelle said.

"But you don't like it either."

"It's just different," Annabelle replied. "It's not awful. It's a lot better than the foster home I could be in, I know that." She looked down at her hands and then ventured a glance up at Billy. "It's just that some days I'm afraid . . . I'm afraid that this is all there is now, and I'm starting to forget what my life was like . . . before."

"I'm sorry about your parents," Billy said. He reached into his shirt pocket and pulled out a cigarette.

"It's okay."

Billy pulled the cigarette away from his lips and said, "It's not okay."

"No," Annabelle said. "But I keep hoping someday it will be."

Annabelle thought that Billy was reaching for his lighter, but instead he placed his big hand on top of her little one and said, "Life can be shit sometimes."

Annabelle nodded, furiously trying to blink away a tear that was threatening to roll down her cheek. It'd been such a long time since she cried. There just didn't seem to be a point to crying, not anymore. But here, in the quiet and safety of Billy's house, his warmth, she couldn't stop herself.

"Hey," he said, sidling closer to her. "Hey now, don't cry." He released his hand from hers and wiped away the wetness with his thumb.

His kindness only made it worse, and Annabelle found herself sobbing into him, each tear more painful than the last, until she was left exhausted and depleted, gasping onto his shoulder while he held her.

When she finally pulled away from him, his shirt was wet, and Annabelle was embarrassed. "I'm so sorry," she said, realizing her voice had gone hoarse. "I didn't mean to . . ."

"Seems like you needed it," Billy replied, his half smile returning. "It's all right. I don't mind."

"I guess I did."

Billy got up and turned the volume higher on the television set and then sat back down. He leaned back against the couch and then slowly, deliberately, pulled Annabelle toward him until her head was against his chest. He didn't say anything to her, and Annabelle didn't want to break the spell they both seemed to be under by speaking, and so she just relaxed against him, breathing his scent until she felt her eyes grow heavy and the world around them disappeared.

It was the banging outside the door that woke her up. It woke all of them up, and Alice jumped up out of a near coma, her eyes wild and hair tangled.

"What in the hell is that?" she asked.

"It's the door," Billy said, groggy. He lifted Annabelle off him and stood up. "It's probably Aaron. I told him to stop by, and he always seems to think that means two a.m."

Alice groaned and lay back down. "Tell him to go away."

The banging continued, even after Billy told whoever was at the door to "Shut the hell up."

Before he could even unlock it, the door was flung open, and the figure of Alice and Billy's father stood before them, furious and gasping. "Where are the girls?" he demanded, stepping over the threshold and into the house. *Where are they?*

Alice jumped up, knocking chips and soda everywhere. "Dad!"

William shifted his eyes from Billy to Alice and then finally settled on Annabelle, who'd yet to get up off the couch. "Get up," he said to her. "Get up right now. We're leaving."

Annabelle stood up, slightly wobbly on her feet, and looked at Billy, whose face had gone from confused to furious in a matter of seconds. "Okay," she said, tearing her eyes away from him to look at his father. "Okay."

"What are you doing here?" Billy asked, refusing to step out of his father's way. "I thought I told you not to show up here."

This time it was William's turn to wobble, and Annabelle realized with frightening clarity that he must be drunk. Of course he was. He was drunk every night by nine p.m., which was why she and Alice thought he wouldn't notice if they didn't turn up at home after dark.

William pointed a finger at Billy, landing it squarely in the middle of the younger man's chest. "Don't you fucking tell me where I can and cannot go," he snarled.

"You're drunk," Billy said matter-of-factly.

William ignored his son and moved past him to Alice. He grabbed her by the arm and pulled her forward before she could get ahold of her cane, which had been a present from her mother, a frivolous expense in her father's eyes, and she stumbled forward, crashing to the cracked linoleum floor on her knees.

Alice let out a sob, and Annabelle could see blood. William turned away from Alice, disgust written on his face, and focused his attention on Annabelle. Before he could get to her, though, Billy launched himself between them.

For a moment, it looked like they might come to blows, and neither one of them spoke. Then William pasted a smile across his skeletal face and said, "I'd rethink whatever it is you're considering, unless you want your PO to know that you've been supplying alcohol to minors." He inclined his head to the empty beer cans. "You'll be back in prison by tomorrow."

The last part of William's sentence ran together so much that Annabelle wasn't exactly sure what he'd said, but she understood what he'd meant. Gently, she touched Billy's arm, squeezing it slightly, and stepped around him. "Why don't you go wait in the car?" she asked William. "I'll get Alice, and we'll be right there."

William glanced from Annabelle to Alice and then back again, his eyes focusing and refocusing on Annabelle. "Hurry up," he said, and wound his way around his daughter, sprawled on the floor, and out of the house.

Wordlessly, Annabelle and Billy helped Alice up, leading her outside into the frosty, early morning air. Together they folded Alice into the back seat; she was still whimpering, but it was softer now, and Annabelle thought that she would probably be all right enough to walk by the time they got home.

As Annabelle moved to slide in beside Alice, Billy held on to her hand, and for a moment their fingers interlocked. "I'll find you this weekend," he whispered.

Annabelle nodded, willing Billy not to let go of her. She wanted to stay right there with him. She didn't want to get into the car with Billy's drunk father.

"Come get in the front," William said to her, rolling down his window to glare at Billy further, and Billy released his hold on Annabelle and disappeared back into his house, leaving Annabelle alone with the older man.

The drive back was mostly quiet. Alice kept to herself in

the back seat, and Annabelle thought she'd maybe even fallen asleep again. A light mist had begun, and William switched on the windshield wipers and then the radio as he rounded the corner to their neighborhood—the kind of neighborhood where the streetlights often went out and the city often forgot about fixing them.

William, in his unsteady way, said, "I missed you at dinner tonight."

Annabelle sucked in air. She didn't like the way he always paid more attention to her than to Alice. She wasn't his daughter. His daughter, in fact, was broken in the back seat because of him, because he'd pulled on her too hard knowing she wasn't all that steady on her feet to begin with. Then he'd left her on the floor to mop herself up. It was his typical way. If he wasn't ignoring his children, he was being cruel to them.

But never, it seemed, to Annabelle. He was always kind to her. He always paid special attention to her.

"We didn't mean to stay out so late," Annabelle lied. "We fell asleep, that's all."

"You didn't look like you were asleep," William countered, slowing the car down to a near crawl. "It looked like you and Billy were pretty cozy there on the couch."

"We were just watching a movie."

William sniffed. "My son is no good. I don't like saying it, but it's true."

Annabelle doubted very much that he hated saying it. "He's doing okay."

"You're young," William replied. "You'll find out soon enough, the way it works."

Annabelle didn't respond. There wasn't any point in arguing, she knew, but she felt like she'd seen enough in her seventeen years—more than enough—to know how the world worked.

"What you need," William continued, "is a real man to take care of you."

He reached out and stroked her shoulder with his thumb and index finger, and Annabelle had to will herself not to flinch as he moved his hand down her arm and laid his palm flat against her thigh.

Annabelle tried to stare very hard at the road in front of them, at the yellow lines bisecting the pavement. If she just concentrated on what was in front of her, they could get home, and she could forget about what was happening. She was afraid to shrug him off, afraid that a commotion might wake Alice, and she'd see. She was afraid, God help her, that if she reacted, he'd set his sights on her in a different way, and she didn't want his cruel attention any more than she wanted *this* attention.

After what felt like an hour, William removed his hand to place it on the steering wheel when he turned in to the driveway, and Annabelle shut her eyes until he was out of the car, leaving both girls to get inside on their own. She sat there for a long time, listening to nothing at all and staring at the front porch until the light went off, until it was safe to go inside.

Chapter 6

Holly woke up before I did the next morning, and when I finally rolled over to turn off the alarm I'd set on my phone, I found a bagel and a glass of orange juice waiting for me on the nightstand.

I sat up and rubbed at my eyes. "How long have you been awake?" I asked.

Holly shrugged. "A couple of hours. I had some work emails to respond to."

I took a drink of the orange juice and got a mouthful of pulp. I swallowed and said, "Thanks for getting me breakfast."

"The continental breakfast isn't very continental," Holly replied. "Powdered eggs and some sad-looking bacon. But the bagels seemed fresh."

"Aren't you going to eat?"

"I had an energy bar in my purse."

Holly was looking at me anxiously, blowing the bangs of her pixie cut out of her eyes, her bottom lip jutting out over her top lip.

"What is it?" I asked. "You're making me nervous just sitting there staring at me. I promise I'll be okay today. I won't fall apart on you during the funeral, if that's what you're worried about."

"It's not that," Holly replied. "I got a call from Christine early this morning."

"Is she all right?" I asked, panic rising in my throat. "Are the kids okay?"

"Everyone's fine," Holly said. "Except that Cora has a stomach flu, and that means Carley is bound to get it. Christine's mother got called into work, and that means Christine doesn't have any help. Two puking kids when you're all alone is an absolutely miserable existence, in case you were wondering."

I wrinkled up my nose at the thought of vomit but tried to make my face look as sympathetic as possible. I loved my niece and nephew, and I loved Holly's kids. But I didn't want to be the one responsible for them 24/7. I was perfectly happy being the "fun" aunt. Why anyone thought having kids of their own was a good idea was beyond me.

"Anyway," Holly continued, "I really need to get back to the city. I know I was supposed to go to the funeral, and I feel just awful for bailing on you, but it'll take me nearly four hours to get back as it is."

I nodded my head and swallowed thickly. I'd be lying if I said I didn't mind going to the funeral by myself, but I knew that was exactly what I was going to have to do—lie. It wasn't Holly's fault. It really wasn't.

"It's fine," I said. "Really, it's no big deal. But how are you going to get home? I need my car."

"I had the guy at the front desk order me a rental," Holly replied, slightly shamefaced. "Are you sure you're going to be okay?"

"Of course," I said. "I'll be fine. I won't know anybody anyway. Nobody will recognize me as the illegitimate daughter of the deceased."

"Don't say that," Holly scolded.

"Just go," I said, urging her up. "Get on the road right now, while it's still early."

"I booked the room for another night," Holly said, giving me a quick hug. "Just in case you're too tired to drive back by yourself afterward."

"You didn't have to do that," I said.

"It's the least I can do for leaving you in the lurch," Holly replied. "Besides, it'll be almost dark by the time the funeral and burial are over. I know how much you hate to drive in the dark."

It was true. My night vision was terrible, and I lived in fear of road construction on the interstate. I sometimes had actual nightmares about running over orange cones that sent me flying into the opposite lane of traffic.

"Thanks," I said. "Text me when you're back safe."

"I will," Holly said. She slung her vintage Louis Vuitton Keepall over her shoulder, the one I coveted and made her promise to will to me upon her death, which at that moment, now that I thought about it, seemed pretty morbid. "And you text me after the service."

"I will."

The door slammed, and I slumped back down into the bed. The mattress was some kind of squishy memory foam, and it made me want to snuggle down and just stay there all day. I realized that I could do just that, if I wanted to, with Holly gone and unable to keep tabs on me. I could order room service and stay in the fluffy bathrobe all day long. I could even rent an expensive in-room movie and charge it to Holly's account. She'd feel so guilty about leaving me that she wouldn't even mention it.

I brought my knees up to my chest and hugged them, feeling guilty for having those thoughts at all. I'd come to Timber Creek for one thing, and one thing only—to go to my birth mother's funeral so that I could finally get the closure everyone else thought I needed. I was a terrible liar. They'd all know if I skipped out.

Besides, I told myself. *It's just for a couple of hours. Nobody here will even know who I am. What's the very worst that could happen?*

I parked just up the street from the church in a bank parking lot. I wanted to make as little an entrance as possible, and I thought maybe I could walk in unnoticed this way. To be honest, I was a little relieved that Holly wasn't with me. It would be easier to blend in. All I had to do was get through the service, and then I could go back to Seattle with my conscience clear.

Simple.

My black combat boots made a pleasant *thunk, thunk, thunk* as I made my way down the street. I'd thought the ensemble I'd picked looked like appropriate funeral attire—black dress, black tights, and black boots. I'd gotten them on sale at the closeout of a store downtown that was a pretty epic rip-off of a 1990s-era Delia's. I'd spent two hours trying on clothes and come home with this outfit and my last credit card absolutely maxed out. My mother, of course, told me I looked like I was headed to the woods for a human sacrifice under the new moon, but I'd ignored her. That morning, however, standing in front of the full-length mirror in the hotel bathroom, I realized she was right. Of course, by then it was too late, and it was either the witch costume or jeans and a wrinkled T-shirt.

Nobody seemed to take too much notice of me, and I managed to get inside the doors without making eye contact with anyone. A woman in cat's-eye glasses and short, spiky red hair handed me a program, and I settled into a chair in the back without looking at the piece of paper in my hand. For a brief moment, I wished that Holly were here to make some bad joke about the people in this town dressing like hillbillies or something to make me laugh. People streamed in slow and steady, and before I knew it, the back row was full and so was the rest of the room.

Eventually a man came to the front of the room, and he started to talk about Annabelle—about what a kind person she'd been and how everyone in the community would miss her. The woman sitting next to me was sniffling, and the man she was with handed her a tissue and patted her leg. I knew that all of this was normal—it was a funeral, after all. The preacher was *supposed* to talk about the dead person like they were Mother Teresa. The people in attendance were *supposed* to cry and be sad. But I couldn't help feeling like the outsider I was: the interloper at an intimate gathering for a celebration of a life well-lived—a life I hadn't been, and now never would be, a part of.

I looked down at the paper in my hand. It was folded into a small square and had a black-and-white photo of Annabelle on the front. She was older than she'd been in the picture my father kept in his drawer, but not as old as she had to have been when she died—thirty, maybe? She was standing beside another woman and grinning into the camera, and she was wearing a baseball cap and holding a huge fish.

She looked happy.

At the end of the service, everyone stood up and sang a hymn posted on the back of the paper with Annabelle's photo. I wasn't much for hymns—my parents were lapsed Catholics who pretty much only went to church on Easter and Christmas, but I gave it my best shot. The pallbearers picked up the casket and carried it down the aisle. The casket was pink, and it had little roses cascading down one side, and the woman next to me whispered, "That looks just like Annabelle," and the man next to her had to give her another tissue.

Bringing up the rear was a face I recognized—the only one I recognized in the whole place: that of the great big hulking Abel Abbott, and when I caught his eyes as he moved past me with the rest of the pallbearers, there was such a look of abject grief in his eyes that I almost burst into tears right there. I wondered how he knew Annabelle. I wondered if he knew who I was, and I wondered, too, why looking into his eyes made me feel the way it did.

CHAPTER 7

I WASN'T SURE WHAT TO DO AFTER THE SERVICE. JUST AS I'D hoped, it seemed like I'd slipped in without being noticed by anyone, except maybe Abel Abbott. But he didn't know me anyway, so that didn't really matter. Still, it felt rude to just leave. There wasn't going to be a graveside, and so people were queuing to hug and greet the family, talking among themselves. There had been something mentioned about a gathering afterward, but I didn't know where it was, and I didn't think I wanted to go to that anyway.

I didn't know what I was waiting for. I hadn't told Alice I was coming, and she was probably the only other person besides Annabelle in Timber Creek who knew I existed. It was petulant, I scolded myself, to be upset that nobody seemed to care that I was there.

Keeping my head down, I moved past the groups of people,

past the tearful woman and the man with the tissues, and to the front door. The cool September air hit me in the face, and I took a big gulp. I'd done it. It was over.

I had my hand on my car door handle when I heard someone calling my name from the direction of the church.

"Maeve? Maeve!"

I looked up, surprised. A woman was running, well, hurrying, toward me. She was a little bit of a person with a mass of bouncy graying curls and a heart-shaped face. She was waving at me with one hand and with the other clutching a thick black cane that touched the ground at the same time as her left leg, which seemed to be a couple of inches shorter than the right.

I arranged my face into a smile and said, "Yes?"

"You're Maeve Stephens, right?" she asked, puffing out bits of air and trying to catch her breath.

"I am," I said. "Are you . . . are you Alice?"

She nodded, and then seemed to wobble on her feet. I put out my hand automatically to help steady her, and she took it, closing her eyes for just a moment.

"Thanks," she said. "My days of Olympic sprinting are over."

I bit my lip to keep from laughing.

"It was a joke, kiddo," she said. She let go of my hand and thumped her cane on the ground. "Obviously."

I started to tell her that I was sorry for not telling her I was coming at the same time she started to tell me thank you for coming, and our words got jumbled up together and an awkward silence ensued.

"Thank you for telling me about the funeral," I said finally.

"Annabelle would have wanted you to know," Alice replied.

I nodded, because I didn't know what to say. I wasn't sure how knowing that my birth mother was dead did me any favors—I mean, I hadn't known her in life, and that wasn't for lack of trying. But that wasn't Alice's fault, and I doubt she was prepared for me to word vomit all my emotional baggage onto her.

"Are you leaving?" Alice asked. "There's a gathering at a friend's house starting about now. We'd love for you to come."

"We?"

"Yes," Alice said, smiling. "It's not far from here. Just a few streets over."

"Thank you," I said, returning her smile. "But it's a four-hour drive back to Seattle, and I should really get on the road."

"You're leaving tonight?"

"I planned on it."

Alice furrowed her brow. "Has anybody else from Timber Creek contacted you?"

"No," I replied. "Why would they?"

"It would just really mean a lot if you could come by for a little bit," Alice continued. "I don't want to put any pressure on you or anything, but it would just be so nice."

I sighed inwardly. But hadn't this been what I'd secretly wanted? And anyway, Holly *had* paid for another night at the hotel. I'd hate for her to waste money. It wasn't like I had a job or anything else pressing to get back to . . .

"Maeve?"

"What?" I broke out of my thoughts and looked over at Alice's expectant face. "Oh, okay," I said. "Yes. I'd love to go."

"Wonderful!" Alice exclaimed. "You can follow me. I'm just parked over there."

I followed her gaze to a slightly rusted 1980s model Volvo station wagon. What was left of the color was yellow, and the back bumper and back glass were absolutely filled with bumper stickers that said things like: "Knit Happens" and "Friends Don't Let Friends Knit and Drive" and a picture of a ball of yarn with "I Like Big Balls" written underneath it.

When Alice caught me staring, she said, "Some people love politics or the fact that their kid is an honors student. Me? Well, I love to knit."

"I can't even sew," I admitted.

Alice patted my arm and then headed off toward her car. "Don't worry," she called over her shoulder. "You can always learn."

ANNABELLE

April 1984

I'M NEVER GOING TO GET THIS," ALICE SAID, EXASPERATED. She held up her naked knitting needles and made a cross with them. "Be gone, Satan!"

Annabelle rolled her eyes. "You should have been paying attention in home ec, but you were too busy trying to figure out how you could stab Eileen Fisher with a knitting needle and get away with it."

"You'd stab her too if she'd told everyone that *you* gave a blow job to Peter Mitchell in the sixth grade."

Annabelle considered this. "It was eighth grade, right?"

Alice threw one of her needles at Annabelle. "You're as bad as Eileen!"

"Look," Annabelle said, bending down to pick up the discarded needle and handing it back to Alice. "It's easy, I promise. You've just got to concentrate."

"I don't know how you can stand Mrs. Porter's class," Alice said, giving a halfhearted stab at the yarn. "All she cares about is preparing young ladies for marriage and *the home*." Alice said *the home* as if she were a middle-aged British woman, which, of course, Mrs. Porter absolutely was. "How do you think she even got here?" Alice continued. "How do you get from one end of the earth to here?"

"The UK isn't the end of the earth," Annabelle replied. "Besides, I like her."

Alice rolled her eyes. "That's because you want to get married and have lots of fat babies with my brother."

"Shhhhh!" Annabelle hissed, her eyes darting around the house. "And I do not."

Alice laughed. "But you do want to have babies one day, don't you? I overheard you telling Mom about it a couple nights ago. You said you wanted babies and your own KitchenAid mixer, whatever that is."

Annabelle felt her cheeks redden. "Someday," she said quietly. "I want a family someday."

But her friend hadn't heard her. "I did it!" Alice squealed. She held up a lopsided stitch, a precarious-looking thing, balanced on the protesting needles. "Look! You better tell Mrs. Porter about this tomorrow, because she won't believe me."

"I will," Annabelle said with a grin. "But you'll have to promise not to threaten anyone with your needles. Not even Eileen Fisher."

Alice set the yarn and needles down carefully on the coffee table and placed her right hand over her heart. "I swear," she said. "I won't stab Eileen Fisher with my knitting needles."

"Or anything else," Annabelle prompted.

Alice removed her hand from her heart. "Now that," she said, "is a promise I can't keep."

CHAPTER 8

I FOLLOWED ALICE UP A FEW STREETS UNTIL SHE PARKED IN front of an immaculately kept Victorian house. I hunched down in the front seat to get a better look through the driver's-side window. There was a huge wraparound porch, more turrets than I could count, and colorful shingles. It was at least three stories tall. It was clear that whoever lived there had painstakingly restored it to its former glory, and it was truly a sight to behold. There were houses like this in Seattle, but I didn't know anyone who lived in one. I felt more than a little bit intimidated. I imagined a little old lady with wire-rimmed glasses and a stern expression answering the door.

"Your mother's house . . . uh, Annabelle's house, is just right up the street," Alice said when she caught me staring. "It's smaller, though, as all the houses up that way are."

I inwardly winced at Alice calling Annabelle my mother but

kept my face blank and scanned the street. "Which one is it?" I asked.

"The one on the corner up there. At the intersection of Maple and Cherry."

"I can't see it," I said, turning back.

"There will be time for all that," she replied, ushering me inside.

Before I had a chance to ask her what she meant, I was greeted by a rush of warm air and the buzz of conversation, and then, as all eyes settled firmly on me, a quieter hum of whispers.

"Do they all know about me?" I asked Alice.

"Some of them," Alice admitted. "And those who didn't know before today will know now." She looked up at me with her bird's eyes and continued, "You look so much like her."

I felt my cheeks warm and pretended it was from the heat of the house. A surly-looking teenager with lots of eyeliner and nearly black hair took my coat. She looked like she would rather be anywhere else, and I knew exactly how she felt.

"Thanks," I said to her, jostling my arms out of my jacket.

"I like your boots," I heard her mumble.

"Oh, thanks," I said. "I got them at this great store in Seattle . . ."

"Thrash," we both said at the same time.

"That's my favorite store," the teenager continued, pushing a mop of bangs out of her eyes. "But my dad thinks it's cheap."

"That's half the fun," I replied. "I got these on sale for like ten dollars."

Alice, who'd been hanging up her own coat, said, "I see you've met Maxine. Maeve Stephens, this is Maxine Abbott. Her dad is Abel Abbott. He owns this house."

"It's Max," the teenager said. "Nobody calls me Maxine except for you, Alice."

Alice ignored Max and pulled her in, while Max protested, for a hug. "Go tell your dad we're here," she said.

Max rolled her eyes in the way only a teenager can and stomped off, leaving us to the throng of people. I looked around the house. All the accents were wood, all the way down to the rich mahogany floors. They shone. I wondered for a minute if maybe I got down close enough, I could see my reflection in them. When I looked back up again, Abel was standing there, his face unreadable.

"Abel," Alice said, putting her hand on one of Abel's arms, which was big enough to be someone else's, some mere mortal's, leg. "This is Maeve Stephens."

I stuck out my hand instinctively, and Abel took it. "It's nice to meet you," I said.

Without returning my greeting, Abel beckoned Alice and me to follow him. Now that we'd officially met, he didn't seem quite as imposing as he had the night before at the bar or earlier this afternoon at the funeral. In fact, I found it quite amusing that such a bear of a man could live in a doll's house like this. Still, I found it puzzling how he fit into Annabelle's life. They had to have been pretty close if he was a pallbearer at her funeral and hosting the get-together afterward, but he was a famous writer, and Annabelle was, well, I didn't know what she'd been, exactly, and once again, that feeling of being an outsider crept over me.

As we waded farther into the vast living area, the whispers quieted, and everyone offered me a sympathetic smile. Actually, I realized, the smiles were for Alice. Some gazes slid over me, but many of them lingered, scrutinizing me before turning away, only to look back again seconds later.

"It's because you look so much like Annabelle," Alice said.

"This is awkward," I replied. "Maybe I shouldn't have come."

"Nonsense," Alice said. "Come on, there are some people I want you to meet."

Alice led me over to a sunroom just off the kitchen, where three women were sitting at a round white table. They looked up when they saw us enter.

"Ladies," Alice said. "This is Maeve Stephens. Maeve, this is Eva, Florence, and Harriett."

Eva was probably about forty and had short, spiky hair. She wore cat's-eye glasses and an outfit straight out of the 1985 Sears catalog. It was the same woman I'd seen handing out programs at the funeral.

The second woman, Florence, looked about Alice's age, although she looked like she came from another plane of existence entirely. Actually, she looked like she ought to be meditating or levitating or something. She was wearing a flowing dress and bangle bracelets, and her graying hair was wound into a loose braid down her back.

The third woman, Harriett, was ancient. I'd never seen so many wrinkles on a face. Her hair was long like Florence's, but steel gray and twisted into a bun. She looked like one of those schoolmarms I'd seen on old television shows. But the smile she gave me was genuine, and I felt myself warm to her immediately.

"Welcome," Harriett said. "Sit down, sit down." She patted the chair between her and Florence.

"It's nice to finally meet you," Florence said. "Thank you for coming."

I tried a smile out on my face, and it probably looked more strained than pleasant, but none of the women seemed to notice. "I'm thankful Alice called and told me, so I could make arrangements to be here," I said.

"Maeve," Alice said. "Aside from me, these women were Annabelle's closest friends."

I wasn't sure what I was supposed to do with that information, so I just kept up my plastic smile. It was starting to hurt my face, and so when Abel came over and put a glass of honey-colored beer in front of me, I thought I might cry with relief.

"Thanks," I said. I put the glass up to my lips and took a long drink.

He gave me a half smile and moved on to a group of people calling his name from the living room.

"Can you believe he's hosting this?" Eva whispered to no one in particular. "I can't believe it."

"He would have done anything for Annabelle," Harriett replied. "Even if that meant opening up his home to the likes of you."

"Were they close?" I asked.

Alice nodded. "Annabelle was good to him when his wife died. I think he's trying to make it up to her, even now."

I stared at the back of Abel's head as it bobbed up and down, the tallest person in the crowd. He didn't look especially uncomfortable to have so many people in his house. Of course, I didn't know him, and he'd looked plenty brooding the night before at Three Sheets.

When he turned, he caught me staring at him, and I swiveled back around to the group of women. "So," I said, trying to ignore the feeling of Abel's eyes on the back of my head. "How did you all know Annabelle? Well, besides you, Alice. I already know you and Annabelle were friends."

"Florence, Annabelle, and I worked at the pillow factory across town before it closed almost twenty years ago," Alice said. "Harriett was our supervisor there, and Eva is her granddaughter."

I nodded now that I understood the connection.

"There was a fire," Eva said, her eyes wide behind her glasses. "That's why the factory closed. Six people died."

"That's awful," I replied.

"It was," Harriett said. "I was less than two weeks from my retirement." She lifted her dress to show two mottled legs. "I was severely burned, but I got out with my life."

"And a lawsuit," Eva said. "Granny sued the pants off the manufacturers of the faulty heating system that caused the fire."

"Little comfort since I can't wear anything but long skirts anymore," Harriett replied. "I used to have great gams."

"You live in a huge house with a gate around it. All that's missing is a moat," Florence replied. "And maybe a dragon."

"You'll have to come to our knitting club," Harriet said, reaching her hand out to take one of mine. "We meet every single week. I own a knitting shop downtown. We could talk more there, you know, about your mother."

"My birth mother," I replied automatically. And then, feeling guilty for how I must've sounded, I said, "I don't think I'll be here long enough to come to your shop. I'm sorry."

"We'd still love to have you," Florence said, brushing right over my comment. "The ladies of St. Francis are always looking for a few good women."

My ears perked up. "The ladies of St. Francis?" I asked.

Florence nodded. "Yes. We're the ladies." She pointed to the women around the table. "It's our knitting club."

"I thought you were some kind of cult," I blurted before I could stop myself.

To my surprise, instead of being offended, the women burst out laughing.

"Oh, honey," Florence said. "Thank you. I needed that laugh today."

"This must be pretty strange for you, huh?" Eva asked me, adjusting her glasses. "I saw you when you first walked into the church, and you looked like you were going to turn around and run right back out."

"I thought about it," I answered honestly. "Like you said, this is all pretty weird."

"Well, we're glad you didn't," Harriett said, shooting Eva a look that clearly told her to shut up. "How long will you be here?"

I shrugged. "Just until tomorrow morning, I think," I said. "Depending on how I feel, I might drive back to Seattle tonight."

The women all exchanged glances.

"What?" I asked.

"You haven't told her?" Eva asked, looking at Alice.

"Told me what?"

"I was waiting for Gary," Alice replied, not looking at me. "Technically, that's his job."

"He's never been able to do his job," Harriett scoffed. "You should know that by now, Alice."

"Can someone tell me what's going on?" I asked, standing up. "Who is Gary?"

"He's a lawyer," Eva replied.

"And he's not a very good one," Harriett cut in.

"Why do I need to talk to a lawyer?" I asked, panic rising in my throat.

Alice shot her friends a look that could have killed them and then turned her attention back to me. "It's nothing like that, I promise," she said. "It's just that, well, Annabelle had a will, and you're named in it."

I sat back down. "I'm what?"

"You're the sole beneficiary," Eva said, matter-of-fact. "You get it all."

"Shut up, Eva," Harriett said. "This isn't your business."

Alice tried to take my hand, but I pulled it away from her. I'd had enough of being touched by strangers for one day. She put her hands palm down on the table instead and said, "Annabelle didn't have much. But she did own a house and she had a little money in the bank. When she made out her will several years ago—we both did, after a woman we went to high school with died suddenly—Annabelle made sure that everything she might have would go to her only child, you."

I inhaled sharply and then let the air out slowly, trying to calm my racing thoughts and racing pulse.

"I'm the executor of her estate," Alice continued. "But I thought it would be best to wait for Gary, Annabelle's lawyer, to speak to you in private, because I didn't want all of this information dumped on you at once." She sent a meaningful look to her friends.

"I'm sorry," Eva said, shrugging her shoulders. "*Somebody* had to tell her before she left town."

"If you want," Alice said gently, "I can go and find Gary right now. I'm sure he's here somewhere."

I looked up at Alice, and try as I might, I couldn't keep my feelings from bubbling to the surface. "I'm sorry," I said. "You can find someone else or sell it or do whatever it is that people without a family do when they die, because I don't want it."

I stood up unsteadily and turned around, praying I could make it to the door and outside before I burst into tears.

CHAPTER 9

ONCE I GOT OUTSIDE, I DIDN'T CRY LIKE I THOUGHT I WAS going to. Instead I sat down on the curb and watched a one-eyed cat in a pink sweater cross the street all by itself, like it was something it did every single day, dressed in its Sunday best.

I didn't even notice when Alice approached me from behind and nudged me with her cane. It wasn't until she cleared her throat that I turned around.

"I can't get all the way down there," she said. "Why don't you come up on the porch so we can talk."

I stood up and followed her.

"I'm sorry you had to find out like that," she said once we were settled in two comfortable rocking chairs on the wraparound porch. "I should have had Gary call you before the funeral."

"It wouldn't have mattered," I replied. "I don't want anything of hers."

"I know you must be angry at her," Alice continued. "Giving you up the way she did. But she never forgot about you. She always loved you."

"If she loved me so much, then why didn't she want anything to do with me?" I asked. I knew it sounded petulant, but I couldn't help it. I *was* angry.

"It had nothing to do with not wanting you," Alice replied. "There were circumstances beyond her control, or even mine, that prevented her from keeping you."

"What circumstances?" I asked.

Alice shrugged. "She had no family, you know. Her parents died when she was fourteen, and she was an only child. My parents took her in, but they didn't have any money to speak of. She was a seventeen-year-old girl who was, for all practical purposes, alone in the world. She wanted better than that for you."

"And what about my father?" I asked. "Did you know him? You were her best friend. Surely you knew who the father of your best friend's child was."

Alice's eyes darted away from mine for the first time in the conversation, and her left hand began to fidget with the grip of her cane. "Not even best friends tell each other everything," she said quietly. "We all have secrets."

I sighed. "I've had a good life. It's not like I wasn't loved and taken care of. I have great parents. I don't hate her for giving me up."

"Then what is it?" Alice asked.

I thought about the letters I'd sent Annabelle—the way they all came back, one by one, without ever even being opened. I thought about the way I refused to acknowledge that my birth mother's refusal to know me had hurt more than I could have ever admitted, to anyone. "It's nothing," I replied. "I'm just incredibly overwhelmed, that's all. I don't want to deal with the responsibility of whatever it is she wanted me to have. Can't you give it to someone else?"

Alice shrugged. "I suppose we can."

"Don't you want it?"

"Listen," Alice replied, ignoring my last comment. "Didn't you tell me during our first conversation that you owed a lot of money?"

"What?"

"When you answered the phone," Alice said patiently. "You thought I was a creditor."

I felt my cheeks grow warm. "Yeah," I admitted. "I lost my job a few weeks ago. I had to move back in with my parents."

"So why don't you just talk with the lawyer? See what you've been given. It might turn out that you can sell the house and use it to pay off whoever it is you owe money to."

"That's your suggestion?" I asked. "To profit off my birth mother's death?"

To my surprise, Alice chuckled. "Well, I wasn't going to put it like that, but, Maeve, she *wanted you to have it.* Whatever you decide to do would have been fine with her, just so long as it was yours."

"I'm leaving tomorrow," I said. "I don't know what I can do before then."

"What if I could schedule a meeting with you and Gary, tomorrow, at Annabelle's house? Just listen to what he has to say and consider your options. You can drive back to Seattle after that."

I sighed. "Okay, fine, whatever."

Alice took that as an invitation to search out the lawyer named Gary and drag him out to the porch where I was still sitting. Trailing him was a tall, thin blond woman. She looked impossibly elegant and out of place, except maybe if she'd been with Abel.

For some reason, I found myself wondering if the blond woman and Abel were an item, until Alice placed her hand on my shoulder and said, "Maeve, this is Gary Johnson. He's the lawyer in charge of Annabelle's estate. I'll leave you two to chat for a minute or two."

I stood up and reached out to take the hand Gary extended. Behind him, I watched Alice take the arm of the blond woman, and together, they walked back inside.

"She's pretty," I said, more to myself than to Gary.

"Who?" Gary asked. "My wife?"

"The blond woman is your wife?" I asked, trying to keep the incredulous tone out of my voice.

The man standing before me wasn't ugly or anything—he was just . . . odd-looking. With his curly red hair and smattering of freckles combined with his crisp black suit, he looked a bit like how I imagined Carrot Top would have looked if he'd picked a nine-to-five job instead of steroid use. It seemed odd that the glamazon I'd just seen could be married to this man, but then again, who was I to be judging anyone? I didn't even have a job, and this guy was a *lawyer*.

"Her name is Yulina," Gary continued. "And she's my wife, yes."

"Cool," I said, hoping he couldn't read the shock on my face. "Anyway, it's nice to meet you."

"I wish the circumstances could have been better," he said, and he flashed me a very white smile.

"So," I said, wanting to get right to the point. "Alice says that Annabelle left me something in her will."

Gary nodded. "Would you prefer to come by my office tomorrow and discuss it, rather than right here out in the open?"

"I'd rather get it out of the way," I said. "Unless she left me a porn stash or something."

Gary's expression didn't change. "No, it's nothing like that," he said. "But she did leave you with nearly everything she owned—her house, her car, what was left in her bank account and insurance policy after burial, her cat, etc., etc. I don't have the list right in front of me, but I can get it and we can discuss further at a more appropriate time."

"Her cat?"

"Yes," Gary said, his lip curling in what appeared to be disgust. "Her cat, Sherbet. He currently resides at her Maple Street house—just up the street. Alice comes by and feeds him, I think. So far he's eluded the live trap. He's a nuisance, according to neighbors."

I wanted to sit down again.

"I know this must be overwhelming for you," Gary continued, as if he sensed that I was starting to panic. "I had planned to call you after the funeral, but of course, that was before I knew you would actually be here today."

"It's okay," I said. "I just don't know how I'm supposed to respond to all of this . . . or what I'm supposed to do."

"Will you be in town tomorrow?" Gary asked.

"I hadn't planned on it," I admitted. "But I do have the hotel room for another night or two, so I guess I could stay. How long do you think all of this is going to take?"

"Let's meet tomorrow afternoon—say, around four o'clock? I can't meet before then, because I'll be in court all day. But if this time is agreeable, I'll show you the house, and we can talk then."

I thought it over. If I stayed another night and then waited around until four p.m. the next day, that would almost inevitably mean I'd have to spend tomorrow night in Timber Creek as well, unless I wanted to drive back to Seattle in the dark, which I *hated* to do. But what were my other options? I knew I couldn't ignore this, even though I wanted to.

"Okay," I said. "I guess I can do that."

"Perfect," Gary said. "The address is 410 Maple. You can almost see the house from here. From where we're standing, it'll be on the right side of the road. If you have any trouble or have any questions before then, let me know." He handed me a slightly bent card from inside his wallet.

"Thanks," I said. As he was turning to walk away, I called after him, "Hey, could you please tell Alice that I had to go? I've got some phone calls to make if I'm going to be staying an extra couple of days."

"Sure," Gary replied, waving to me over his shoulder. "Take care."

I walked to the curb and stood for a few more seconds before I pulled my keys out of my pocket and slid into the seat of my car. I rested my head against the steering wheel and again resisted the urge to cry.

CHAPTER 10

"W HAT DO YOU MEAN SHE LEFT YOU A HOUSE?" MY mother asked on the phone that evening. "A whole house?"

I rolled my eyes, even though she couldn't see me doing it—well, probably because she couldn't see me doing it. "A whole house, Mom," I said. "And a car too, and I guess what little bit of money she had left after the funeral and burial were paid for."

"Well, that was kind of her, don't you think?" my father replied, ever the diplomat. He'd clearly been listening in from his office on the other side of the house.

"It's just a lot to deal with," I said. "And I'm not sure I want the responsibility of sorting out what's left of someone else's life."

Both of my parents were silent for a second, and then my

mother said, softly, "Well, maybe she'd planned to contact you, but she died before she got the chance."

I sighed. "You're right," I said. "I'm sure you're right, but I'm overwhelmed, and I want to come home."

"Then come home right now," my mother replied. "You don't have to stay there. We can call our lawyer right now and have her contact this Gary person."

"Thanks, Mom," I said. "But I think I need to at least see Mr. Johnson tomorrow and go over everything with him. Then I'll come home."

"Do you want one of us to drive up and be with you?" my father asked. "We could both come, if you need us."

"It's okay," I said.

"Call us as soon as the meeting is over," my mother said.

"I will," I replied. "I promise."

I ended the call and flopped down on the hotel bed, stomach first. I had text messages from Holly and Eli to answer, but I couldn't rally the energy at the moment. I thought back to a story I'd written when I first started working for the *Lantern*. It had been a profile of a new Mariners shortstop who'd worked his way up through high school, college, and AAA baseball, before finally being drafted entirely too old, at thirty-six, to play pro baseball. The player, whose name escaped me and who had lasted only a couple of seasons with the Mariners, had been one of the most optimistic people I'd ever met. He'd reminded me a lot of Eli, both in personality and in circumstance when he'd been younger. The difference was that this guy had spent his entire life in the foster care system and never been adopted.

I remembered wondering how someone whose life had been so hard, so unfair, could turn out the way he had. My editor had called it "strength of character," and I'd used the term in my story. Ever since that interview, I'd wondered what my life might've been like if my birth mother kept me instead of putting me up for adoption. For all intents and purposes, I'd had an idyllic childhood. I'd been raised by two parents who loved me, gone to good schools, and had plenty of food to eat and a refrigerator that was always full. I'd basically been given every opportunity a kid could be given to succeed.

And yet here I was, thirty-six and a complete and total mess. There were people in the world who could go through enough hardship for ten people and still rise to the top, while I couldn't even get up off the bed and return a couple of text messages. Clearly my strength of character needed a little work.

Groaning, I rolled over onto my back and opened the text from Holly. It read: *Call me when you can. Sorry I couldn't be with you today. Have you seen any more of Abel Abbott? I'm telling everyone I met a famous author. Christine is jealous.*

I grinned, despite my mood. I was sure Christine was jealous. She was one of those crunchy granola outdoor types who probably owned every single book Abel Abbott wrote, just like my brother.

Before I could stop myself, I opened an Internet search on

my phone. I typed in "Abel Abbott" and waited for the results. After a few unsuccessful attempts to connect and a call to the front desk for the Wi-Fi password, my search returned thousands of hits. I ignored the voice of my freshman English professor in my head telling me that Wikipedia was not a credible source and clicked on Abel's Wikipedia page.

Professionally, Mr. Abel Joseph Abbot was the author of five nonfiction titles, all of which were *New York Times* Best Sellers. The majority of what he'd written had been translated into dozens of languages and was even the inspiration for a short-lived television series. His biggest seller was his autobiography, entitled *Dead of Winter*.

I scrolled down to read about his personal life. He was born in the Midwest and was the oldest of two. His brother, Arden, was two years younger. His parents had been survivalists, leftover hippies from a bygone era. Abel and his brother spent their formative years living in the Canadian wilderness. When he'd been twelve years old, his parents were caretakers of a small piece of land in Canada. The Canadian winter, often brutal, had been especially so that year. An unexpected blizzard in April prompted Abel's parents to leave him and his brother at the cabin where they lived to make the trek into the nearest town for supplies. Their parents never returned, and the brothers were forced to stay in the cabin and forage for food and fuel until they could be rescued nearly a month later. They never found the bodies of their parents.

Abel and Arden were sent to live with their grandparents

in Seattle, a huge change from what they'd been used to their whole lives.

"It was a hard time," he'd said in an interview with *GQ* magazine. "I was a kid trying to keep it together for the sake of my brother, and at the end of the day, all I wanted to do was disappear. Since I couldn't do that, not really, I spent most of my time outside, trying to remember everything my parents taught me about survival and living off the land."

There were more quotes from him about writing that I scrolled past, hoping to get to the good stuff. He'd been married at twenty-two years old to a woman he met in college named Claire Hunter. Together they'd had one daughter, and they'd lived much the same life that Abel had known as a child, since both he and Claire were avid outdoorspeople. At the end of the page there was a small paragraph about his wife falling ill after the birth of their daughter. They'd given up their rugged lifestyle for the comfort of small-town living in Washington State. The paragraph ended by saying that Claire had died when their daughter was just two years old.

I spent another hour perusing various websites and articles about Abel, hoping to find more information, but they all gave the same basic breakdown. His last interview was given not long after his wife died, and the interviewer asked Abel what, if anything, he had to say to his readers.

"Tell them," he said, standing up and thus signaling the end of the interview. "Tell them they can all go to hell."

Since that interview, he'd stayed out of the public eye. Little was written about him except for a small blurb about his wife's death, which gave no further information about how she died. There were three more articles begging the question—"What happened to Abel Abbott?" All the articles ended the same way—requests for an interview with the famed, and now reclusive, writer had been denied.

I was sure Holly had plans to get me to ask him for an interview at *Bitch Rant*, and I had a feeling she was going to be sorely disappointed in his response. Besides, I really doubted I'd ever see him again. I had one more day in Timber Creek before I beat the pavement back to Seattle, and after the last experience, my days of mingling with any man in the spotlight were over—sexy famous writers included.

CHAPTER 11

I WOKE UP LATE THE NEXT MORNING AND ORDERED ROOM service on Holly's dime. She'd called me the night before, and when I recounted to her the day, she told me to order dinner on her. I'd fallen asleep before I got the chance, and I figured breakfast was as good a time as any.

After that I did something I hadn't done for a long time—I lay in bed and watched bad movies on the Lifetime network until I fell asleep crossways, on top of the covers, wearing only a T-shirt. The next time I opened my eyes, my phone was ringing. It was a number I didn't recognize.

"Hello?" I croaked.

"Maeve?" the man on the other end asked. "Is this Maeve Stephens?"

"Yeah," I said, sitting up. "Yes, this is she."

"Maeve, this is Gary Johnson. I thought we were meeting at four p.m. today at Annabelle's house?"

"Oh shit!" I said, jumping up. "Shit, shit. I'm so sorry."

There was a pause, and then Gary said, "When do you think you can be here?"

"Give me ten minutes."

I threw on the least wrinkled clothing I could find in my suitcase, and I pulled my hair back into a bun and threw my deodorant into my purse. It was nearly ten after five before I pulled up next to the house on Maple Street. It took me three wrong turns to find it. Parked in the only parking spot was a sleek gray Lexus SUV, its windows tinted black.

When Gary saw me pull up, he and his wife stepped out of the Lexus and waved. "I was starting to think you stood us up," he said. He was smiling broadly, but he sounded slightly annoyed. His curly red hair was slicked back, and his freckles appeared almost glowing.

"I'm so sorry," I said.

"I want you to meet my wife," Gary said. "Maeve, this is Yulina."

"It's nice to meet you," I said, reaching out my hand to her.

"It is nice to meet you too," she replied in a thick accent that I couldn't quite place. "I can see Annabelle in you. The resemblance is very strong."

I smiled, because it was the only polite thing I could think of to do. "I've heard that before," I said. "But I have to say, it always surprises me to hear it."

"Yulina and I have dinner reservations at six o'clock," Gary cut in. "They'll give our table away if we're late."

"Oh," I said. "I'm sorry. I didn't mean to hold you up. I fell asleep in the hotel room."

"No worries," he replied, relaxing his jaw.

I don't know what I expected to see, but the neat little bungalow had not been it. Alice had been right, though—the houses on this side of the street were a lot smaller. There was a narrow sidewalk leading up to the green-painted privacy fence, which matched the green-clapboard-and-rock exterior of the house.

"This is an old part of the town," Gary continued. "Not a bad part, because there aren't really any bad parts of Timber Creek—some of them are just dingier than others."

"Yes," Yulina replied, speaking up. "And Mr. Abbott is quite close."

"You ready to go inside?" Gary asked, jangling the keys in my direction.

Just as Gary opened the door, an orange shock of fur bolted past us and right through the threshold, knocking Gary off his feet so that Yulina had to steady him.

"Damn cat," Gary said under his breath.

"That is Sherbet," Yulina said. "He is Annabelle's cat."

"Damn cat," Gary repeated. "Alice tried to take him home with her, and he just came right back again. Causing a ruckus all over the block."

Yulina nodded. "Alice comes by to feed him, but he will not leave this house."

"That's a stupid cat, if you ask me," Gary replied.

"He has a broken heart," Yulina said. "Even cats can have broken hearts."

Gary rolled his eyes and looked to me for a response, but I looked down at my tennis shoes. "Anyway," he said, allowing me to step inside first. "It's a cute little place. Annabelle bought it twenty-five years ago, and she's been fixing it up ever since. Property values stay high in this area because of the bigger houses down the street."

I stepped inside and looked around. The front rooms—a living room, dining room, and kitchen—were small but cozy. There was a worn couch and an armchair facing an older television set. In front of the armchair was a TV stand, and I realized that this was probably where Annabelle ate her meals. I was prone to this behavior as well, living alone, a fact that irritated my mother to no end. She was convinced the reason I'd failed to find myself a husband was because I ate from a TV stand instead of at a table that I didn't even own.

Beyond the living room was the dining room, and instead of place settings on the table, there were skeins and skeins of yarn in baskets. When Yulina saw me staring at them, she said, "Annabelle loved to knit. She was in a club that met downtown at the yarn shop."

"Alice told me," I said. It sounded like something an eighty-year-old grandmother would do after church on Sundays, and I couldn't really picture Alice, full of spit and vinegar, sitting still long enough to knit. "I guess she's in some kind of club?"

"St. Francis," Yulina replied.

"That's it," I said. I was starting to think that everybody knew about these women but me, and I still wasn't entirely sure that they *weren't* a cult.

Yulina rolled a piece of fuchsia yarn between her fingertips. "Do you knit?" she asked.

"No," I replied, trying not to laugh. "I mean, I've never really tried."

"I am sure Alice could teach you."

"Oh, I'm not going to stay," I said, taking a step back. "I've been here a day too long already."

Gary nodded. "Of course, you have a job back in Seattle. And a nice boyfriend, I'm sure." He gave me a wry smile. "Pretty girl like you ought to have a boyfriend."

Beside me Yulina flinched, almost imperceptibly, and I hoped Gary's comment hadn't made her uncomfortable. I liked her, and even though I had zero intention of staying in Timber Creek, I didn't want to make enemies before I'd at least had a chance to make them on my own merit.

"What is it that you do?" Yulina asked, turning to me. "Your career?"

I swallowed. "Well, I worked for a newspaper until a few weeks ago," I replied. "It closed down, so I'm temporarily out of a job."

"Does your boyfriend work?" Gary asked.

"No," I said, wishing he would shut up about my boyfriend. "I don't have one of those either."

"So what's keeping you in Seattle?" he wanted to know. "A mortgage?"

"No," I said once again, feeling my cheeks begin to burn. "I'm living with my parents right now."

Yulina turned away from Gary, shaking her head slightly, and I left them to wander down the hallway. There were two bedrooms on one end with a hallway bathroom and another bedroom at the other end with a bathroom of its own. Like the front rooms, these rooms were also small and sparsely decorated. I opened the door to the bedroom closest to the bathroom and flipped the light switch.

It was clear this had been Annabelle's bedroom. Unlike the rest of the house, this room was stuffed full of things—more yarn, three dressers, a writing desk, and a four-poster bed. For the first time since I entered the house, it felt like I was intruding on someone's private and personal space, and I fought the urge to back out. The only thing that stopped me was that I knew if I left the room, I'd have to face Gary and Yulina and their barrage of questions about my nonexistent life back in Seattle.

I walked over to the bed and put my hand on the frayed patchwork quilt covering it. It looked like a quilt my mother had showcased in one of the guest bedrooms. As a child, I'd loved to play in that room and with the quilt, even though my mother told me hundreds of times that the quilt was an antique and not to be played with.

When I was about eight, I snuck into the room with a bottle

of cherry-red nail polish, intent on making my toenails match the cool teenage neighbor's across the street. She'd been my babysitter the night before and told me that the *only* acceptable color on toenails was red. Feeling very grown-up, I sat down at the edge of the bed and positioned my feet onto the folded quilt and began to paint my toenails. As I painted, the bottle next to me tipped over and spilled the cherry-red nail polish all over the quilt. I didn't notice until I was finished, and the nail polish was all but dry.

My mother, who was furious when she caught me, told me the quilt had been in our family for generations and that I'd spoiled an heirloom. She said I was too young to understand, but that one day when I had children I'd know the importance of preserving history. At the time, I'd been more hurt that she told me I was too young to understand something rather than sorrowful I'd ruined the quilt.

Now, looking at Annabelle's quilt, I wondered if she'd kept it on her own bed for everyday use because she'd had no children to spill nail polish onto important things. The quilt, along with everything else in her house, had been safe from sticky little hands.

"I see you found Annabelle's bedroom," Yulina said from the doorway. "It was her favorite room of the house."

I turned, startled by the interruption. I'd forgotten about the two people I was with, and it took me a moment to respond. "You must have been very good friends with her," I said, "to know so much about her."

Yulina looked over her shoulder before entering the room. "She taught me to knit when I was pregnant with my daughter," she said. "I wanted to knit a blanket, but I did not know how. My English was not good. She helped me with that also."

I wanted to ask Yulina where she was from and how she came to a small town like Timber Creek instead of one of the larger cities like Seattle, but Gary found us before I had the chance.

"So," he said, wrapping one of his arms around Yulina's waist. "What do you think of the place?"

"It's fine," I said, stepping away from the bed and the quilt.

"Well, it's yours," Gary replied. "If you think you want to sell it, I can get you in touch with a real estate buddy of mine."

"Give her time, Gary," Yulina said, breaking away from his embrace. "This must be very overwhelming for her."

"It's okay," I replied. "I haven't given it too much thought, to be honest."

"Of course," Gary said, bobbing his head up and down. "But if you don't mind, my wife and I need to skedaddle. We're already late for dinner."

I took the keys from Gary's outstretched hand and, after locking the door, shoved them into my pocket. "Thanks for showing me the house tonight," I said. "Can I come back anytime?"

"Pretty much," Gary replied. "There will be some more paperwork, but the house is titled to you upon death, so it really is yours now."

As Gary hurried out to the car, Yulina grabbed my hand and

held me back. "Do you really think you will sell this house?" she asked.

"I don't know," I said.

"Annabelle wanted you to have it."

"*Annabelle* didn't know me," I replied, sounding terser than I'd wanted to. I took a deep breath. "I'm sorry, but you were right, all of this is a bit overwhelming."

"I understand," Yulina said.

"Do you?" I asked.

"In a way," she replied, a small smile playing at her lips. "In a way."

I looked away from her and across the street, where the porch light of one of the houses illuminated two figures standing on the front steps. I couldn't make out their features, but one of the figures was tall, with broad shoulders—a man, I could tell. He was standing over a smaller figure, a woman, and he was nodding, with his arms crossed over his chest. The woman wasn't yelling, but she didn't sound happy either.

When Gary honked at us, causing Sherbet to jump up and run between my feet, both the man and the woman turned to stare at us. Their conversation paused, and I was caught between wanting to squint to see them better and wanting to look away, embarrassed I'd been caught staring.

I reached down and ran my hand along the length of Sherbet's body, in an attempt to reroute my focus. From the corner of my eye, I could see the woman still looking at us, one hand on her hip and the other pointing at our side of the street.

"Time to go," Yulina said.

"Are those the neighbors?" I asked.

Yulina nodded. "Yes," she said. "Look out for the fat one."

"The fat one?" I asked.

"The woman, Beryl," Yulina said, her tone dripping with disdain. "She is trouble."

Before I could ask anything else, Gary honked again, and Yulina jumped.

"We are going to be late," Yulina said. "Gary hates to be late."

"I'm sorry," I said. "I hope the restaurant doesn't cancel your reservation."

"I hate that restaurant," Yulina replied, leading me off the porch. "The bread tastes like feet."

I stifled a giggle. "Why don't you tell Gary you don't like it?"

Yulina waved one of her hands in the air. "He knows."

CHAPTER 12

I WATCHED THE SUV DRIVE AWAY AND THEN SAT DOWN ON the porch steps. I felt exhausted. All I really wanted to do was crawl into bed and pretend I was having a bad dream. I wanted to pretend none of this had ever happened, and although I had no intention of showing it to Annabelle's friends, or anyone in this damn town for that matter, I was secretly seething that she'd put me in this position.

She'd never wanted to know me when she was alive, and it didn't matter to me what kind of excuses my parents made for her—she hadn't wanted me, and she hadn't wanted to know me. Why, then, was I sitting on her front porch? Why, then, had she left me everything she owned, including another actual living being?

Sherbet rubbed up against my legs as if reading my mind, and I absently reached out to stroke him. He really was a beautiful cat, with his soft orange fur and strange green eyes. I stood up and went back onto the porch and opened a black trash can that read "cat food" in pink spray paint. Sure enough, there was food inside. I put the food in the bowl on the porch for Sherbet, who gladly began snapping it up.

"Excuse me?"

I looked up to see a man standing in the yard, just beyond the steps. He was wearing a pair of ripped, stone-washed jeans and a black T-shirt. He had a shaggy salt-and-pepper beard, and I couldn't tell, just by looking at him, if he was homeless or a hipster. In one hand he held a leash that was attached to a giant white dog.

"Uh, hello," I said. I backed up a bit toward the door. I knew it was locked, but for now it was the only direction I could go. "Can I help you?"

The man held up the leash and said, "Are you the animal lady?"

"Am I the what?"

"The animal lady," he repeated. "You take animals for people who can't care for 'em no more, right?"

I looked around to see if someone was playing a joke on me. Alice, maybe? Surely this guy was joking. He had to be.

"No," I said. "I'm not the *animal lady*. I don't know what you're talking about. I'm sorry."

He held up a card with an address scrawled on the back and said, "This ain't 410 Maple Street?"

"It is," I replied patiently. "But I'm not the person you're look-ing for."

"Is there someone else here who's the dog lady?"

I sighed. "No, there's no one else here. It's just me."

He took a step toward the porch, and for a split second, I regretted telling him I was alone.

"Look," I said. "You're probably looking for Annabelle, right?"

"That sounds like the name they give me," he said. "She don't live here?"

"No," I said. "Well, she did live here, but she died last week. I'm sorry."

"They told me a lady at this address could take my dog," the man persisted. "Been damn near three weeks ago, but I didn't need to find her a home until now."

"I'm really sorry," I repeated. "I don't know what else to tell you, except I'm not the person you're looking for."

"What am I supposed to do with her, then?" he asked. "You gotta pay twenty-five dollars to surrender to animal control."

In the distance, I saw Abel standing in his front yard, a rake in his hand, staring at us. When the man and dog advanced again toward the porch, I saw him throw down the rake and trot toward us.

"Please take her," the man was saying. "I can't have her at my new place. She's a good girl, really."

"I can't," I said. "I can't have her where I live either."

"You don't live here?"

"No," I said. "I don't, and I'm sorry, but I really need you to leave now."

"Hey, Maeve," Abel said, reaching us. "How's it going? Is there something I can help with?"

The man held up his hands and took a step back, the dog following loyally behind him. "Naw, it's all good."

I felt a wave of guilt watching the man and the dog walk off. The dog was big, but she looked sweet, if maybe a little skinny. I wondered where they were going and what the man would end up doing with her. I didn't want to think about what could happen if he didn't find someone to take care of her.

"What was that about?" Abel asked, pulling me out of my thoughts. "Do you know that guy?"

"No," I said, looking at him. "I don't know anybody in this town."

"You know me," Abel replied, a sly grin spreading across his face.

"I don't *know* you," I said tartly. "You're an *acquaintance*."

"Well, I guess that means you're not interested in coming over for a drink?" Abel asked. "I just brought home a couple of growlers from a local microbrewery."

I tried to appear uninterested, but a drink sounded so good that I could practically feel my mouth watering. I crossed my arms over my chest and said, "Why are you being nice to me? Aren't you supposed to be some kind of hateful hermit?"

"Hateful hermit?" Abel scratched at his black beard. "That sounds an awful lot like a band I was in in college."

"Oh yeah?" I asked. "I think maybe I saw them once. They were pretty shitty."

Abel opened up his mouth and let out a guffaw, flashing me his perfect white teeth. It was startling to see them up against the dark thicket of hair, almost like a bear getting ready to pounce . . . if the bear happened to be muscled and tattooed and utterly gorgeous.

"So," Abel said, angling his head toward me. "How about it? You in?"

I looked back at Annabelle's house one last time. "Sure," I said. "It's not like I have anything else better to do."

"I'm going to pretend you're more excited than you are," Abel replied, beckoning to me to follow.

"I'm actually really excited about the prospect of a drink," I said. "It's been a rough few days."

"I have to say," Abel said as we walked toward his house, "I was surprised to see you here."

"Where?" I asked. "At Annabelle's house?"

"Timber Creek," Abel replied. "I hadn't . . . I mean, I didn't know Annabelle had been in contact with you."

"So you knew about me?"

"I knew Annabelle gave a baby up for adoption when she was seventeen," Abel said, his tone guarded. "All she ever told me was that you lived in Seattle with a nice family."

"Well, that's all true, I suppose," I conceded. I waited for him to open the door, and I walked inside. "But we weren't in contact with each other."

"So you didn't know about her?"

"I did," I said, stepping into the now familiar hallway. "But like I said, we weren't in contact."

Abel looked at me as if he wanted to say something else, but instead he led me into the kitchen, pulled out a cloudy brown jug from the refrigerator, and held it up to me. "Do you like IPAs?"

"Yes," I replied. I sat down heavily on one of the bar stools facing him and rested my arms against the cool granite countertop. "Fill 'er up."

"That's all you need to know before you agree to drink it?" Abel asked.

"At this point I'd drink rubbing alcohol," I quipped. "But truly, I don't think I've ever met an IPA I didn't like."

"Same," Abel said. "This is my particular favorite. A couple buddies of mine brew it. They just got started a few years ago, but the beer is great, and I'm not just saying that because I hold stock in the company."

"You own stock in beer?" I asked, impressed. "Cool."

Abel handed me an overfull glass and said, "They needed a few investors back when they were first starting out. One of them—they're twins—is married to my wife's best friend. She's the local veterinarian."

"Your wife is the local veterinarian?" I asked without thinking. I regretted it as soon as the words were out of my mouth.

His face closed off. The transition was slight, but not so slight that I didn't notice it. Abel took a drink of beer. "No," he replied. "I should have said that the local veterinarian *was* my wife's best friend. Claire, that was my wife, has been dead nearly twelve years."

"I'm so sorry," I said. "I didn't mean to—"

"It's fine," he said, cutting me off in a tone that told me it most definitely *was not* fine.

An awkward silence settled and hung between us, both of us gulping our beer so quickly that Abel had refilled both our glasses before I even realized it. After a few minutes, I couldn't stand it anymore and said, "So, your daughter . . . Maxine, is it? Where is she?"

"Studying," Abel replied. "She thinks I don't know that the boy she's studying with is her boyfriend."

"I remember those days," I said.

"Oh, you do?" Abel asked, an amused glint in his eye.

"It's just being a teenager," I said. "Or weren't you ever one?"

"I might've been," he replied.

"Well," I continued. "Teenage girls don't like their parents to know when they've got a boyfriend."

"Your parents," Abel began. "They live in Seattle?"

I nodded. "Yep. That's where I grew up."

"You've always lived there?"

Again I nodded. "Yep."

I knew better than to ask him, well, anything about his parents, and I should have known better than to ask anything about his wife too. It seemed as if there were lots of things Abel Abbott didn't like to be questioned about.

"So," Abel continued. "What did you think of Annabelle's house?"

"It was cute," I said. "It actually looks a lot like my old apartment back in Seattle. I guess she passed down her inability to decorate."

"She never was one for having stuff lying around she didn't need."

"Except yarn," I interrupted. "Her entire bedroom was full of yarn."

"Okay," Abel replied. "That's true. I think between her and Alice, they own more yarn than the entire knitting store downtown."

"What's the deal with their weird secret society?" I asked.

"St. Francis?" Abel asked. "It's hardly secret."

I sighed. "You know what I mean. Everybody talks about it like it's the illuminati or something."

Abel shrugged. "It's just a bunch of women knitting," he said. "Seems pretty ordinary to me."

"Fine," I said. "Knitting seems like such an old lady thing to do, though. I mean, Alice isn't that old, and I guess Annabelle wasn't either."

"I guess they've been doing it since they were kids," Abel replied. "I heard Alice talking about it once. Besides, the knitting club that they're in does lots of good for the community."

"Doesn't Alice seem a bit, I don't know, tough to be in a knitting club?"

Abel laughed. "She is tough. I guess she's had to be, the way she grew up, especially with her leg the way it is. People weren't very understanding of physical disabilities like hers when she was a kid. At least, that's the way she tells it."

"Didn't she and Annabelle grow up in the same house?" I asked. "I mean, after Annabelle's parents died?"

"I imagine Alice will tell you this in her own time," Abel replied, pouring us our third beer. "But Alice's father was an alcoholic, and he could be abusive. It's not really a secret, so I don't mind telling you that part, but I know it was hard on Alice and her brother and Annabelle, even though she never talked about Alice's father."

I sat back. "Was he abusive to Alice? To Annabelle?"

"I don't know," Abel replied honestly. "Neither one of them ever talked about that."

"Are Alice's parents still alive?" I asked.

"No," Abel said. "Alice's father was gone before I moved to town, and her mother died a couple of years ago. She still lives in the house where she grew up, though. I help her out some-times, with yard work and keeping the place up. It's a little run-down."

Before I could ask anything else, Abel's phone began to ring, and he excused himself to answer it. After a few minutes, my glass was empty, and he still hadn't returned, so I began to wander around the living room, which was a large open space just off the kitchen.

The fireplace at the end of the far wall had a broad white mantel above it full of pictures. There were pictures of Max at every stage of life, and an especially cute one of her in a bathing suit and a pair of oversized rain boots, holding a fish nearly as big as she was. At the end of the mantel, all crowded together, were three pictures. All three of them featured the same slim blond woman, a woman I could only assume was Abel Abbott's dead wife—Claire. The first picture was of Abel and Claire on their wedding day, the second was of Abel and Claire when Claire was heavily pregnant, and the third was of a smiling Claire holding a tiny, wrinkled baby.

I was still staring at these pictures when I heard Abel walk into the room. I counted to five before I turned around, guilty for wandering off and snooping into what I knew was a private and painful part of his life. Again, that feeling of being an interloper in someone else's life was ever present, and I didn't like it.

"I should probably go," I said. "It's already getting dark, and I can barely find my way around in the daylight."

"Do you want me to drive you?" Abel asked. "You've had three pints of beer."

"So have you."

"Two," Abel corrected me. "And I'm bigger than you are."

I rolled my eyes, but I knew he was right. "Just call me a cab," I said. "I'll be fine."

"I have to go and pick up Max anyway," Abel replied. "That was her on the phone. She's had a fight with that boy, and she's crying and carrying on about something I don't understand. I told her to give me half an hour."

"They'll probably have made up by then," I said.

Abel let out a long-suffering sigh and replied, "It's always something."

I followed Abel to the front door, grabbing my purse from off the table as we went. He led me around the back of the house to an old garage with a manual door. He lifted it up to reveal an older model Jeep.

"Brakes on the Tahoe need fixing," he said. "I didn't get to it today, so we'll just have to take Old Faithful."

I stood aside as he fired the Jeep up and backed it out of the garage, and he barely stopped it long enough for me to jump inside. It was a rickety ride back to the hotel, and it was entirely too loud inside the Jeep to talk, and for that I was thankful.

When we pulled into the parking lot, Abel cut the engine, and I looked around, realizing something. "I never told you where I was staying," I said. "How did you know?"

Abel looked at me and gave me another disarming smile. "Everybody knows where you're staying," he replied. "You've been the talk of the town since you got here."

"Is that stereotype really true?" I asked. "Small town, big gossip?"

"I'm just glad they've all got something better to talk about than me," Abel said. "It's too bad you're leaving tomorrow."

"Another rumor you heard?"

"So you're staying?"

I don't know why I did it, but right then I wasn't sure what to say, so I simply shrugged and slammed the door closed. He drove away, rolling the window down slightly to wave at me as he went.

Once Abel was out of sight, I turned to go inside and nearly tripped over a dark shape at my feet. After a few seconds of forcing my eyes to focus, I realized to my astonishment that it was Sherbet at my feet, staring up at me with his odd-colored eyes.

"What are you doing here?" I asked, bending down to him. "I thought you never left the house?"

In response, Sherbet rubbed himself up against my out-stretched hand. I stayed there, squatted in the parking lot, for a few more minutes before I stood up, feeling the world swirl around me as I did so.

"I think I should stop drinking beer with men I don't know in towns I don't know," I said to Sherbet. "And now I've got to go inside. I guess you'll have to find your own way back home."

I didn't even get two steps forward before Sherbet was in front of me again.

"Go," I said, in a fruitless attempt to shoo him away. "Please! Go home!"

Sherbet continued to follow me, and I realized he was going to follow me all the way into the hotel. I couldn't imagine that the night clerk would appreciate a cat following me inside, but I wasn't sure how to get him to go away. I didn't want to stomp my foot or be mean. I guessed, technically, he was my cat, and therefore my responsibility.

I pulled out all the odds and ends from my purse and shoved

them down into my pockets and made as much room inside as I could. Then, as carefully as a relatively sober person could, I picked Sherbet up and set him down into my bag. I thought he might jump back out, but instead he curled into a ball and began to purr.

"What do you know?" I whispered to my bag as I stepped in through the sliding double doors. "Maybe I am the animal lady after all."

CHAPTER 13

I WOKE UP THE NEXT MORNING WITH THE PLASTIC HOTEL room service menu stuck to my face. I sat up and peeled it from my cheek. Sherbet was curled up next to me, snoring, which was all he'd done since I'd brought him to the hotel room the night before. He'd jumped right up on the bed, scratched at one of the pillows, and settled in for the night.

I'd never had such an agreeable bedmate.

With a groan, I forced myself out of bed and trudged over to the coffeemaker. It was one of those one-serving coffeemakers with the little cups, and I heard my sister-in-law's voice in my head telling me how wasteful and terrible for the environment they were. The thought made me want to make six cups of coffee. Instead, I made just one cup and sat back down on the bed. Sherbet stirred and settled himself down on my lap.

I hadn't even had my first sip when my phone started ringing, startling us both out of our pleasant company. Sherbet jumped out of my lap and disappeared under the bed. I figured my mother was the disturbing force, and so I reached over to the nightstand and picked up my phone. It wasn't my mother. It was Eli.

"Hello?" I croaked into the phone.

"Mae?"

"I think so," I said. "Although I'm so hungover, I'm not entirely sure."

"Hi, Maeve," Kate said, her voice sounding annoyingly awake. "We're *all* in the car this morning."

I sighed. This was my cue to stop talking about being hungover, and probably my dose of karma for thinking a hateful thought about her so early in the morning. Rowan had already learned more than one questionable phrase from me over the years. "Hi, Kate," I replied.

"We're calling because Rowan has something she wants to tell you," Eli said. "She said she couldn't wait until you came home."

"Well, you better tell me what it is," I said. I took a sip of my coffee and reveled in its deliciousness. "What's so important that you couldn't wait, Rowan?"

There was a flourish of whispering on the other end of the phone, and then my niece said, "Mommy and Daddy are having a baby! A *girl* baby!"

I raised the cup at the same time I dropped my phone, and in my surprise, I spilled the coffee, the scalding liquid soaking through my T-shirt and burning my chest. I let out a string of curse words and jumped up in a furious attempt to remove my shirt.

"Mae?"

My brother's voice floated up to me from my phone on the floor.

"Mae? Are you there?"

I winced and bent down to pick up the phone. "I'm here," I said. "I'm sorry. I spilled my coffee."

"Don't use those words at school," Kate said to Rowan. "Any of them. They're bad words."

"I know," Rowan replied, and even though I couldn't see her, I knew that she was rolling her eyes at her mother, and the thought brought temporary comfort to my now inflamed chest.

"I'm so happy for you guys," I managed to say through the pain. "Kate, I just saw you five days ago. You don't even look pregnant!"

"I know," Kate said. "I'm just fifteen weeks. We had some genetic testing done, and the tests told us the gender."

"Is everything all right?" I asked.

"Fine," Eli replied. "Everything is just fine, but Rowan couldn't wait to tell you. We're telling Mom and Dad later to-day."

"That's wonderful news," I said. "I can't believe you're having another one."

"Mommy and Daddy said I could name her," Rowan squealed.

"Oh really?" I asked. "Mommy and Daddy said that?"

"Uh-huh."

"And do you have a name picked out yet?"

There was a pause, and then Rowan replied, "I'm thinking Vampirina or Princess Twilight Sparkle."

I covered my mouth with my free hand to tamp down the giggle that threatened to escape. Vampirina and Princess Twilight Sparkle were both cartoon characters that Rowan loved. I was a little more partial to Vampirina, myself, but I wasn't about to say that in front of Kate. "Those are both great choices," I said, still choking back a laugh. "Thank you so much for calling and telling me about this."

"Don't tell Mom and Dad," Eli said. "We want it to be a surprise."

"We're having a gender reveal tonight on Facebook Live," Kate continued. "So don't say anything on social media either."

I rolled my eyes. I'd never understood gender reveals. Nobody cares that much about the stupid gender of a baby that they want to take time out of their day to watch you shoot a balloon filled with colored sand or whatever it was that people did during those ordeals. My mother told me when Kate was pregnant with Theo that the reason I didn't understand was because I didn't have a child of my own. I guessed she could be right.

"Mom!" Rowan said. "Why do we have to wait? I want to tell Nana and Papa now!"

"It's just a little while," Kate replied.

"But *I* want to tell them."

"You can wear your Big Sister shirt."

Rowan sighed and the call dropped. I didn't try to call back. I knew that the morning drive was not long enough for Kate to convince Rowan that the gender reveal was a better idea than allowing their oldest child to burst in and proclaim, "It's a girl!"

Rowan and I, much to Kate's dismay, were a lot alike. I'd always been good with children, but when Rowan was born, the bond was immediate. I wondered sometimes if Kate wasn't a bit jealous of our relationship. Kate ended up defending herself against the both of us more often than she probably should have had to.

Once, several months ago, I'd been out to dinner with Eli, Kate, and Rowan while my parents watched Theo. He'd been a newborn, and Kate, a bona fide germophobe, refused to take him out in public until he was at least two months old. Rowan and I voted for pasta, and Kate and Eli wanted to try the fancy new sushi place in downtown Seattle. While Rowan and I both loved sushi, I knew that the wait would likely be an hour or two, and neither Rowan nor I was interested in *that*. As the four of us sat in the car arguing over where to eat, Kate turned exasperatedly toward Eli and said, "I can't believe how alike those two are. I mean, they aren't even related."

Kate realized what she'd said the minute the words were out of her mouth. From the back seat, I could see my brother's jaw set in a hard line, and we drove in silence the rest of the way to the Italian restaurant. The next day, Kate called to apologize, and I could tell from the tone of her voice that she and Eli must've had a horrible argument about it when they got home the night before.

I told her not to worry about it. What she'd said had been insensitive, but Kate hadn't meant to be cruel. She'd said it without thinking. She and I weren't best friends, but she loved my brother, and I knew she'd never say anything to hurt him or me or anyone else, really, on purpose. But her words stung, and Eli knew it. Now that Eli had children, he had a family by blood, and he was keenly aware that was something I didn't have. He worked hard to make sure I never felt left out, but it wasn't as if I could forget the truth.

I got up from the bed and rummaged around in my suitcase to find a clean shirt. I should have hung my clothes in the closet the night before, but I'd been too tired, and now everything I'd brought with me was wrinkled. I laid out a pair of jeans and a T-shirt on the bathroom countertop and shut the door, hoping the steam from the shower that I was about to take would release the wrinkles. If I showed up back at home in wrinkled clothes, my mother would think something awful had happened that I wasn't telling her and grill me about why I couldn't be bothered to look presentable out in public, rather than what it was—sheer laziness on my part.

I was happy for Eli and Kate. Really, I was. Ever since we were kids, Eli had wanted to have a big family. He spent more time thinking about weddings and families than any girl I knew, and Kate was from a big family already. She was in the middle of seven children. Both Eli and Kate worked hard to have a stable and successful life, and for the first time, I began to think about how different our lives had become.

It was true—getting married and having a family hadn't been on my radar. I'd never thought about having a job that made money, saving for my future, buying a house, or taking summer vacations to the beach. It wasn't my style. Still, I wanted . . . something. I wanted something so special that it warranted a phone call early in the morning. I wanted to have something that was mine, just mine, that I could feel proud of and want to share with my family. Maybe I didn't want exactly what Eli had, but I wanted some variation of it.

I stepped into the shower and let the water warm me from head to toe, careful not to let it touch the tender skin on my chest from the spilled coffee. As I lathered my hair, it occurred to me that I'd begun to see everything in my life as temporary. My job, my apartment; my baseball player boyfriend was a lot of fun but not forever—as I'd recently and publicly become painfully aware. Even my visit to Timber Creek was simply a thing I had to get through while I was waiting for my Real Life to begin. I was thirty-six years old.

Wasn't it time my Real Life started?

Maybe I wasn't looking at my visit to Timber Creek the right way. Maybe it was an opportunity. Maybe I was being given a chance to start over in a new place. Hell, I owned a house here, didn't I? I didn't have to go back to Seattle right away. I could stay for as long as I wanted, and I didn't have to wait for anything.

I thought about my parents, about how my mother would react to the news that I was considering staying in Timber Creek indefinitely. I thought about Rowan too and about how she would be upset if I missed important moments in her life because I was nearly four hours away. But the truth was that four hours was hardly a continent. I'd never lived more than an hour from my family, not even during college. Surely everyone, save for Rowan, could understand my need to try something different.

I could hear Holly in my head asking me how I was going to deal with not only inheriting the house of my dead birth mother but also living in it. The truth was that I didn't know. Looking at the house hadn't been so awful, and I liked Sherbet the cat. Besides, Annabelle had left me the house for a reason, hadn't she?

I got out of the shower, grabbed a towel, and then realized that the clothes I'd laid out were still just as wrinkled as they'd been when I pulled them out of the suitcase. Not great, but it would have to do, and for now, telling the rest of my family about my decision to stay would just have to wait.

CHAPTER 14

I TRIED TO IGNORE THE QUESTIONING LOOKS THE ELDERLY
woman driving me gave me as we drove along. I wondered
if she thought I'd brought someone back to my room for the
night and was now doing the walk . . . uh, drive, of shame. It
would be a lie to say that I hadn't at least *thought* about what it
might've been like to have Abel in my room, but this cranky-
looking lady didn't need to know that. I thanked her when she
dropped me off, and I slid into the front seat of my car and
plugged in the directions to Gary's office.

To say that Gary was surprised to see me was an understatement. I waited with the receptionist while he finished up with
a client, a rotund woman who loudly proclaimed as she was
leaving that she would "take that cheating bastard for all he's
worth" and winked at me.

"What are you doing here?" Gary asked. "After showing you the house last night, I figured you'd be on the interstate back to Seattle before daylight."

"I thought about it," I replied, sitting down on his leather couch, the cushion still warm from the behind of the soon-to-be divorcée. "I'm going to stay awhile longer, I think."

"Oh?" Gary seemed surprised at my admission.

I shrugged. "At this point I don't have much to lose."

"So you'd like to take possession?"

"I would."

Gary stared at me for a few seconds before unlocking the middle drawer of his desk and pulling out a thick manila envelope. "There will be more where this came from," he said, nodding toward the envelope. "Get the rest back to me when you can. Nothing in here will have to be notarized."

"Thanks," I replied. "I appreciate everything you've done for me and . . . for Annabelle."

Gary waved one hand in the air. "It's nothing, really," he said. "Like I told you, Annabelle and I went way back. But if you ever decide to sell, promise me you'll give me first shot. That house would be great for rental income."

I nodded. "I will."

"Good," Gary replied, standing up. "I hate to cut our visit short, but I've got a midmorning appointment."

"No problem." I stood and followed him to the door. "Thanks for seeing me on no notice."

"No worries," he said.

"Did you make your reservation?" I asked. "I'm sorry that I was late meeting you."

"Barely," he replied. "Yulina spent entirely too much time chatting with you. It's not your fault."

"She was telling me a bit about Annabelle, and it sounds like they were good friends. They were in a club together?"

"Oh, that stupid St. Francis." Gary rolled his eyes. "I had to put a stop to that. No husband likes to come home from work and hear about all the gossip his wife heard from the town busybodies. They can't leave well enough alone if you ask me. It's going to get them into trouble one day."

I felt my left eyebrow tick up a couple of notches and replied, "Well, thanks again for the help."

Gary gave me a distracted wave as I left the room, his nose already buried in the vast pile of paperwork spread across his desk. I showed myself out, clutching the manila folder, and headed for the house on Maple Street.

When I got to the house, it was midmorning, and Alice was already there, waiting on me. I'd called her on my way to Gary's office, and she'd agreed to meet me. When I opened my car door and Sherbet jumped out, Alice said, "Well, I'll be."

"He must've followed me to my hotel or something," I said.

"I had to shove him down into my bag to get him up to the hotel room."

"That cat stayed with you in a hotel room?"

I nodded. "He did. The only thing I can figure is that he must've jumped up into Abel's Jeep last night when he took me back to the hotel. Slept all night and ate sausage for breakfast."

Alice smiled knowingly at the mention of Abel's name, but she didn't comment on it. "Sherbet's always been an unusual cat," she said finally. "Annabelle used to take him for walks on a leash like a dog."

"Are you kidding me?" I began to giggle. "I used to see that sometimes in Seattle in the apartment building where I lived. I thought only hipsters did that to be ironic."

Alice shrugged. "I don't know what a hipster is," she said. "But I do know that Sherbet must have taken a shine to you, and that's a good thing, because he can be a real asshole when he wants to be."

"I guess that's something we have in common," I said.

Alice let out a croak of a laugh. After a few minutes of Sherbet purring up against her leg, she said, "So, when you called, you said you thought that you might stay here awhile?"

"I was thinking about it," I replied. "It's not like I have anything compelling back in Seattle."

"Annabelle would be glad to know that you're not going to sell right away," Alice said approvingly.

"I'm not doing it for her," I said, sounding harsher than I

meant to. Softening my tone, I continued, "Look, it's not that I'm not appreciative, but she never showed any interest in knowing me when she was alive. I just don't understand why she would leave everything she had to me in death."

Alice fixed me with one of those birdlike stares. It wasn't an unkind gaze. It was more thoughtful, and for a moment, I could see her as a young woman—without the glasses and gray tinge to her hair, without the fine lines around her eyes and mouth, and it occurred to me that she must have been quite pretty in a delicate way that, even now, she tried to hide. "It was a complicated thing," she said finally. "Giving you up."

I sighed. "It doesn't matter. It's mine now, I guess."

Alice touched my shoulder and then with a sly grin said, "I've got a key Gary doesn't have, you know."

"You do?"

"I've got two," Alice replied. "Come on."

I followed Alice down the porch steps, and around the side of the house to where a ramshackle shed stood. Honestly, I thought it might collapse at any second. "What's in there?" I asked, taking a step back. "It looks like it might fall in."

"It's sound as can be," Alice replied, pulling a key from her cardigan and holding it up to me. "This key right here, the silver one, is the key to the shed."

"What's the other key for?"

Alice grinned. "That's the key to your mother's prized possession."

I took the keys and put the first one into the lock and popped it open. After the dust cleared and I'd finished hacking up at least half a lung, I squinted into the darkness. "I don't see anything," I said.

Alice brushed past me and reached inside the shed and felt along the wall. A few seconds later, light bathed the room.

"It's a car," I said.

"She's a beauty, isn't she?"

I nodded. The car, a Volkswagen Beetle, was in pristine condition. It was the old body style, the first body style, and it was a powder-blue convertible. I wanted to get in and drive it right that second. "It's beautiful," I said.

"Most people don't take the time to restore a classic like this," Alice continued. "It's not practical for Washington, especially in the winter, but your mother loved that car. That's where most of her money went."

I ran my hand along the hood. The metal was cold beneath my touch. "The engine is in the back, isn't it?" I asked.

"It is," Alice replied.

"My brother had a friend in high school with one like this," I said. "It wasn't a convertible, and it wasn't in great shape. But it's how I learned to drive a standard."

"You have a brother?"

"An adopted brother," I said. "He's four years younger than I am."

"How lovely," Alice said. "My brother was five years older than me."

"Was?"

"He died," Alice replied. "A long time ago."

"I'm sorry," I said.

Alice waved her hand in the air. "It was a long time ago," she repeated. "Before you were born."

"Still," I said. "I'm sorry. I can't imagine losing my brother."

Alice smiled at me. "What's his name?" she asked.

"Eli," I replied. "He's a dentist in Seattle. He's got two kids—Rowan and Theo—and they just called this morning and said another is on the way."

"I'm glad you've got family," Alice said. Her voice was wistful, and I could tell she meant what she said. "Family is important."

"You and Annabelle were like family," I said.

"We were."

I kept my focus on the car. It really was beautiful. Sure, it wasn't a Mustang or a Corvette, but there was something special about it, nonetheless. It was chilly outside, but not too chilly to take a spin around town with the top down midday.

"Do you want to take it for a spin?" Alice asked, jerking me out of my daydream. "She hasn't been started in a while, but I bet she still runs like a top."

"Really?" I asked.

"As long as you'll let me drive," Alice replied. "I've got a few errands to run. You might as well come with me . . . I mean, if you want to."

"I don't have anything else to do," I said.

"Grab the keys," said Alice. "Let's go."

CHAPTER 15

I STARED OUT THE WINDOW AT THE HOUSES AS WE PASSED them by, and Alice tapped the steering wheel with her fingers to the beat of some seventies disco song I'd never heard. My mother hated disco. She listened to fifties bubblegum pop almost exclusively. I wondered idly if Annabelle liked disco. Surely if Alice liked it, Annabelle had too.

I noticed as we drove that the houses were looking older and less well kept. Some of the houses down Argyle Street, where we turned off, were abandoned. At least, they sure looked that way.

"Where are we going?" I asked.

"To my house," Alice replied.

She pulled the car into the driveway of a shotgun house the color of mud. Despite the run-down condition of the house, there were beautiful mums planted in the flower boxes in the windows and what looked like a new fence going in around the back.

"I know it's not much," Alice said. "But I grew up in this house."

"The flowers are pretty."

Alice smiled. "My father built this house before my brother was born. It's cheap and drafty. But it's been home for a long time."

I got out of the car and followed Alice to the front door. She went inside and motioned me inside when I hesitated. "I can wait out here," I said.

"Don't be ridiculous," Alice replied. "Come."

I followed Alice into a small living room with shag carpet, two threadbare recliners, and an old box television set sitting on the floor. There was a little dog asleep in front of it, and when the door closed behind me, it looked up and started to growl.

"Oh, hush, Mitzi," Alice said. "We aren't here to bother you."

"That dog does not look happy to see us," I said.

"That dog isn't happy to see anyone," Alice said. "She's half-rabid, I swear. She keeps escaping from the yard and terrorizing the neighbor's children. Animal control came last week and said I had to put a fence up or they were going to cite me."

"She doesn't look like she could do much damage," I said.

"She won't bite, but she growls and barks and scares people,"

Alice said. "She was my mother's dog, and I know she's basically the worst dog to have ever lived, but I promised my mother I'd take care of her."

"So you live here alone?" I asked. I already knew the answer, but I didn't know what else to say.

Alice nodded. "My father has been gone for a long time, but I lost my mother two springs ago."

"I'm so sorry," I replied.

"It's okay," Alice said, dismissing me. "She'd been sick for a long time. Early onset dementia. It was just her time."

Alice led me into the kitchen and motioned for me to sit down at the table.

"Annabelle grew up across the street," Alice said. "In the house where the children Mitzi doesn't like now live. Her parents and my parents were good friends. After Annabelle's mom and dad died, my parents took her in. We were fourteen. She lived with us until . . . well, until she got pregnant with you."

"Was your father mad Annabelle got pregnant?" I asked.

"My father was mad about a lot of things," Alice said, somewhat dismissively. "He was angry in general."

"Did your parents send her away when they found out?"

Alice shook her head. "No," she said. "They never found out."

I was about to ask her why not, when there was a knock at the front door. I peered around the kitchen opening to see Abel Abbott standing in the doorway. He was dripping with sweat, despite the relative coolness of the day. His white undershirt clung to him, and a flannel shirt was wrapped around one arm.

"I snagged my arm on a damn nail," he said, stepping into the house. "Do you have a first-aid kit?"

"It's in the bathroom," Alice said, jumping up. "I'll be right back."

Abel came into the kitchen and sat down beside me. "Hello again," he said.

"Hi," I said.

"I thought you were leaving."

I shrugged. "I'm not sure my car would even make it back to Seattle," I replied.

Abel laughed. It was a hearty laugh that reached all the way up to his eyes. Then he winced as he rested his arm down on the table.

Alice returned with the first-aid kit and set it on the table between us. "Abel, that looks bad," she said. "Maybe you ought to go to the ER."

"Is there a *nail* in there?" I asked. I leaned over to inspect his arm.

"Nail gun mishap," he said.

"Do you want me to drive you to the ER?"

"I'm not spending all day in there," Abel said. "I can get the nail out. Do you have any tweezers in that kit?"

Alice dug around in the kit and produced a metal pair of

tweezers. "The kit is a bit old," she admitted. "I don't know how sterile everything is."

"Do you have a lighter?" I asked.

"In the top drawer," Alice replied, pointing to a cabinet by the kitchen sink.

I took the tweezers from Alice and fished the lighter out of the drawer. "Just a second," I said.

"What are you doing?" Alice asked. "You aren't going to use that to pull out the nail, are you? I really think he needs to see a doctor."

"It'll be fine," I said. "I used to do this all the time at the newspaper where I worked. The building was half-condemned, and people were forever stepping on nails. Nobody could afford to go to the doctor without health insurance."

"And everybody just trusted you to pull rusty nails out of their feet?" Abel asked. "I hope you gave them a tetanus shot while you were at it."

"They got a tetanus shot down at the mobile vaccination clinic," I said, sitting back down next to Abel to inspect his arm. "And they trusted me, because I was in nursing school for a semester back in college."

"Just a semester?" Abel asked.

"Yeah," I said, taking hold of Abel's wrist with one hand and poising the tweezers above the nail with the other hand. "As it turns out, while I'm fine with blood and guts, I have a terrible bedside manner."

"Ow! Fuck!" Abel yelled, jerking away from me as I plucked the nail from his forearm. "Jesus, you could have warned me!"

"What fun would that have been?" I asked. I held the bloody nail up for him and Alice to see. "Besides, I was afraid you'd squirm."

Abel accepted the alcohol Alice handed to him and said, "I don't think I need stitches."

"Of course you don't," I said. "But you probably *do* need a tetanus shot."

"I had one a couple of years ago," Abel said. "My daughter pulled a board from her tree house and left it lying in the grass. I didn't see it and stepped on it."

"I remember that," Alice said, placing gauze and medical tape over Abel's arm. "I'm sorry about this, but you know how much I appreciate this, right?"

Abel nodded and stood up to give Alice a hug. "I know," he said. "And you know I'd do anything for you and Mitzi."

At the sound of her name, Mitzi jumped up, ran up to Abel, and practically leaped into his arms. He held her up to his face, and she licked his nose, making happy little grunting noises the whole time until he put her down.

"Mitzi loves Abel," Alice said matter-of-factly, when she caught me staring at the scene, openmouthed. "She loved my mother and she loves Abel; everybody else gets barred teeth and barking."

Outside, there was a crack and then a yell from behind the house. Abel let out a curse and ran out the front door. Alice and I followed him outside to where a man was standing on the other side of the newly posted fence with a sledgehammer.

"You're on my property!" the man yelled, raising the sledgehammer above his head and bringing it down onto the already splintering wood. "I warned you!"

"Mr. Rose!" Alice said. "What are you doing?"

"I warned that boy," the man, whose name was apparently Mr. Rose, said. "I warned him yesterday he was on my property!"

"The fence isn't on your property, old man," Abel said. "You got the survey same as Alice over here did."

"That survey is a steaming pile of bullshit!" Mr. Rose spat. "You're damn near five inches on my property!"

"Mr. Rose," Alice pleaded. "You can't just come out here and smash my fence."

"Like hell I can't," Mr. Rose said. "You sent this behemoth of a man to intimidate me."

Abel sighed and pressed his fingers into the bridge of his nose. "Mr. Rose, you've known me for years. You know that I help Alice keep the house up. Why would I want to intimidate you?"

Mr. Rose was no longer paying attention to Alice or Abel. Instead he was concentrating on me, his bushy eyebrows knitted together. He let the sledgehammer fall to the ground as he said, "My God. You look just like Annabelle."

"Maeve," Alice said, taking hold of my shoulder. "This is Silas Rose. Silas, this is Maeve Stephens, Annabelle's daughter."

I stuck out my hand automatically. "It's nice to meet you," I said.

Silas blinked. And then, remembering his manners, took my hand. "I'm sorry, I didn't know Annabelle had a daughter."

"I was adopted," I said. I'd realized by now that this was something I was going to have to get used to saying.

"But you look so much like her," Silas replied.

"She didn't adopt me," I said. "She gave me up for adoption."

Now Silas looked really confused. "I don't understand," he said. "Annabelle never would've done something like that."

Beside me, Alice stiffened. "That's a discussion for another day," she said.

"It's okay," I said, hoping to break the tension. "Really. I have great parents."

"I just thought I knew her, is all," Silas continued. "I never figured she had a kid."

"I never figured she wanted a kid," I said, only half joking. I could feel Alice's eyes boring into my back, but I didn't turn around to look at her.

Just then a woman came flying down the steps of the house next door. She was wearing a hot-pink terry-cloth robe that scarcely covered her behind. In one hand she held a lit cigarette, and in the other, a cordless phone. I recognized her instantly as Charlene, the woman I'd met at Three Sheets the other night.

"Daddy!" she said, hurrying over to us. "What are you doing? You said you were going on a walk."

"You didn't notice he had a sledgehammer in his hands?" Abel asked, holding the instrument up for Charlene to see.

Charlene glared at Abel. "I didn't see him at all," she said. "I was in my room, getting ready for my date tonight."

"They're on my property," Silas said, but with much less gusto than he had before.

"Daddy, we've been through this," Charlene said, sighing heavily. "You have the survey." Then, turning her attention to me, she said, "Oh, hey, Maeve. What are you doing here?"

"You've met her?" Silas demanded, looking at his daughter. "You met Annabelle's daughter and didn't tell me?"

"I didn't hardly have the time," Charlene replied.

"Are we good here?" Abel asked. "I'd like to fix this damage before I have to pick the girls up from school."

Silas looked from Charlene to Abel, and then to me. "I still say you're on my property," he said.

"Is the fence going to hurt anything, Mr. Rose?" I asked, glancing up at Abel. "If Abel doesn't get the fence up, Alice will have to give her mother's dog, Mitzi, away."

Silas's face softened. "Well," he said. "I would have appreciated being consulted is all."

"Why don't we just quit for the day?" Alice asked. "Abel, you can't work with that arm the way it is. I demand you see a doctor before you come back here."

Abel opened his mouth to protest, but Alice gave him a look so fierce, he decided against it. "Fine," he said. "I'll go home and get cleaned up."

"Good idea," Alice replied. "And, Maeve, we need to get to lunch."

Silas took my hands in his. "It was a pleasure to meet you, Maeve."

"I'm sorry about that," Alice said as we walked away from Silas and Charlene. "Silas is a bit of an old coot. I should have known he'd try to start trouble when we began to build the fence."

"But he and Annabelle were friends?" I asked.

Alice nodded. "Silas was five years older than us in school. He's always been an odd duck, but your mother had a way with him. She had a way with all people, really, but people like Silas, like Abel, were drawn to her."

"Abel?"

"Oh, Abel isn't anything like Silas," Alice said. "But he's got a temper on him. He's never been one for small talk or formalities. And since his wife died, it's only been that much worse."

"Charlene told me he gave up writing to be a handyman," I said.

Alice laughed. "Well, 'carpenter' is more like it, but he's a jack-of-all-trades, really. He's good with his hands. He's been good to me," Alice said. "He's been good to my mother. I suspect it was because he admired your mother so much."

I didn't say anything as we got back into the car. It felt overwhelming and strange to be here, almost in place of Annabelle. Everyone seemed to love this woman whom I'd never met but was related to by blood and the rather broken bonds of daughterhood. I was in her house, taking care of her business, meeting her friends, and now sitting in the passenger seat of her car. Always before, being adopted was just something that had happened to me. It wasn't something that I thought had any effect on who I was or what I'd become. But now, sitting next to Alice, driving down the roads of a town that I might've called home if things had been different, I wasn't so sure.

ANNABELLE

April 1984

ANNABELLE STUDIED A SPOON AS SHE MADE HER WAY around the table, setting the pieces of silverware in their proper places. Judging from the spots on everything, Alice had been the one to wash them.

Behind her, humming about the stove, was Alice's mother, Lillian. She was a slight woman, like her daughter. Annabelle was sure she'd been a beauty in her time, but now she was as faded as the blue knit shawl she wore. To Annabelle's eyes, she looked at least twenty years older than she was, and Annabelle figured that had a lot to do with the way William acted when he got drunk. She'd still not been able to get that conversation out of her head or the feel of his hand on her leg to go away. He'd not said anything to her since that night other than a few pleasantries in passing, but she felt his eyes on her all the time, and she wondered if Lillian and Alice noticed.

"Stop looking at the silverware like you think I washed it," Alice said, coming in through the doorway. "Mom did it, not me."

Annabelle grinned. "I don't believe you."

"She knows I wash dishes better than that," Lillian said, flipping over a pork chop. "Where is your father? Dinner will be ready in five minutes."

"He's in the garage," Alice replied.

Annabelle looked over at Alice. They all knew that William being in the garage was code for drinking.

"Do you want me to go get him?" Alice asked her mother.

"No," Lillian replied. "I'll go. You just stay here and watch the meat."

Alice nodded and took over at the stove.

"Did he have a bad day at work?" Annabelle asked.

Alice nodded. "He got laid off at the factory," she said.

Annabelle stopped setting the table. "What?"

"Got caught with whiskey in his coffee thermos," Alice said. "He says it's because the foreman doesn't like him, but I poured out his coffee after he gave me his lunch pail. It almost made me puke."

"What will he do now?"

"He'll find another job," Alice replied. "He always does, but he's blaming Billy over this one. Says he poisoned the foreman against his own father."

"I'm sure that's not true," Annabelle replied. "He'd never do that to you or your mom."

"Or to you," Alice said.

Annabelle didn't respond. The yelling coming from the garage was getting louder and louder, and both girls went to the doorway to listen.

"Should we go and check on them?" Annabelle asked.

Alice shook her head. "We need to get dinner on the table," she replied. "If we don't, it will be worse for her."

"Finish with the table," Annabelle said. "You always burn the pork chops."

A few minutes later, Lillian limped back into the house, missing a shoe and her cheeks tearstained. Behind her came William. He sat down in his chair at the head of the table and said, "Go get cleaned up, Lillian. You look like hell."

Annabelle lay awake late that night, tucked into bed and staring out the window facing the street. Every once in a while a pair of headlights would shine into the room, illuminating the twin bed where Alice was sleeping. Usually the two friends stayed up late into the night talking, but Alice had a cough that wouldn't go away, and Lillian had given her cough syrup with codeine. She'd been asleep since eight thirty p.m.

Lillian was asleep in her bedroom, and William was passed out in the recliner in front of the television set—his nightly ritual. Sometimes he would still be there in the morning when Alice and Annabelle got up for school. Annabelle thought that was probably the reason he got fired from the factory. She knew a few boys who hadn't been able to keep their jobs after high school graduation, because they couldn't get to work on time. They'd complained about it at parties—high school parties—and Annabelle always wondered why being an adult was so hard for some people. She couldn't wait to graduate and get a job. She couldn't wait to be on her own.

Just then a car drove down the street and stopped just past the old oak tree in the front yard. The headlights went off and then on and then back off again. Annabelle threw off the covers and stuffed her feet into her tennis shoes. As quietly as she could, she opened the window and climbed outside.

Billy was waiting in the car, and he opened the door when he saw her coming.

"Hey," he said. "I'm sorry I'm late. I got caught up."

"With what?"

"Joe and a couple of the other guys from the plant are having a party," Billy replied.

"Are we going?" Annabelle asked.

Billy shook his head. "It's not your type of party, trust me."

"Well, where are we going?"

"Back to my place?"

Annabelle shifted in the seat. "Okay."

"We don't have to," Billy said quickly. "We can go somewhere else. It's okay."

"No," Annabelle replied. "I want to. It's just the last time we were there—I don't know, I don't want your dad to come busting in again."

"I thought you said he was passed out?"

"He is."

"He won't wake up again. The only reason he came by that night is because he'd been at the bar drinking and came home and you and Alice weren't there," Billy said. "Once he's in that chair, believe me, he's not getting out again."

"Alice said he got fired today," Annabelle replied. "Did you have anything to do with it?"

Billy sighed. "He came to work drunk, Anna," he said. "I could have told him to go home, and I could have covered his shift, but I didn't."

"That doesn't mean it's your fault he got fired."

"He won't see it that way," Billy replied.

"Are you going to be okay?" Annabelle asked, putting her hand on his arm. "He and your mom had an awful fight before dinner."

"About him losing his job?"

"I don't know," Annabelle said.

"Did he hurt my mom?" Billy asked, pulling into his driveway.

"She went to bed right after dinner," Annabelle replied. "She seemed pretty shaken up."

"I'll go by the grocery store and check on her tomorrow," Billy said. "She won't want me coming by the house. At least not for a while."

Annabelle got out of the car and followed Billy to the door. "I'm sorry it is the way it is," she said, taking hold of his hand. His eyes looked so sad, and all she wanted to do was wrap herself around him and tell him everything was going to be okay, even if they both knew it wasn't true.

"I'm not sorry," Billy said, pulling her closer to him. "I've got you, and that's the way it is for me. Nothing else matters."

"I'm glad I've got you too," Annabelle whispered against his chest, and then she allowed herself to be pulled inside, where their own private world awaited them.

CHAPTER 16

LATER THAT DAY, AS I TOLD MY MOTHER I PLANNED TO stay in Timber Creek, I paced in the hallway of the house, opening up random drawers and looking inside them, lifting up towels in the bathroom, and smelling old perfume bottles. As I'd anticipated, my mother was less than thrilled with my decision.

"Why do you need to stay?" she asked. "Is there something you aren't telling me?"

"No, I'm telling you everything," I said, sitting down on the side of the bathtub. "It's just that I think it would be a good idea to spend some time here. Maybe clean out the house and get it ready to sell. I don't know. I want some time here. That's all."

"Well, I can't say I understand," my mother replied.

"I don't need you to understand," I said, sighing heavily. "I just need you to support my decision."

"Fine, fine. Do you need your father and me to come up one day next week and bring you some things?" my mother asked. She was clearly upset, but I could tell her resolve was waning.

"I already talked to Eli. He's going to bring me some clothes on Friday. Kate is visiting her sister in Albuquerque for a week, and she's taking Ro and Theo. So he's got a couple of days. He may bring Dad along, but there really isn't any reason for you to come. I know you don't like to leave the city."

"I know Kate is going to be gone," my mother said stiffly. "My daughter-in-law tells me about her plans before she makes them."

I sighed. "Mom, cut me some slack. It's not like I planned on my birth mother dying and leaving me all of her worldly possessions. This is new for me too."

"It's fine," I heard my father say. It made me laugh that he was listening on his phone in his study. Some things never changed. My father continued, "Don't worry about your mother. You know how she gets."

"This doesn't have anything to do with her," I said. "I'm not trying to make her upset."

"That's precisely the issue," he replied. "It's got nothing to do with her."

By now my mother was probably huffing down the hallway to call Kate on her cell and complain about how she wished her daughter was as easy to deal with as her daughter-in-law.

"Will you make sure the first two drawers in my dresser are packed?" I asked. "And the shoes and dresses in the closet."

"I will," my father replied. "If you'll make sure to stay in Timber Creek as long as you need to stay and promise not to worry about us here in Seattle."

"I'll try," I said. "But I can't make any promises."

"So, how are things?" my father asked.

"Alice invited me to some knitting circle thing Annabelle used to be a part of," I replied. I thought about telling him about meeting Abel, but I didn't really know how to say it without it sounding like I'd been stalking him or something. All our meetings had been by chance, and he was nothing more than an interesting acquaintance.

"That's nice," my father replied. "I'm sure she's thrilled to get to know you."

"It's just so weird," I said. "Being here. I feel like an interloper in someone else's life."

"Try not to think of it that way," my father replied. "You're learning more about yourself, and you know, even though I'm very sorry for the circumstances, I don't think that this could have come at a better time in your life."

"Well," I replied. "I can be an unemployed loser anywhere, I guess."

"Don't you dare talk about yourself that way!" my mother cut in. "You are *not* a loser!"

"I better get going," I said. "I called in an order to the restaurant down the street, and it's about time to pick it up."

"June!" my father said. "Hang up the phone!"

I listened to them argue back and forth for a few seconds,

smiling to myself at the familiarity of it all, before I pressed the end call button and set the phone on the coffee table, my stomach rumbling. I guessed tomorrow I'd go grocery shopping so that I wouldn't be ordering from Three Sheets every single night. I'd made up a bed in the spare room at the end of the hallway—on the opposite side from the master bedroom. The house was surprisingly barren with the exception of the overfull master, and I didn't want to go back in there. Not only would the room have to be cleaned out before I could sleep in there, but it also felt too much like I was intruding on a space that wasn't mine. It was easier if I just shut the door and pretended like the house had only two bedrooms instead of three.

I picked up my keys from next to my phone and stood. That burger was sounding better and better. Three Sheets was less than two blocks from the house, and when I stepped outside, it was surprisingly cold. Sherbet began to rub up against my legs, and I took a cursory look around the neighborhood. All the houses looked like this one, older, but nice and neat, except for a few across the street. One of the houses was a smaller version of a Victorian-style house with peeling siding and an overgrown lawn. There was a rusted van in the driveway, so I assumed someone lived there, even though there were no lights on inside. The house next to it was split up into a duplex, with two front doors. It also had peeling siding and an overgrown lawn, and two of the windows on the right side of the duplex were busted out. There was an errant tree branch across the roof.

It was already dark by the time I made it the couple of blocks to Three Sheets. The same bartender as before greeted me with an eye roll when I told her I'd placed an order to go.

"Give me a sec," she said.

I sat down at the bar and glanced around. It wasn't as crowded as it had been on Saturday. I figured it was probably the sudden cold snap keeping people at home inside their houses. In the corner, however, Abel sat in the same spot I'd seen him in the other night. He looked up and caught my eye, and I gave him a little wave.

"Don't waste your time," the bartender said, heaving a white plastic bag up onto the bar. "He's not interested."

I stared at her in a vain attempt to keep my neck from reddening. "What are you talking about?"

"Don't take it personal," she said. "Abel Abbott ain't interested in nobody."

"Okay," I said. "Thanks for the tip."

"I'm just giving you some friendly advice. Don't waste your time."

"I didn't know you were friendly," I said, grabbing my food and putting some cash on the counter. "Keep the change."

I started to walk away, but stopped at the door and turned around, glancing between the bartender and Abel. It irritated me that she thought I was interested, and it irritated me even more that she thought she could tell me who I should and shouldn't waste my time on. If anybody was my friend in this damn tiny town, it was Abel Abbott. Ignoring her stare, I sauntered over to where Abel sat and set my food down on top of his table.

"How's that arm?" I asked.

He gestured to the chair across from him, and I sat down.

"It's fine," he said. "Alice called me four times this afternoon until I went to urgent care. They gave me some antibiotics and a butterfly bandage. I don't think I needed either."

"Do you help her out a lot?" I asked.

"From time to time," Abel replied.

"That's nice of you," I said.

Abel shrugged. "What did you order?"

"A burger and fries," I said. "The food here is fantastic."

"Go ahead and eat," he said. "It's only good when it's hot."

"You sure?" I asked. "I don't want to interrupt you."

Abel waved to one of the waitresses and held up two fingers. "Might as well have some company."

I opened the plastic bag and dug in, trying not to feel self-conscious as he watched me while I chewed.

The waitress came over and set two dark-colored beers on the table. Abel shoved one over to me. "Try it," he said.

I swallowed and took a sip. "Tastes familiar," I said.

"Better not drink three this time."

We sat in silence for a few minutes while I ate, and I glanced around the bar. Several of the patrons were looking in our direction, and the waitress who'd served us was at the bar talking to the bartender. I shoved a few fries in my mouth and tried to ignore it.

"So," I said, after I'd finished every last fry, "have you heard that I'm your new neighbor?"

Abel set down his beer glass and looked at me. "So you're staying?"

I shrugged. "For a little while, at least."

I prepared myself for the storm of questions that were sure to follow—*What about your life back in Seattle? Don't you have a boyfriend? A house? A job?*

Instead, Abel simply said, "Well, then welcome to the neighborhood."

"I feel like people are staring at me," I said, glancing around. "I don't feel very welcome."

"That's because they are," Abel replied. He took a long drink of his beer.

"Why?"

"You're new in town, for one," Abel replied. "And for another, you're sitting with me."

"Your table off-limits?" I asked. "I didn't see a sign."

"What did the bartender tell you about me before you came over here?" Abel wanted to know. "I bet she told you something to the effect of, 'Don't even try,' right?"

I stared at him from over the top of my beer glass. "More or less."

"That's what I thought."

"I'm confused," I said, sitting up a little straighter in my chair. "Aren't you some kind of famous writer and thrill seeker? I figured you'd be the town hero."

"Town disappointment is more like it."

"I doubt that," I said.

Abel let out a throaty chuckle before downing the rest of his beer. He stood up and placed a crisp twenty-dollar bill down onto the table. "Thanks for the company," he said. "But you got some sound advice earlier—don't even try. I'm a lost cause."

I threw a tip down on the table and followed him out the door while the barmaid stood behind the bar. I didn't know it was possible to want to slap someone I'd just met, but she was pretty high on my list right then.

The crisp air hit me right as I exited the bar, and it felt good against my beer-warmed cheeks. "What is your problem?" I yelled at Abel. "You going for some dark-and-mysterious vibe?"

He turned around, a smile inching up on his face, although he was doing his best to contain it. "You aren't buying it?"

I waited for him to jog back to where I was standing. "Nope," I said.

"I guess I'll have to work a little harder at it, then," Abel replied. He took a step closer to me.

"You probably should." All my instincts told me to answer his step toward me by closing off the space between us, but I knew that I shouldn't. I didn't know him, not really, and the last thing I needed was to get involved with another quasi-famous guy with no concern for anybody other than himself, especially if this quasi-famous guy fancied himself the dangerous type.

The door to the bar opened, and a wave of people spilled out onto the sidewalk, laughing and joking with one another. One of the men in the group stepped off the curb and stumbled forward, crashing into me as he struggled to gain his footing. I pitched forward and fell into Abel, who caught me by the arms before I face-planted onto the parking lot.

"Sorry, lady!" the man called over his shoulder as he staggered after his friends.

"Watch where you're going, jackass!" Abel yelled. "Are you all right?" he asked me.

"I think so," I said.

"You're, uh, you're losing your jacket," Abel replied. He reached over to pull my hoodie back over my shoulder, and my body responded with an involuntary shiver when his hand brushed my bare skin.

I was getting ready to apologize and blame my reaction on the wind chill when Abel grasped at the fabric of my hoodie and pulled me closer to him. When he looked down at me, I saw his teeth graze his bottom lip, and that was all the invitation I needed to reach up and draw his mouth down to mine.

When he finally pulled away from me, we were both breathless.

"I should go," I said, fumbling with the zipper on my hoodie to keep from looking at him.

"Me too," Abel replied. "I'll, uh, I'll see you around."

Chapter 17

Sherbet was on the porch when I got back to the house. He was lying in front of the door, cleaning himself, as I stuck my key in the lock. When I opened the door, he shot inside.

When I hesitated at the threshold, the cat looked at me as if to say, "Well?"

I stepped inside, and he jumped up onto the couch and resumed his cleaning.

It had been an interesting day in Timber Creek, that was for sure. I supposed sitting on a ragged couch with a strange cat was the least of it, so, after taking a quick shower, I changed into my old, ratty sweatpants and a city-league softball shirt I'd stolen from Eli and plopped down onto the couch, but I couldn't get my mind off Abel, which annoyed me.

To keep myself from overanalyzing everything, I scrolled

through my phone, logging into various social media networks to see what I'd missed, to keep myself from dwelling on a man other women told me to stay away from and of whom my own heart told me to be wary.

Besides my family, the only people I'd really been close with were Holly and Christine. I'd always kept to myself, preferring to stay in rather than go out, a piece of my personality that my mother was forever lamenting. Judging from the worn spot on the couch where I sat, Annabelle had been like that too.

As I scrolled past the posts of people I didn't really care to interact with, I stopped on a picture of Eli's on Instagram. It was of his new bookshelf, which took up an entire wall of his study. He'd had it built-in, and he had one of those ladders that I'd seen only in the Beast's library in *Beauty and the Beast*. He and Kate stood next to it, grinning proudly. "Finally finished!" the caption read. I enlarged the picture to get a better look at the books just behind them on the top shelf. All of my brother's books were in alphabetical order, which meant that Abel Abbott wrote the very first books on the bookshelf. I'd never read them, but I knew the titles well. They were Eli's favorites.

It occurred to me that I should probably have told Eli about Abel the last time we talked. He probably would have been more excited about packing up my clothes and bringing them to me. As it was, he was less than thrilled about the eight-hour round-trip, and he'd told me as much. He didn't get many days off, because he often volunteered at the low-cost clinic downtown. I made a mental note to tell him the next time we talked.

He'd agreed only because he was worried about me, and I felt bad for taking advantage of that fact. I was fine, I guessed, for the most part. Still, he knew what it was like to lose a birth mother. Eli encouraged me, the summer I was sixteen, to reach out to Annabelle, and I don't think he'd ever quite forgiven himself. He told me later that he thought if I could connect with my birth mother, then maybe he wouldn't miss his own quite so much.

After all my letters came back unanswered, he'd been angry, and I'd caught him one night in his bedroom, furiously writing in his notebook. One of the unopened letters was propped up against the lamp on his desk.

"What are you doing?" I asked him, angry that he'd taken one of the letters out of the trash. "That's not yours!"

As I went to grab the envelope, I glanced down at Eli's notebook and saw Annabelle's name. I saw the words he'd written after it, and I was surprised a kid his age knew them.

"I was just . . ." Eli trailed off, and I noticed his cheeks were tearstained.

"Are you all right?" I asked. "What's wrong? Why are you crying?"

"I'm not crying," he replied stubbornly.

I knelt down in front of him and looked him in the eyes. "I know what you're doing, and I love you for it," I said. "But it's okay. She doesn't want to know me, and neither one of us can bully her into it."

"It's not fair," he'd said. "It's not fair that she gets to be alive and my mother is dead. She doesn't deserve it."

I hugged him close to me while we both cried, and I promised myself right then and there that I'd never contact Annabelle again.

The next morning, I found the letter ripped to shreds and thrown in the hallway bathroom's trash can. We never talked about that night, but I wondered if he sometimes thought about it the way I did—on nights when the memories he never got to make with a family that didn't exist were nearly too much to accept.

Chapter 18

THE NEXT MORNING, I WOKE UP WITH A START, THE FEEL-
ing of being smothered pulling me out of sleep. I bolted
upright, and Sherbet clung to my chest like Velcro, a displeased
meow emitting from his throat. I managed to pry him off me
without losing any skin, and he sat at my feet, alternating between vocalizing his displeasure and purring. Groaning, I
forced myself out of bed and padded into the kitchen, scoop-
ing up a bit of the cat food I'd brought in from the porch and
pouring it into an empty bowl for Sherbet. He wasted no time
and began to eat. I silently cursed him for waking me up at the
crack of dawn—my phone screen read six thirty a.m.—but I
decided that I might as well start the day by picking up around
the house.

By midmorning I'd managed to clean the kitchen and rid
it of all the spoiled food. There wasn't much by way of food to

begin with, and I found it interesting that in practically every drawer, there was a set of knitting needles. There were knitting needles in the silverware drawer, in the pantry, and even one very cold pair of metal knitting needles in the freezer. I put the collection in the middle of the dining room table.

In the spare bedroom, I discovered a huge pile of blankets in the cedar chest, and underneath the blankets, I found more skeins of yarn. I was beginning to wonder if Annabelle had done anything other than sit in her house and knit. Sherbet made himself a bed on one of the blankets, and so I left them all out on the floor as I continued to make my way through the house. There was a large bookshelf in the other spare bedroom. It was so crammed full of books that I couldn't even see what the titles to any of them were until I started pulling them off the shelves.

There were all kinds of books on the shelves, and most of them appeared to have been read multiple times. Some of them looked waterlogged, like they'd been read in the bathtub with a good glass of wine—really, in my opinion, the only good way to read. The majority of the books were nonfiction true-crime books. There were a few women's fiction novels with cutesy covers. There were books of poetry and short stories, and there were several classic gothic novels like *Wuthering Heights* and *Dracula*.

Toward the middle of the bookshelf, sandwiched in between books about John Dillinger and the Dillinger Gang, were two of Abel Abbott's books. I picked one of them up and turned it over in my hands. It was clear the book had been read, because there were creases in the spine. But it wasn't beat up like the others. I opened it up to the title page and was surprised by what I found. There was an inscription to Annabelle.

> *For Annabelle,*
>
> *Thank you. Your kind words and understanding ears were what I needed to get through my darkest days.*
>
> > *Always,*
> > *Abel*

I stared at the ink-smeared words for a long time, trying to figure out exactly what it was they meant. The other book had a similar note. I remembered Alice mentioning the day before that Annabelle had been friends with Abel, a fact that I found odd yet interesting. I took both books and set them in the middle of the table along with the yarn and knitting needles.

I'd just piled everything up nice and neat on the table when I heard a knock at the door. Half expecting to see a Jehovah's Witness at the door with a pamphlet for the Watchtower, I opened it up to see Yulina standing there, a nervous smile on her face.

"Hi," I said, stepping back to let her inside.

"I hope I am not intruding," she said. "Alice told me you were still here."

194 ANNIE ENGLAND NOBLIN

"Of course not," I replied. "Come in."

I wondered why Gary hadn't told her I was still here, but figured that maybe Alice had gotten to her first.

She gave me a hesitant smile. "I cannot stay long. My mother-in-law has Ani, and I need to pick her up soon."

"Ani?"

"My daughter," Yulina explained. "She's two. Her name is Anichka, but we call her Ani."

I motioned for her to sit down on the couch. "Anichka," I repeated. "That's . . . Ukrainian?"

Yulina's face lit up. "Yes. It is both Hebrew and Ukrainian," she said. "How did you know?"

"My father worked with a man who was originally from Ukraine," I replied. "His wife was named Anichka. I was friends with their daughters before they moved out of state."

"I am from Ukraine," Yulina said. "Originally."

"Where in Ukraine?" I asked.

"You've heard of Chernobyl nuclear disaster, yes?"

"Yes," I replied. "You're from *there*?"

I tried not to sound too incredulous, but I wasn't sure that I was entirely successful. I'd first learned about the Chernobyl nuclear disaster when I was in junior high. I'd always found it fascinating, especially because I knew people from Ukraine when I learned about it. My father, however, told me never to ask my friends, the two daughters of the man he worked with, about it. He said it might be too difficult for them to speak about, although I couldn't imagine why. They'd been children when it happened, and lived far away from the disaster site. As an adult, though, I understood his hesitation and was glad I'd never stuck my foot in my mouth by asking nosy questions.

"I was born in Pripyat," Yulina continued after a short pause. "It was the city built to house the power plant workers. My father was one of them."

"I read about that place," I said. "In a global history class I took in junior high."

"My father died the day of the disaster," Yulina said. "My mother, sisters, and I were relocated to Slavutych."

"I'm so sorry," I said. I reached out to her and stopped myself just in time when I saw her stiffen. "I can't imagine how terrible that must have been for your family."

Yulina shrugged. "I was not yet two, so I did not get a chance to know him," she said. "My mother remarried a kind man. I had a good life."

I wanted to ask her what brought her to the United States and ask her about how she met Gary, but I didn't want to pry, especially after her admission about her father. Instead I said, "Do you miss it? Ukraine?"

The wistful look on Yulina's face faded and her eyes became hard. "No," she said at last. "This is my life now."

"That's a good way to look at things," I said. "I should give that philosophy a try. Because I don't have any idea what my life is right now."

"It can be hard to tell sometimes," Yulina said. "Life is not always what we think it will be."

"That's for sure," I muttered. "If someone told me even two weeks ago that this is where I'd be right now, well, I wouldn't have believed them."

"I wanted to become a scientist," Yulina said. "But my marks were not high enough. When I met Gary, I thought I could come to this country and go to school."

"Did you?" I asked. "Go to school?"

Yulina shook her head. "Gary did not like that idea."

I bristled. I didn't want her to think I was judging her, although it was hard for me to understand how in the twenty-first century, women were still accustomed to being told what they could and could not do by their husbands. "How did you and Gary meet?" I asked instead of saying what I was thinking. What did I know anyway? It wasn't like I was the authority on healthy relationships—quite the opposite, in fact.

Yulina smiled. "Now that is an interesting story."

"I've got time," I said.

"My best friend Irina met a man through a matching service," Yulina replied. "He is a doctor from Los Angeles. I did not like Irina meeting men this way, but I understood it. She came back for a visit two years after meeting her husband and brought their son. She was happy, and I was not happy living in Ukraine. She encouraged me to sign up for the program."

"So you decided to give it a try?" I prompted after Yulina became quiet. "And that's how you met Gary?"

"I met another man," Yulina said. "Gary's friend from Seattle. One of his trips to Ukraine, he brought Gary with him."

"And you fell in love with Gary?" I asked.

"Gary's friend was married," Yulina said. "Gary told me on their last night in Ukraine. I was heartbroken, but Gary was kind. I married him six months later and moved here, to Timber Creek."

"Do you still speak to Gary's friend?" I asked. "Is he still married?"

"He and Gary are no longer friends. I do not know what happened to him."

I watched Yulina's face as she spoke. The pain in her eyes was palpable. She must have really cared for this friend of Gary's, and I wondered if she'd married Gary by default or if she really loved him. I couldn't imagine how hard it would be to move to another country with a man I barely knew and a culture I didn't understand. It was hard enough being four hours away from everyone I loved. How would I cope on a different continent? On impulse, I reached out and tried again to take her hand. "I'm sorry," I said. "For the ache that must have caused."

Yulina recoiled, and my fingernails snagged the cotton of her long-sleeved shirt instead. Before she managed to pull the fabric back down over her right wrist, I caught the blue-green hue of a healing bruise. It was huge. "Yulina," I gasped. "What happened?"

Yulina sat on her hands, casting her eyes down to the floor, where Sherbet was fast asleep at our feet after finishing his second helping of cat food. "It is nothing," she said, in a voice so tremulous that it was barely audible. "Anichka is in a phase.

She likes to bite. The doctor, how do you say . . . pediatrician . . . said it is quite normal."

I nodded. "My niece, Rowan, was a biter," I said. "She bit me so hard on the back of my thigh once that she drew blood. My brother wanted me to bite her back, but I could never bring myself to do it."

"Me either," Yulina said, relaxing a bit. "She's just a child."

"My nephew has never done anything like that," I continued. "He must take after my brother, and not my sister-in-law, because I'm almost positive that Kate would encourage it if it was suggested in any of her parenting books."

Yulina gave me a tight but grateful smile. "I should go," she said. She reached down into the purse she carried on her shoulder and pulled something out of it. "These are the purpose of my visit. I wanted to bring these to you."

I looked at the pair of knitting needles she held in her hands. "What are those for?"

"Annabelle gave them to me," she said. "They were my first set. They are bamboo." She ran one of her long, thin fingers along the needles. "They will be easier to use as a beginner. They catch the yarn. It is easier to keep these from slipping."

"I don't knit," I said to her. "I've never even tried."

"I know," Yulina replied. "Alice told me. I thought you might want to take these to the meeting tonight."

"Oh, I don't think I'm going to that," I replied. I'd forgotten all about it. "I can't imagine that I'd be any good at knitting. I'm sure they won't want me to join their group."

"You should go," Yulina said, pressing the knitting needles into my hands. "It will be good for you."

I looked down at the knitting needles. They were beautiful. "Are you sure you don't want to keep them?" I asked.

"I do not use them anymore," Yulina said.

"But Annabelle gave them to you."

Yulina smiled. "They are mine to give to you," she said. "Annabelle, I think, would want it this way."

"Thank you," I said. "That's really kind of you."

"You are welcome."

I walked Yulina to the door and watched her walk down the steps. "Wait," I said, calling after her. "Yulina, hang on a second."

She turned around. "Yes? What is it?"

"Can you point me in the direction of the nearest supermarket?" I asked. "Most of the food left in the house was spoiled, and I don't have anything here to eat. I'm going to gain ten pounds this week if I don't stop ordering takeout from Three Sheets."

Yulina smiled. "I am going to the store myself," she said. "Would you like to join me?"

"Oh yes," I said. "Thank you. Can you give me five minutes to change?"

"Of course," Yulina replied. "I will wait in the car."

CHAPTER 19

TWENTY MINUTES LATER, YULINA AND I WERE INSIDE A Food Lion on the other side of town. I didn't usually do a lot of grocery shopping. When I'd lived in Seattle, I'd just bought enough food for a couple of days at a time, because if I didn't, I ended up deciding halfway through my shopping trip that I wanted to eat healthy. This prompted me to spend half my paycheck at Trader Joe's on avocados and various other fruits and vegetables that went bad before I could eat them and sat in my fridge until my mother came over and cleaned them out.

"What is it that you are looking for?" Yulina asked. "I created a list, but now I do not know where it is."

"I don't know what I'm looking for," I said. "You should try making a list on your phone, though. That's what I always do."

Yulina laughed and pulled an old Nokia flip phone from her purse. "With this?"

I stared at her phone. It looked like the exact phone I'd had when I was a junior in high school. "*That's* your phone?"

"I have had it since I moved here," Yulina replied.

"Why don't you get a new one?" I asked. "I'm not trying to be rude, but Gary is a lawyer. Surely you two can afford it."

"Gary does not want me to have a phone," Yulina said, shoving the phone back into her purse.

I stopped pushing my cart. "What?"

Yulina shook her head. "He is afraid I will not pay attention to Ani if I have one."

"That's ridiculous," I replied.

"I am used to it."

"You shouldn't have to be," I said.

"It is what it is," Yulina said. "Besides, he does not know about this phone. I keep my own secrets."

"What does he expect you to do when you have an emergency?" I asked. "I know that people survived before cell phones, but honestly, I don't know how."

"He knows where I am all the time," Yulina replied. "I am expected at home at a certain time. If I am not at home, he will come looking."

"Does he know where you are now?" I asked.

"He knows I have gone to the market, and I will pick Ani up from his mother's house at four p.m. I will be home by four thirty p.m."

I pushed my cart ahead and turned down the aisle with all the frozen food. I wanted to tell Yulina that what she'd just described didn't sound at all like a healthy relationship. In fact, it sounded downright unhealthy. But I didn't want to make her upset with me. I liked Yulina, and I hoped we could be friends. Besides, I didn't have a single clue what a healthy relationship looked like. To my knowledge, I'd never been in one, and it wasn't like I was about to start anytime soon—not so long as I kept on kissing men I'd just met in parking lots.

"Yulina?" I reached into one of the freezers to grab a box of cherry Toaster Strudel. "Did Annabelle think you had a good relationship with Gary?"

"No," Yulina said simply. "She did not."

"Is that why you left St. Francis?"

"It was time for me to concentrate on my family," Yulina said. "Annabelle understood."

"I don't even understand why Annabelle would keep him as her lawyer if she felt that way," I said. "It just doesn't make any sense."

"Maeve," Yulina began. She reached out and grabbed the metal of the cart. "I should not have said anything to you. Think nothing of this conversation. I'm very tired today. I did not mean to speak that way about Gary."

"Are you sure?" I asked.

"I am sure," she said. "He is a good father. He takes care of Ani and me. I would not want you to think bad things about him."

I sighed. "Okay," I said. "It's forgotten."

Yulina's face brightened. "Thank you."

My own phone began to ring, and I fished it out of my pocket. It was a number I didn't recognize, but it had a Timber Creek area code. I answered it, remembering that I'd given Alice my number the day before.

"Hello?"

"Hello, Maeve?" Alice asked. She sounded far away. "Are you there?"

"I'm here," I said, holding up a finger to Yulina, who nodded and wandered off to another aisle. "Is everything all right?"

"Oh, everything is fine," Alice said. "I was on the phone with Ruthie Wiles, and she said that she saw you just now over at the Food Lion."

I looked around the aisle where I was standing. I was completely alone. "What?" I asked.

"My friend Ruthie says you're at the Food Lion. I guess you were coming in as she was going out," Alice explained.

"I don't know anybody named Ruthie," I said.

"She saw you with Yulina," Alice said, sounding slightly frustrated. "Anyway, I have a dilemma, and I was wondering if you could help me with it."

"Uh, sure," I said, still confused.

"Well, I'm caught up at my house having some boards replaced in the front porch. I am completely out of Diet Coke, and if I don't get some caffeine soon, I may beat someone to death with my cane. I called Ruthie to see if she could stop by, and she said she was just leaving, and she was in a hurry to get on over to the hospital to see her new baby granddaughter, but that she'd just seen you going into the Food Lion with Yulina."

By this time, Yulina had returned and was staring at me curiously, no doubt because of the look on my face. "Okay," I said to Alice. "You might want to have your issues checked out by a therapist, though. That can't be healthy."

"Diet Coke is better than a shrink," Alice replied, her tone sardonic. "Diet Coke doesn't talk back."

I laughed. "Do you want me to bring them to you?"

"If you could run them over to my house, that would be great," Alice replied.

"Okay," I said. "Sure, I can do that."

"You are a lifesaver," Alice replied. "Thank you so much."

I hung up the phone and looked over at Yulina. "That was the strangest conversation I've ever had in my life," I said.

"Is everything all right?" Yulina asked.

"Alice called me. Some woman saw me here and told Alice about it, and now Alice wants me to get her some Diet Coke," I replied.

Yulina grinned. "Ruthie Wiles, that old busybody."

"You know her?"

"I know everyone," Yulina replied. "Timber Creek is a very small village. It is strange at first, I know, but you will get used to it."

"I don't know about that," I said.

"The first week I was here, a woman I had never seen before

came up to me and invited me to a barbecue while I was standing in line for medicine at the pharmacy. I went home and told Gary about it. I thought the woman must have been crazy or mistaken me for someone else. Gary laughed at me for half an hour. He said to me, 'Welcome to small-town life.'"

"That sounds less like a welcome and more like a hostage situation," I muttered.

"Like I said," Yulina replied. "You will get used to it, but you might want to avoid kissing Abel Abbott in front of the wide-open door at Three Sheets. Lillie the bartender saw it all, and she is telling everyone."

Yulina dropped me off at the house, and I carried my groceries inside, put them away, and then headed back out again to Alice's. I took at least two wrong turns, but I finally found the right street. Timber Creek was a cute little town, and I found that I enjoyed driving around and looking at the neighborhoods. I felt safe no matter which street I took, no matter which way I turned, which was quite different than it was in Seattle. I'd never lived anywhere before where it didn't really matter which route I took home from work at night.

I pulled into the driveway and grabbed the twelve-pack of Diet Coke from the front seat. When I knocked on the door, nobody answered, so I knocked again and waited for a minute more before Alice finally answered.

"Sorry," she said, her voice thick. "I lay down for a few minutes, and I guess I dozed off."

"That's okay," I said, handing her the drinks. "Here you go."

"Come in," Alice insisted. "Let me get some cash for you."

"Oh, it's okay," I said, but Alice wasn't listening.

Alice led me into the kitchen, hunting for her purse. When she realized it wasn't in the kitchen, she told me to hang on while she went to look for it in the bedroom.

I stood in the kitchen for a minute, listening, and then wandered out into the living room. Mitzi, the dog, was in the recliner. I hadn't even noticed her when I walked inside, and I was glad she hadn't woken up. I had no interest in being attacked by a two-pound ankle biter.

There were a few pictures hanging on the wood-paneled wall behind the recliner, and I stepped in closer to get a better look. The first photo was a wedding picture of a man and a woman who I assumed had to be Alice's parents. The picture was in black and white, and they were both smiling for the camera, their dark eyes happy. Hanging next to that one were two baby pictures, head shots, of a boy and a girl—Alice and her brother, Billy. There were a couple of other grainy family pictures, but they were hard to make out. I resisted the urge to take one off the wall to see it better. Billy, I could tell, looked quite a lot like his father—dark hair and dark eyes. In his baby photo, he had full lips and a dimple in the side of his left cheek. Alice was fairer, with dark blond hair and blue eyes. She looked like their mother.

"Those are my favorite pictures," Alice said from behind me, causing me to jump. "The basement flooded several years ago when my mother was still alive and they were in storage, but I managed to save them. I know they don't look great, but I like knowing they're here, on the wall."

"Why did your mom put them in storage?" I asked.

Alice shrugged. "I think they made her sad to look at, with both my dad and Billy being dead."

I nodded. I thought I could understand that, but it broke my heart for Alice, knowing she didn't have any family left and now she'd lost her best friend. Pictures seemed like a pretty hollow substitute.

I got into my car and let out a breath I hadn't known I'd been holding. All I wanted to do was go back to the house on Maple Street, get something to eat, and take a nap. And that, I decided, was exactly what I was going to do.

CHAPTER 20

ABOUT AN HOUR BEFORE IT GOT DARK, I SAT OUTSIDE ON the front porch with Sherbet, drinking a cup of coffee. On the porch, there was a small folding table and two brightly colored chairs on either side. I'd settled myself in the pink chair, and the fat orange cat lounged idly in the green one.

Beryl, the woman in the two-story gable-front house across the street, was outside. She appeared to be in her mid-fifties, and her graying mullet told me that she'd stopped paying attention to fashion trends somewhere around 1985. She was tall and broad, and she was wearing a long muumuu the color of my chair with purple flowers around the hem.

I knew all of this, because she'd been standing on the sidewalk in front of her house scowling at me for the last five minutes. I'd tried smiling and waving, but that was apparently not the response she'd been looking for.

I drained my coffee cup and stood to go back inside. My hand was on the door handle when I heard the woman yell, "That cat is messin' up my flower beds."

I turned to face her. "I'm sorry, what?"

She took a step off the sidewalk and into the street. "I said that cat is messin' up my flower beds. That big orange one."

I looked over at Sherbet, but he'd somehow managed to disappear. "Traitor," I mumbled under my breath.

"What did you say?"

"I apologize," I replied, amplifying my voice. "He's, um, he's not really my cat."

The woman shoved her hands into the pockets of the muumuu. "You been feedin' him, ain't ya?" she asked.

"Well, yes," I said. "But I—"

"That makes him yours," she replied, cutting me off. "You feed him, and then he comes over to my flower beds to take a shit."

I wasn't sure how to counter that. It hadn't occurred to me where the cat might relieve himself. I thought for the first time that perhaps I should invest in a litter box. For lack of a better response, I said, "I'm sorry."

Her scowl deepened. "I musta called the city a hundred times when that Annabelle turned up dead," she said. "They told me ain't a damn thing they can do about it. Said I had to catch him in the act."

I looked back to the door, wondering if she would follow me into my house if I ran inside and shut the door.

"I had me a security system installed," she continued. "I got a camera right on them flower beds."

Because I couldn't help myself, I turned back around and replied, "Did you catch him?"

She shook her head, the "party in the back" portion of her hair fluttering around her shoulders. "If you don't put an end to it," the woman replied, "I will."

"Well," I said, shrugging my shoulders and giving her my sunniest smile. "Good luck with that."

I turned back around and opened the front door. Faster than lightning, Sherbet shot between my legs and inside the house. I looked at him as he settled himself on the floor and went to licking himself.

"And where have you been?" I asked him.

Sherbet glanced up at me, and I could have sworn he was giving me a wry smile. I sincerely hoped that on his way to wherever he'd been going, he'd taken a moment to stop and smell the flowers on the other side of the street.

The St. Francis Knitting Shop was located downtown, just about a block from the house on Maple Street. I considered walking, since it was so close, but the blast of cold air that confronted me when I stepped out onto the porch that evening was enough to send me straight to my car. I stared longingly at the shed, where I knew the Volkswagen was parked. I was dying to drive it, but tonight probably wasn't the night.

Instead, I took my own car downtown and parked on the street, amazed and thrilled I didn't have to pay a meter for the parking spot. I had to try not to laugh out loud at the sign, which was a picture of St. Francis, the patron saint of animals, holding what appeared to be a hairless dog in a sweater. It was a sweater not unlike the one I'd seen the cat wearing on my first night in Timber Creek.

It was still a few minutes before seven o'clock, so I got out of my car, stuffing the knitting needles from Yulina in my back pocket, and went inside to take a look around. I had to admit, there had been so much buildup about the club that I couldn't wait to see what it was all about, even though I knew it was probably just as Gary said—a bunch of women sitting around and gossiping about the town. I wasn't even sure how anyone was able to knit and talk at the same time, let alone gossip about anyone.

The shop was small, with rich wooden floors and exposed brick walls. It looked like it had probably looked when the building had first been built, which gave me a little thrill. I loved it when older buildings survived being modernized or—worse—demolished altogether. Inside, the air smelled of floor polish and wool, and the walls were filled with rows and rows of yarn and knitting needles. There was no one in the shop, not even behind the register on the right-hand side of the room, so I wandered around looking at all the shop had to offer.

I was reaching up to touch a particularly enticing piece of yarn when I felt someone tap me on my shoulder.

"Excuse me?" a woman's voice behind me said.

I turned around. "Hi," I replied. I'd expected to find Alice or someone who looked like they worked at the shop, but instead I found a harried-looking woman with a baby on her hip. "I'm sorry," I continued. "Am I in your way?"

The woman glanced around the store before shifting her gaze back to me. "No," she said. "I, um, I need to knit my husband a scarf."

"Oh," I said. "Okay."

We stared at each other for a few uncomfortable moments before the woman leaned in and whispered, "Can you help me?"

"Oh, I don't work here," I said. "And trust me, you don't want my help knitting anything."

The woman took a step back from me and said, "I just saw the knitting needles in your back pocket and thought . . ."

"She can't help you," called a voice from the back of the shop. "But I can."

Florence swanned into the room, all smiles and gold jewelry. She wore a gauzy dress that hung on her frame like a tent, and she was barefoot. I curled my toes inward from inside my boots. Even with fuzzy socks, my feet were cold just looking at hers.

"That's okay," the woman said. "I can come back."

"Nonsense," Florence replied. "Now, you'd like to knit a scarf for your husband, is that correct?"

The woman nodded.

"Follow me over to the register," Florence said. "I'll get you one of our starter kits. Inside you'll find everything you need to begin."

The woman shifted the baby to her other hip and complied, taking a second to glance at me once more over her shoulder.

"Now," Florence began. "My name is Florence. If you have any questions, my number is on a card inside the kit."

"Okay," the woman replied. She took a brown paper bag with twine handles from Florence. "Thank you."

"About how long do you think you need to get the scarf finished up?" Florence asked.

"A couple of weeks," the woman replied. "Not more than a month. I'd like . . . well, I'd like to have it finished before Halloween."

"Oh, that's plenty of time," Florence said. "Promise you'll call or come see me if you have any more questions?"

The woman nodded again.

"Great, then you're all set!"

"What do I owe you?" the woman asked.

"Starter kits are always free," Florence replied, giving her a wink.

The woman hesitated. "All right. Thank you again."

The woman hurried out of the shop, followed by Florence, who turned the sign around from "Open" to "Closed." Then she turned off the lights above the front door and faced me.

"Come on," Florence said, pulling me along with her toward

the back of the store. "Everybody but Alice is already here. She's late most of the time, so we just start without her."

I followed Florence beyond the main part of the store. To my surprise, there was a little apartment in the back. It was cozy, with deep red accents and a thick carpet in front of a fireplace. There were two other women seated on an antique couch, their knitting needles poised. They looked up when we walked into the room.

"Thanks for inviting me," I said, and sat down in the chair to the right.

I remembered just a split second too late that I had a pair of knitting needles in my back pocket, and when I sat down, the tops of them dug right into my back. I jumped up, yelping a curse word.

All three women stared at me, and I was frozen for a second. Slowly I reached behind me and pulled the knitting needles from my pants pocket and held them up.

"I forgot I had these," I said, sheepish. "Whoops."

"She stick them in her back pocket?" a familiar voice behind me said.

I turned and saw Alice standing in the doorway to the apartment. She had one hand on her cane and the other on her hip.

"She did," Florence replied.

"Just like Annabelle used to do," Eva said.

"She also curses like Annabelle used to," Harriett said.

I sat back down in the seat and muttered, "I didn't have anywhere else to put them."

"Let me see those," Alice said, coming over to inspect the needles. She took them from me and held them up for the others to see. "You remember these, right? Annabelle gave them to Yulina."

The women all nodded.

Alice handed them back to me and sat down in the chair nearest to the fireplace, while Florence sat down on the floor, crossing her legs one over the other the way Rowan did during reading time at the Seattle library.

"How are you finding Timber Creek so far?" Eva asked me. "Quite a switch from Seattle, I'd expect."

I nodded. "It's a change, that's for sure."

"Do you have plans to stay?" Harriett asked. "In the house?"

"I plan to stay for a while," I said. "I don't know how long."

"You're single, then?" Harriett continued, her eyes not on me but on her knitting. It looked like she was knitting a baby sweater of some kind.

"I am," I replied. "I'm also jobless, and up until a few days ago, I was living with my parents. Those are usually the next two questions I'm asked, so I figured I could just get it out of the way right now."

Harriett looked up at Alice and raised an eyebrow.

"Not too many single men in Timber Creek," Eva said. "Trust me, I'd know."

"I'm not looking for a man," I said.

"All right," Florence said, giving Eva and Harriett a stern look. "That concludes the question-and-answer portion of the evening."

I gave her a grateful smile. "I really do appreciate being invited to be here tonight," I said. "I'm still just very uncomfortable being here, in Annabelle's hometown."

"That's understandable," Harriett said. "I truly cannot imagine how you must be feeling right now."

"Confused, mostly," I said.

"Do you know how to knit?" Eva asked, pointing at my knitting needles. "Those are good needles to begin with."

"That's what Yulina said," I replied. "She came by the house today. She said she used to be in this . . . club, or whatever it is, and she said she wanted me to have these needles. I guess Annabelle gave them to her."

The women shared a glance with one another, and then Florence said, "Your mother gave those to her when she first started with us. We miss them both, your mother and Yulina."

"At least we can see Yulina at the supermarket," Harriett grumbled. "Gotta die to see Annabelle."

"Well, you're not far off," Eva said, a sarcastic grin on her face.

Harriett pointed her knitting at Eva and replied, "And I'm going to haunt you first."

All four women began to laugh, and I felt myself relax a little. I sat back in the chair and eased the death grip I had on the knitting needles. "So," I said. "Is this like a club? Do you just sit here and knit?"

Florence reached into a basket by her chair and held up what looked like another baby sweater. "We mostly sit here and enjoy each other's company," she said. "But we also work on these."

"Baby clothes?"

"That's not for a baby," Harriett said, shoving her own knit concoction at me. "It's a sweater. Flo's is for a cat, see?" She pointed to Florence. "It's smaller and shorter. This one here that I'm working on is for a dog."

I stared at them. "You're making clothes . . . for animals?"

"Well, somebody has to," Harriett replied.

"It's starting to get cold out there," Eva said. "We can't have the animals of Timber Creek freezing to death every time they go outside."

"I saw a cat in a sweater my first night in town," I said. "I thought I was hallucinating."

"Big cat?" Florence asked. "Black and white?"

I nodded.

"That's Cyclops," she said. "He's my cat. I got him from your mother five years ago. He tends to wander."

"Cyclops?"

"He's just got the one eye," Florence replied, one of her hands moving up to her face.

"I noticed that," I said.

"You noticed the sweater, too, right?" Eva pointed out. "See, not only does it keep the animals warm, but it's free advertisement for the shop."

"So you just go around putting sweaters on random animals?" I asked. I was starting to wish I'd hallucinated the cat. The reality seemed far stranger.

"Well, of course not," Harriett replied, looking at me as if

I had two heads. "We give them away here. People love them. It's our trademark."

"The dog on the sign is supposed to be my dog, Iggy," Eva said. "But I messed up and sent the designer a picture of him when he was a puppy and had mange. He's really a Jack Russell, but he looks like a Mexican hairless instead. Flo won't change the sign because it's too expensive. I can't even look at it. It's too embarrassing for Iggy."

I had to bite my lip to keep from laughing. It was clear this was a source of contention for Eva and I doubted she'd appreciate that reaction. Instead, I attempted to wade back over into neutral territory. "Maybe I can knit one for Sherbet," I said hopefully.

The women all began to laugh, and Florence said, "You can, but he won't wear it. Poor Annabelle had to take him to the vet once because he tore a sweater she made him to shreds and then got stuck in it. She couldn't even get him out with scissors!"

I couldn't help but laugh along with them, thinking about Annabelle's strange cat stuck in a sweater.

"Goodness," Harriett said after we'd all calmed down. "We're running out of time. We better get started if we want to reach our quota by the end of the week."

I watched as the women resumed the projects in their laps. They chatted among themselves for a few minutes before Alice looked over at me and said, "Would you like me to show you how?"

I shrugged. "You're welcome to try," I said.

"I brought this," Alice said, taking a ball of yarn out of her bag. "It's smooth and lightweight. It will be good for you to start with. The color is light, so you can see your stitches."

"Okay," I said. "Thanks."

"Watch me," Alice said, kneeling down beside me. "The first stitch is called the slipknot."

"Like the band?"

"Like the stitch," Harriett said.

I watched Alice work and tried to emulate her. After a few unsuccessful attempts and a few curse words under my breath, I created something similar to what she showed me.

"Well," Alice said, standing up. "That's probably enough for tonight. I'll teach you how to cast on at the next meeting."

"You'll come back, won't you?" Florence asked. "Next week?"

"I'll try," I said. "But if I'm going to stay here, I'm going to have to find a job. I might end up having to work nights."

"What are you qualified to do?" Eva asked. "I teach second grade at the elementary."

"I'm not qualified for that," I said with a laugh. "I have a degree in English. My last job was as a sportswriter for a now bankrupt newspaper. I wasn't especially great at it."

From the corner of my eye, I saw Florence and Alice holding a silent conversation with each other. After a few minutes, Alice nodded her head.

"Maeve," Florence said, stepping up to me and touching my arm. "Would you be interested in a little part-time work here at the shop?"

"Really?" I asked. "But I don't know anything about knitting. It took me twenty minutes to make a sloop knot."

"Slipknot," Eva and Harriett said at the same time.

"See?" I said. "I doubt you want my help."

"Oh, ignore them," Florence said, waving her hands over at the two women. "I can teach you what you need to know, and I promise not to leave you alone up front until you know enough to help a customer."

I took a deep breath. "Well," I said. "Okay, thank you. That would be great."

"Come by tomorrow," Florence replied. "After lunch sometime, about one o'clock. I'll show you the ropes."

"Sounds good," I said. "I'll be here."

I walked out of the store and into the frigid night air. I couldn't believe how cold it had gotten just in the four days I'd been in Timber Creek, but I also knew that Washington weather was like that, especially the farther north a person went. Suddenly, sweaters for cats weren't sounding quite as crazy as I'd originally thought.

CHAPTER 21

Sherbet was watching me from the window when I pulled into the driveway. He put one paw up against the screen, and I realized he was probably mad at me for not letting him out before I left. I wasn't used to having a cat, but I'd read somewhere that outside cats lived only half as long as inside cats. I'd made the decision to make him stay inside, and now I wasn't so sure it'd been a good one. I couldn't have him clawing up the couch or doing whatever it was that angry cats did when their caretakers were neglectful.

I was just starting up the steps when I saw something move in the shadows next to the rosebush. I caught a flash of white, and when I stepped closer, I realized it was a dog. And it had been tied to the porch railing. It was shaking and whining, and it took me exactly two seconds to figure out that it was the same dog that had been with the man who showed up my first day at the house.

He'd gone and tied his dog to the porch and left it there. Rather, she'd been padlocked by a chain to the porch.

"Shit," I muttered to myself.

As I knelt down to pet her, I noticed something that I hadn't noticed on Monday. The chain around her neck had rubbed the skin raw, and she was bleeding.

I touched my fingers to the cold metal and realized just how heavy and tight the chain really was. Since it was padlocked, there wasn't any way for me to unlock it without a key. As I sat there, wondering how I could get the chain off her neck, I had an idea.

"I'll be right back," I whispered to her.

I stood up and hurried behind the house, fumbling with my keys. I remembered seeing a toolbox in the garage. After a few minutes of rummaging around, I found a rusty pair of bolt cutters. I wasn't entirely sure they would work, but they were better than nothing.

By the time I got back to the dog, she'd stopped whining and was now licking me and wiggling so hard I couldn't get a decent grip on the chain.

"Hold still," I said.

I picked up the chain and went to cut the part around her neck when I realized that if I freed her, she might run away. Instead, I counted back a few links and settled the chain into the bolt cutters. The cutters were so rusty, I could barely close them, let alone cut the chain. After ten minutes, my hands were starting to look like the dog's neck, and I was cursing myself for refusing to go to the gym with Kate.

"What in the hell are you doing?"

I sucked in a breath of cold air so quickly that I thought my lungs might freeze. I dropped the bolt cutters and squinted into the dim light my phone provided, at the windows of the house next to the tree. It took me a moment to realize that the voice was coming from the street.

I bent down to pick up the bolt cutters and looked up to find Abel Abbott staring at me, his hands shoved lazily down into his jeans pockets.

"What are you doing here?" I demanded.

"What are *you* doing here?" he shot back.

"I *live* here," I said.

"I was out on my porch when I heard noises coming from this lot. I was afraid someone was trying to break into your house," Abel replied. "But I can see now it was just you and that dog making all the noise."

"She's hurt," I said, pointing the bolt cutters at the dog. "And I think she's been abandoned. I couldn't let her suffer. I was trying to cut the chain, but these damn bolt cutters don't work for shit."

I handed the bolt cutters over to him and took hold of the chain, so he could get a better grip. It took a couple of tries, but eventually I heard the snap of the chain.

I pulled lightly on the chain, and the dog stood up and followed me. I hurried up the steps. We burst through the door in time to see Sherbet disappear into the laundry room.

I looked down at the dog; I was still holding the chain she was attached to. "Oh my God," I said. "What kind of an asshole *padlocks a dog to a porch*?"

"Someone who's desperate," Abel replied. "I recognize this dog from the other day. I'm sure the man thought he had no choice."

"That's ridiculous," I said. "How can this even be in the column of choices?"

Abel stepped inside and closed the door. "We need to get that chain off from around her neck," he said.

I looked down at the dog. She was staring up at us expectantly, and the wounds around her neck were even more apparent in the light. "Okay," I said. "Can you do it with the bolt cutters?"

"I think so," he said.

I knelt down on the floor next to the dog in the most soothing manner I could muster. "It's all right," I said to her. "Nobody is going to hurt you."

She licked my face, and in a second, it was over. The huge chain fell to the floor and the dog, sensing she was now free, flopped down on the floor and rolled over on her back.

"What kind of dog do you think she is?" Abel asked. He scooted the chain over to the wall with his foot. "Maybe a boxer?"

I shook my head. "I don't think so. She's bigger than a boxer."

"True," he said, crossing his arms over his chest.

"Well, whatever she is, what am I going to do with her?" I asked, plopping myself down on the floor next to her.

"I think we better clean her neck up a bit," Abel said.

"The chain really did a number on her," I replied. "I don't understand why someone would just move off and leave their pet."

"If she was chained up outside, she wasn't treated like much of a pet," Abel said. "Do you have a washcloth?"

"I think so." I stood up and padded to the bathroom and opened up the cabinet. I pulled out a washcloth and wet it with warm water. "Will this work?"

Abel took the washcloth from me and patted it around the dog's raw neck. "I think you'll need to take her to the vet," he said. "She may need an antibiotic or something."

"Oh, I can't keep her," I said.

"You may have to," Abel said. He handed me the blood-soaked washcloth. "Unless you're going to turn her loose in the streets."

"I'm not going to do that," I said. "I figured I'd take her to the shelter tomorrow."

"They'll euthanize her if nobody comes for her after three days," Abel said. "And if you found her tied up on your porch, nobody is going to be coming for her."

I felt my pulse tick up a notch. I hadn't considered that. I hadn't considered anything, really. I'd just wanted to get the dog out of the freezing cold. I was looking down at her, the way she was wagging her tail and looking up at me as if to say,

"Thank you," and I knew that I couldn't just take her to the pound and leave her.

"I can't let her die," I said finally. "I guess I'll find a vet tomorrow and take her."

"Dr. Langley at the Timber Creek Animal Clinic is good," Abel said. "I told you about her earlier, at my house that night. She'll get you right in."

"Thanks," I replied. "I guess I might as well empty what's left in my bank account."

Abel cocked an eyebrow, but he was too polite to say anything, and I felt my face warm at my outburst. He glanced around the house. "I haven't been here in a long time," he said. "It still looks the same."

"Annabelle wasn't much of an interior decorator," I replied. "Most of her possessions consist of yarn and books."

Abel walked over to the table and picked up the copies of his books I'd placed there earlier that day. He turned them over in his hands. "I forgot I gave these to her," he said. "It's been so long ago."

"I found them on her bookshelf," I said. "What you wrote on the inside was nice."

"She was a good woman, Annabelle," Abel said.

"That's what everyone keeps telling me."

He handed the books to me. "Are you angry with her?" he asked. "For all of this?"

I shrugged. "If I say yes, then I'm speaking ill of a dead woman," I replied. "If I say no, then I'm lying."

"What are you angry about?"

"I don't know," I admitted. "Lots of things."

Abel nodded. "I can see how you would be."

"I have good parents," I said quickly. "I have a nice family. I really couldn't have asked for anything better. I don't know," I finished. "It's complicated."

"Nearly everything is."

We looked at each other for a long moment before the dog licked my hand, and I realized we'd gone from friendly conversation to awkward silence. I cleared my throat. "Well, uh, thank you again," I said. "For helping me. I'd probably still be out there if you hadn't stopped."

"I have a feeling you would have figured it out," he said. He bent down and gave the dog's head a scratch. "Listen, about last night . . . I, uh, well, I'm sorry."

"What are you sorry for?" I asked. "I kissed you, remember?"

"But I didn't stop you," Abel replied. "And I should have."

I felt my chest tighten. "It's okay. I should have stopped myself."

"It's just that I'm not looking for a relationship or anything right now," he said. "And I'm sorry if I gave you the wrong impression."

I rolled my eyes. "It was a kiss, not a proposal. Besides, I feel the exact same way. I just got out of a relationship, and it wasn't a good one. The last thing I need is to be getting involved with someone else."

"With that baseball player?" A hint of a smile played on his lips.

"Has everybody seen that damn video?" I asked, raising my hands up to the ceiling. "I wish whoever posted that to You-Tube would just die in a fire already."

"Well," Abel replied. "For what it's worth, it's really his loss."

"It doesn't feel that way," I admitted. "But I appreciate you saying it."

"Shit outfielder, too."

"Well, that much is true."

Abel shifted on his feet. "So, friends, then?"

"Absolutely," I replied, sticking out my hand. "Friends."

"Good night, Maeve," he said, releasing my hand.

"Good night."

I followed him to the door and locked it behind him. When I turned around, Sherbet had reemerged and was sniffing around the dog. The dog, in turn, was on her belly, attempting to lick Sherbet. I watched them for a bit as they danced around each other and then headed off to the bedroom to change into my pajamas. To my surprise, the dog followed me, her entire body wiggling anytime I reached down to pet her.

"How could anyone leave a sweet girl like you out in the cold?" I asked her.

She licked my hand, and I sat down next to her for a while, petting her. She settled down in my lap, and I rested my hand on her head. This had absolutely been one of the strangest days of my life. I'd hoped that staying here would give me some time to rest and figure out what I wanted to do with my life, but so far, I had more questions than I had answers. I knew that Abel was probably right about just being friends. It had been stupid for us to make out in public like teenagers, and apparently people had seen it happen. Despite the glimmer of excitement I'd had coursing through me all day, I wasn't ready for a relationship either.

I stood up and left the dog asleep on the floor. I took a shower and pulled on the pajamas I'd been wearing for the last few nights, making a mental note to wash them the next day. When I settled down into the bed, I pulled out the knitting needles and practiced the stitch I'd learned. I fumbled around for what felt like an hour before I finally got the hang of it. I could understand why Annabelle and her friends found knitting soothing. For a while, at least, I didn't think about anything except making a slingshot.

The next time I looked up, both the dog and the cat had somehow managed to jump up on the bed without my noticing.

"What are you two doing?" I asked them. "I didn't invite you up."

They looked at me expectantly, their eyes round and pleading.

"Fine," I sighed. "Go on. Get comfortable."

The dog settled in at my feet and Sherbet nestled himself on the extra pillow beside me. In a matter of days, I'd gone from being completely alone to being responsible for two lives. I decided not to tell either of them about the fact that I'd once killed a cactus in college. Besides, it hadn't really been my fault. Holly kept moving it around the apartment, and I kept bumping into it on my way to the bathroom in the middle of the night. If anybody was to blame, it was her. She'd bought the damn thing.

"We'll go get you a harness and a leash tomorrow," I said to the dog. "And some food. And I guess whatever we need to make your neck better."

At my feet, the dog began to snore, and I put my knitting away and scrunched down into the covers.

I began to mentally calculate how much it was going to cost and wondered if Florence might give me an advance on my first paycheck. I'd spent nearly a hundred dollars on food today, and there was no way I could ask my parents for money. They'd already bailed me out enough as it was, and even though I knew they'd help, I also knew my mother would tell Kate. That was the absolute last thing I wanted.

I lay back and listened to the rhythmic breathing of the two sleeping animals on my bed, thankful that we were all three warm and safe in our borrowed bed. I lay there for half an hour before switching on the light and navigating myself around the animals in an effort to get out of bed. I padded back into the dining room and retrieved one of Abel's books, his autobiography, and poured myself a glass of water.

I set the water on the nightstand and slid back into bed, opening the book to chapter 1: "When Winter Comes."

ANNABELLE

June 1984

ANNABELLE SIGHED AND SAT DOWN ON ONE OF THE metal chairs in the break room. In the month since graduating from high school, she'd been working nearly every day at the pillow factory, the early shift, and sometimes the late shift if she could manage it. She'd been saving her money, as much as she could, for an apartment.

After William was fired, he'd showed up and caused a big scene with Billy, right in the middle of the production line. The foreman fired Billy on the spot, and since then, he hadn't been able to find any work because of his record. He'd been couch surfing for weeks, and Annabelle was starting to worry about some of the people he was staying with. They threw big parties all the time, and Billy didn't like her to go, and Annabelle knew why.

She was afraid he was using again.

She had other things on her mind too, things she didn't want to say aloud, afraid speaking about them would make her fears a reality. She wasn't sure how things had gotten so complicated so fast, but all she wanted to do was sink down into a bed—any bed—and sleep for days at a time. She was so tired. Some nights she fell asleep before dinner and didn't wake up again until a wave of early morning nausea hit her, and she was locked in the bathroom until it was time to leave for work.

"What are you thinking about?" Alice asked, sitting down beside her friend. "You look like you're about to burst into tears."

Annabelle blinked hard and tried to smile. "I'm just tired," she said. "I shouldn't have worked a double yesterday."

"Why *are* you working so much, anyway?" Alice wanted to know, handing Annabelle a Pepsi from the vending machine. "You planning on moving out?"

"Eventually," Annabelle replied. "Aren't you?"

Alice shrugged, and then she looked down at her hands. "Somebody has to take care of them, you know? Especially now that Daddy doesn't have a job."

"But that's not your responsibility."

"I can't let them lose the house," Alice said. "And that's exactly what will happen if it's just Mama bringing in income. You and I both know that Daddy will never work again."

Annabelle nodded. "I know."

"Hey," Alice said suddenly, sitting up. "Can I ask you something?"

"Sure." Annabelle took a sip of her Pepsi. "Shoot."

"Are you seeing my brother?"

Annabelle almost choked. "What are you talking about?"

"Don't pretend to be stupid," Alice replied, rolling her eyes. "Better yet, don't pretend that *I'm* stupid."

"I don't think you're stupid," Annabelle replied. "Has your father ever asked you about me and Billy?"

"He asks me nearly every day," Alice replied, shifting her eyes away from Annabelle.

"And what do you tell him?"

"I tell him you've never, ever said anything to me about it."

Annabelle nodded. "And that's the way it's going to stay."

CHAPTER 22

I STOOD IN FRONT OF ANNABELLE'S BEDROOM DOOR, STILL dripping from my midmorning shower. I couldn't find towels anywhere, and the two I'd already used were sitting in the laundry room, still wet, smelling slightly of mildew. I figured that the rest of them had to be in the master bathroom, which meant I had to go inside Annabelle's room.

I felt silly for being hesitant. It was just a room, after all. I pushed open the door and hurried inside, eager to find something to dry off with. In the bathroom, I found several fluffy pink towels that still smelled like fabric softener, and I wrapped one around my middle and used another for my hair.

Since I hadn't gone through the bedroom during my cleanup the day before, everything in the bathroom was untouched. It looked like Annabelle had just stepped out and would be right back, for all this bathroom knew about it. There were odds and ends of drugstore makeup strewn across the countertop. There were random bottles of shampoo and shower gel in the shower, and there must've been at least six different types of hair dryers and detangling sprays, and I suddenly realized where I'd gotten my easily tangled hair. I tidied up but didn't throw away anything except a couple of empty toilet paper rolls, and then padded back out into the bedroom. Still in my towel, I meant to hurry out of the room before my hair began to dry, but a picture sitting on the nightstand caught my eye.

It was Annabelle—young and pretty, standing between a woman who looked like her and a man with dark hair and dark eyes. I realized almost instantly that the people with her had to be her parents. Annabelle couldn't have been much older than twelve or thirteen, from the look of her. I picked up the picture frame and stared at it, unconsciously tracing over their faces with my forefinger. I'd never seen my grandparents before. I wondered what they'd been like, and then I realized with a sharp intake of air that I would never know. I would never have the opportunity to ask the one person who should have been there to tell me. I felt a flash of anger that was soon overshadowed by guilt, knowing that my hurt would only hurt my parents if they knew. They'd given me everything, and here I was crying over dead people I didn't know.

I set the picture down like it was a hot potato and hurried out of the room.

Sherbet gave me a cursory glance when I returned to the spare bedroom to get dressed and then promptly went back to sleep. The dog, however, upon hearing my sniffling, opened her eyes and sat up, tail *thump*, *thump*, *thump*ing against the bedpost at the foot of the bed. I leaned over to inspect her neck, and she rolled over, tongue lolling out of the side of her mouth.

I couldn't tell that her neck looked much better, but at least she hadn't bled any more during the night and that disgusting chain was off her. I reached over to rub her belly, and she wiggled her way right off the bed and onto the floor.

Something small and white on the navy blue bedspread caught my eye. I took a step closer to check it out and saw what looked like several tiny grains of rice near where the dog had been sleeping. I reached down and picked one up to inspect it, rolling it around on the tip of my finger.

To my absolute shock and horror, the grain of rice began to *move*. I screamed and shook my finger, but the rice creature stayed stuck. The dog began to jump around and bark at my feet, her tail wagging so furiously that I tripped over it and fell crashing to the floor, causing the rice creature to come unstuck and land directly on my cheek. I sat on the floor for a few seconds, too stunned to move. Eventually I gained my bearings and scrambled up.

I picked the rice creature off my face and ran to the bathroom, chanting, "Ew, ew, ew," under my breath.

After I flushed the rice creature down the toilet, I rummaged around in the kitchen and found a pair of rubber gloves underneath the sink. I tied a T-shirt around my face and went back into the bedroom to do battle.

Ten minutes later, I'd cleared the bedroom of the creatures and put the bedspread into the washing machine. After a scalding shower, I collapsed onto the couch and called the vet clinic. Becky, the perky receptionist, assured me that both the rice creatures and the wounds on the dog's neck could be taken care of and gave us the first available appointment for later that afternoon.

"What's the dog's name?" she asked.

I looked down at the dog. I didn't have the faintest clue what her name was. I wondered if she'd ever even had a name at all.

"Her name is . . ." I trailed off, struggling to come up with something.

"I'm sorry, honey, I didn't catch that," Becky replied. "Her name is what?"

The dog sat at my feet, her tail wagging slightly every time we made eye contact. After a few seconds, she put her paw on my leg, and then her tongue fell out of her mouth and she began to pant, the sides of her jowls turning up slightly so that it looked like she was smiling. Unable to resist, I gave her head a scratch and said into the phone, "Happy. Her name is Happy."

I took a quick trip to the only pet store Google told me Timber Creek had to offer and bought a harness and a leash for Happy. I didn't want to put a collar around her neck because of the wounds, and the salesclerk said a harness was the best option.

All they had left in her size was a Burberry-inspired harness with red rhinestones around the sides. The matching leash, of course, also had rhinestones. It looked like something Dolly Parton might pick up at Nordstrom.

While I was there, I bought dog food and bowls, as well as food and bowls for Sherbet and a litter box and litter, since he seemed to be content staying inside, and the thought of another verbal evisceration by my neighbor across the street truly frightened me. The salesclerk also talked me into a collar with a little bell for Sherbet. I walked out of the store with what I was sure was going to be an overdraft on my checking account, and my panic multiplied when I realized that I'd also have to pay for a vet visit less than an hour later.

I'd just rounded the corner at the top of the hill on Maple Street when my car began to make a sound I'd never heard before. It was a knocking sound somewhere under the hood, and it got louder and louder until all of a sudden the car stalled, right as I was perched on the top of the hill, the nose of my car pointed dangerously downward. Before I could do anything about it, my car began to coast down the hill. I resisted the urge to close my eyes and hope for the best.

Instead, I managed to steer the car into the driveway, and it rolled to a stop. I might've overshot the driveway and crashed right into the house if not for the large tree in the yard. I bumped against it and the scraping of the metal against the trunk of the tree brought out several neighbors, who stared at me in confusion.

I sat in the car for a few minutes trying to recover, hoping that everyone else would just go back inside. When they didn't, I grabbed the bags from the passenger's seat and got out.

"I'm fine," I said, giving those watching the show a little wave. "Sorry for the noise. There's something wrong with my car."

"You sure there ain't somethin' wrong with your drivin'?" Beryl asked. "Ten and two, that's the way to do it."

I closed my eyes and willed myself to give her a polite smile. "I'll take that into consideration next time," I said.

"That's good information," the old man two houses down hollered. "Especially for women. You've got such small hands!"

"Oh God," I muttered.

I gave the old man another wave and hurried up the steps. I just had about ten minutes before I needed to take Happy to the vet, and I still wasn't sure how the harness I'd bought was supposed to work, but when I stepped inside the house, all thoughts of the vet and the harness were forgotten.

Happy sat on the couch, what was left of a roll of toilet paper hanging out of her mouth. The rest of the toilet paper was littered on the floor, along with a half-eaten area rug and the contents of the trash can. From the bedroom, Sherbet yowled like he was being skinned alive. I opened the door to the room, and he came flying out to inspect the damage. After a few seconds, he looked up at me as if to say, "If you'd left me out to supervise, none of this would have happened."

I set my bags down on the coffee table. I didn't have time to deal with the mess. I didn't have time to think about my car.

I'd just have to take the Volkswagen, despite the fact that I'd realized the tags were expired when Alice had driven it.

I cut the plastic off the harness and coaxed Happy into it. She immediately flopped onto the floor and wouldn't move. I was just about to give up on the entire day and crawl back into my rice-creature-infested bed when Happy saw the leash in my hand and jumped up. She barked and sat and allowed me to clip the leash to the harness.

"Come on," I said to her. "If we don't hurry, we're going to be late."

Happy's nervous excitement turned into sheer panic when I opened the passenger's side door to the Volkswagen. The door protested being opened, and the hinges squeaked. Happy began to back up and wiggle out of her harness, a high-pitched whine emitting from her throat.

"It's okay," I said to her, but she was nonplussed by the outstretched door and wouldn't move past it. I realized that she'd probably never been in a car before, and I didn't blame her for not wanting to get into a vehicle that sounded like that. I wasn't even sure I wanted to get inside.

When she continued to refuse to budge, I sighed and threw my purse and phone into the driver's seat. Then I gave her a pat on the head and lifted her underneath her belly into the passenger's seat. Happy didn't protest, but I could tell the sensation of being picked all the way up was new to her, and she craned her head back to stare at me.

When I shut the door, she put her paws up on the window,

and before I could make it to the driver's side, Happy climbed over and was waiting for me.

"Scoot over," I said.

Happy cocked her head to one side and stared at me.

"Over!" I said again.

We went on like that for nearly five minutes before I gave up and sandwiched myself between the door and her. By the time I got the car started and into gear, and gave a joyous yelp that the car not only started but had a full tank of gas, Happy was sitting on my lap. I peered around her in a ridiculous attempt to both drive and see the road at the same time.

We'd already been honked at by four cars and nearly smashed by a semi as I pulled into the veterinary clinic. Thankfully, Happy was much easier to get out of the car than she was to get into it. She jumped out and practically dragged me to the door. The woman at the front desk looked up at us when we barged through.

"Hi," I said. "My name is Maeve Stephens. I have an appointment today for Happy." I pointed down at the dog. "She's got a wound on her neck."

"I've got you checked in," the woman said. "I'm Becky. We spoke on the phone. You can go ahead and have a seat, and we'll call you back when Dr. Langley is ready."

"Thanks," I said.

There was only one other person in the waiting room, an elderly woman holding a cream-colored cat. I sat down in an orange plastic chair across from her. Happy settled in at my feet, and I picked up a magazine about shih tzu on the table beside me. When I looked up a few minutes later, the woman across from me was sobbing.

"I'm just not ready," the woman said, her head buried in the cat's fur. "I'm just not ready."

I looked around the room to see if she could be talking to anyone else, but Becky was no longer behind the desk. It was just the two of us.

"Are you talking to me?" I asked.

The woman looked up and blinked. She looked surprised to see someone. "Oh, honey, no," she said. "I was talking . . . well, I was talking to myself, I guess."

"Oh," I replied. "Okay."

"Today is my last day with her," the woman said, nodding down to the cat she was holding. "I don't know what I'm going to do."

"I'm so sorry," I said. I shifted in my seat. "Is she sick?"

The older woman shook her head. "No, she's just very old. She's nearly twenty-two."

"Wow," I said. "I didn't know cats could live that long."

"She was just a kitten when I got her," the woman said. "But now she can't walk anymore. She can't eat. It's time. I know it is, but I don't want to say goodbye."

"I'm so sorry," I said again.

The woman looked up at me and tilted her head to one side. "Do I know you?" she asked. "You look familiar to me, but I can't place you."

"No," I said. "I'm new here."

"Are you sure we've never met?"

"Fairly certain."

"Hmmm," the woman said. "Well, I'm all out of sorts today. I don't know which way is up."

I shifted uncomfortably in my seat. I knew why I looked familiar to her. It seemed almost mean not to tell her, especially when she was so obviously distressed. "I think you may have known my birth mother," I said. "Annabelle Lake?"

The woman's eyes lit up. "Annabelle was your mother? I didn't know she had any children."

I nodded. "Yes, well, she had me very young, and I was adopted as an infant. I grew up in Seattle."

"You look just like her," the woman said.

"That's what I've been told," I said.

"She gave me Tapioca," the woman said.

"She gave you what?"

"My cat," the woman replied. "My husband, Roger, had just died. She knew I was grieving, he died so young, and she offered me a kitten she'd saved from the side of the road. Poor thing almost froze to death before she found her. I kept telling Annabelle no, but Annabelle knew just what I needed, even when I didn't. She was just that kind of person."

"That was nice of her," I said. "I guess she was pretty good with animals."

"She was good with people too," the woman said. "She was a good person."

I nodded. More and more, this seemed to be the kind of response I encountered when someone told me about Annabelle. I grudgingly admitted to myself that this was a good thing.

"Mrs. Newhart?" Becky asked, appearing from around the corner of the hallway. "Dr. Langley is ready for you and Tapioca."

"I need more time," Mrs. Newhart said, her eyes going a bit wild. "I'm not ready."

"We'll go," I said, standing up. "Happy and I can go back, if that's okay, and give Mrs. Newhart a little more time."

"Of course," Becky said, giving me a relieved smile. "Take your time, Mrs. Newhart."

Happy and I followed Becky back around the corner into the hallway, all the way down to a door on the left. Becky motioned for us to go inside, and I gave her a nervous smile before entering the room.

Behind a metal table stood a woman wearing a white coat and blue latex gloves. With her long blond hair swept up into a bun, delicate bone structure, and tall frame, she looked more like the picture of a veterinarian you'd see in a magazine than an *actual* veterinarian.

"Ah," she said when she saw us. "You must be Happy and Maeve."

"Yes," I said. "Thank you so much for getting us in today."

"I'm Dr. Ash Langley," she replied. "And it was no problem at all. We had a cancellation."

"I cleaned her up a little last night," I said, motioning to the dog. "But I'm afraid she could have an infection."

"Let's have a look, shall we?" Dr. Langley asked. She motioned for Becky to come into the room, and together they lifted Happy up onto the table.

Happy went flat as her paws touched the table, and she looked at me, her eyes wild.

"It's okay," I said to her, reaching out to rub one of her ears.

"She's a rescue?" Dr. Langley said.

"A what?"

"I'm assuming you rescued her? I assume you didn't allow her neck to get this way on purpose."

"Oh," I said. "No, some guy chained her to the porch."

Dr. Langley raised an eyebrow.

"He came by a few days ago and asked me to take her. He thought I was someone else. I told him I couldn't, and then I came home last night and there she was—chained to my porch."

"Annabelle's porch?"

I nodded.

"Well, it's a good thing you got the collar off when you did," Dr. Langley replied. "Much longer, and the chain would have been embedded in her neck."

"That sounds bad," I said.

"It can be," Dr. Langley said. She inspected the sensitive skin around Happy's neck. "It looks like the chain rubbed her skin a bit raw, but I don't think it's anything a topical cream and a few days of antibiotics can't fix. Her ears and her teeth look good too. Her ears are dirty, but they're not infected or inflamed."

I sighed with relief.

"Becky mentioned that you thought she might also have worms?"

"Is that what they are?" I asked. "Those wiggly rice things?"

Dr. Langley laughed. "Tapeworms," she said. "We'll take a fecal sample and treat her for the worms. I'd also like to take a blood sample to rule out heartworms and get her started on heartworm preventative as well as a flea and tick medication. We can do a rabies and the seven-way shot today, and you can bring her back next week for everything else. We don't want to do too much and overwhelm her system."

"Okay," I said. "Whatever you think we need to do."

Dr. Langley pulled out a small white device that looked like it had a tiny spoon on the end. She walked around behind Happy, and I turned my head as she inserted it, feeling worse for Happy than I already did. Then she and Becky held her while they took a blood sample.

"I'll be right back," Dr. Langley said. "You're a brave girl, Happy."

Becky took off her gloves and threw them into the trash. "She's a pretty dog, this one," she said.

"What kind of a dog do you think she is?" I asked.

"Some boxers do have long tails, but this girl right here is an American bulldog," Becky replied.

"That's what I thought."

Dr. Langley breezed back into the room with two green bottles and a tube in her hand. "She's got pretty much all the worms, except heartworm, which is good news," she said.

"Great," I replied. "I don't even want to know how many worms there are."

"She'll be fine," Dr. Langley replied. "I'll send this stuff up with Becky, and she can explain to you how and when to apply the cream and give the medication." She held up the bottles. "Don't be overwhelmed. It's pretty easy. The heartworm prevention as well as flea and tick prevention is up front too."

I shifted from one foot to the other. I didn't want to have to ask the question I was about to ask, but I had to know before I got to the front desk and had a heart attack. "Can you tell me about how much all of this is going to cost?" I asked. "Will I need to pay for it all right now? I feel terrible for asking, but I just moved here and haven't started working yet."

Dr. Langley glanced over at Becky, who shrugged. "I thought you already knew," the veterinarian said.

"Knew what?"

"The bill has been paid," Dr. Langley replied. "Abel Abbott called this morning and took care of it."

Chapter 23

I RUSHED INTO ST. FRANCIS WITH HAPPY AT MY HEELS, nearly an hour late. I'd had to get out of the car at the house for a few minutes to let Happy do her business, and then I had to go inside and give her the first round of medication. I was beginning to think that along with unemployment and a dwindling bank account, being late was an all-too-familiar theme in my life. I couldn't decide if I was thankful or annoyed that Abel had paid the bill. I knew I couldn't have afforded it, but I also knew I was going to have to thank him . . . again, and that galled me.

Florence was behind the counter at the front of the store when I got there.

"I'm so sorry," I said, in between gulps of air. "I had to take the dog to the vet, and I couldn't leave her at home by herself, because earlier this morning she destroyed a rug and nearly twelve rolls of toilet paper."

"That's your dog?" Florence asked.

I bent over to catch my breath and said, "Kind of."

"I don't know what that means, but I know better than to ask any questions. Annabelle was forever showing up with random animals."

"Please let me make it up to you," I said.

"Oh, child, stop," Florence replied, waving a bangle-clad arm in the air. "It's fine. But if that dog is going to be here, we need to get her a sweater. Something, at least, to distract from that gaping neck wound."

I looked down at Happy. She was thin for a dog her size, but she still weighed nearly fifty pounds. "Do you have one big enough for her?"

"Of course," Florence said. A few seconds later she emerged with a huge bright purple sweater. "I think this ought to do the trick. And it'll come down far enough that it won't bother her neck."

I bent down and released the leash and removed Happy's harness. Thrilled to be free, she wiggled her way over to Florence.

"Isn't she a doll?" Florence said, reaching down to cup Happy's face in her hands. "Such kind eyes. I can tell she's got an old soul."

"What's an old soul?" I asked.

"This isn't her first life as a dog," Florence replied. "She's been here many times before."

I cocked my head to one side. I couldn't tell if Florence was joking or being serious. "Well," I said. "I don't know what her previous lives were like, but this one has been pretty terrible."

Florence eased the sweater over Happy's head, careful to avoid the wounds on her neck. Then she put each one of her front paws through the leg holes and slid it on over Happy's body. "I have a feeling it's about to get better for her," Florence said.

I thought Happy might not like the sweater, but instead of being bothered by it, she seemed to revel in wearing it, prancing around the front of the store while her nails clacked on the hardwood. I had to admit, she looked adorable.

"We'll have to get her a bed and a water bowl if she's going to come to work with you," Florence replied.

"She doesn't have to," I said quickly. "I just brought her today, because I'm not sure what to do with her while I'm gone."

"She can come," Florence replied. "It'll be nice to have a store mascot other than that awful hairless beast Eva calls a dog."

"Thanks," I said, unable to hide my grin. "And I'm really sorry for being late. It won't happen again."

"I know it won't," Florence said. "Would you like to come in a little later tomorrow?"

"Tomorrow my brother and father are bringing some of my belongings up from Seattle, but I can come in anytime on Saturday," I said.

"No worries," Florence replied. "We're having our annual

sale on Saturday, but you're probably not ready for that level of insanity. Besides, the girls always come in and help me during that time."

"Are you sure?" I asked. "I can come in if you need me to."

"We'll just play the first couple of weeks by ear," Florence replied. "Now, why don't I give you a little tour and introduce you to our merchandise?"

"Okay," I said. "That would be great." I followed Florence over to the wall of yarn I'd been admiring the night before.

"We have all different kinds of yarn. They're separated by weight," Florence said. "The weight and type of yarn are on the cards next to the yarn, so it won't be too confusing for you to find what a customer needs."

"Oh great," I replied, inspecting one of the cards.

"Now, the lace here on top is a zero in weight," Florence continued. "You might use it to knit a doily or something like that. Then at the bottom, you've got your weights five and six, which are the bulkiest yarns. You could use it for a thick scarf or a throw."

I squinted at the yarn.

"You've got your wool, your mohair, your cotton," Florence said. "And of course angora, alpaca, silk, nylon, and polyester."

"I'm glad you have the labels," I said. "It would take me forever to memorize it all."

"Once you learn it by touch," Florence replied, "you won't need the labels. It'll come more quickly than you expect, I promise."

"Because Annabelle was good at it?" I asked.

"Oh, goddess, no," Florence said. "Your mother was terrible at remembering the names. She'd just say something like, 'I need that yarn, you know, the one made from the animal that looks like the llama.'"

"Alpaca?"

"That's the one," Florence said, laughing. "All she had to do was look at the ball band. Even if we didn't have little signs, the ball band tells you everything you need to know, including the fiber content, weight, amount, care instructions, suggested needle size, gauge, and dye-lot number."

"I'll do my best not to screw it up," I said.

"You were a reporter before this, right?" Florence asked. "Working here should be a piece of cake."

"I was a sportswriter," I replied. "And I wasn't particularly good at it."

"Well," Florence said. "What are you good at?"

"I don't know," I said.

"What's your passion, then?"

I shrugged.

"You don't have a passion?" Florence asked me, slightly stunned. "Everyone has a passion, Maeve."

"Is this shop your passion?" I asked.

"One of them," Florence said.

"My degree is in English literature," I said. "English is about the only thing I've ever been any good at. My mother wanted me to be a lawyer like her best friend's daughter, but I'm not . . . controlled enough for that."

"Your passions don't have to be limited to what you've accomplished in school," Florence replied. "When you were a little girl, what did you want to be when you grew up?"

"I wanted to be a raptor," I said.

Florence coughed. "You mean the dinosaur?"

I nodded. "In the first grade, we had to draw a picture in art class of what we wanted to be when we grew up, and I drew a raptor first. Then I looked around the room, and everybody was drawing normal things like doctors and teachers, so I copied off the boy next to me and drew my raptor with a stethoscope."

At that Florence burst out laughing. She laughed until she had tears running down her cheeks, and I had to offer her a tissue.

"That's wonderful," she said at last. "Simply wonderful."

"I've never been very practical," I muttered.

"Thank goddess for that," Florence said, giving my arm a squeeze.

She led me past the front part of the store down a small hallway to the left. "Back this way there's a small meeting room," she said. "I rent it out for special occasions, but mostly people use it for their own knitting clubs. The Girl Scouts use it once a month and so does the Catholic Ladies Society."

"I didn't realize knitting was so popular," I said.

"You'd be surprised," Florence replied. "But they don't all use it for knitting. If they do, the room is free. If not, I charge them twenty-five dollars."

"That's cheap," I said. "I can't think of a single place in Seattle you could rent for less than a few hundred."

"This isn't Seattle," Florence said with a wink. "Besides, I don't care a wit about the money, and people sure do appreciate having a place to go."

"I bet."

"Most of these groups meet at night," Florence continued. "From four o'clock until about seven o'clock. I'd like for you to work some evenings during those meetings. Would that be all right with you?"

"Sure," I said. "I'm happy to work anytime you need me."

"Wonderful," Florence said. "Alice used to come and help me, but she hasn't been able to help as much."

"How come?" I asked.

"That old house," Florence replied with a sigh. "She refuses to let it go. She spends every dime she has on fixing it up, but the problem is that there is always something that needs to be done."

"Why does she care about the house so much?" I asked, hoping I wasn't asking too many questions.

Florence shook her head and then seemed to spend a few seconds deciding whether or not it was safe to tell me. "It's all she has left," she said at last. "Of any of them."

"That's so sad," I replied.

"It is," Florence agreed.

I could tell there was something Florence wasn't telling me. I wanted so badly to ask what it was, but the door chime rang, signaling a customer. A look of relief passed across Florence's face that was so brief, I almost didn't recognize it.

"We better go see who that is," Florence said.

We hurried up to the front in time to see Harriett stroll through the door, followed by a somber-looking Max.

Florence looked down at her watch. "What on earth?" she asked. "Max, shouldn't you be in school?"

"Guess who went and got herself suspended?" Harriett broke in, glancing over at Max disapprovingly. Then she took Max's chin in one of her hands and said, "Look! Just look at that split lip!"

"What?" Florence gasped. "Max, you didn't."

Max ignored the two older women and dropped her bag on the floor. "Whose dog?" she asked.

It took me a moment to realize that I should be the one answering. "Oh, mine, I guess. She's mine."

"What's her name?"

"Happy."

"She does seem pretty happy."

"Max," Harriett broke in. "What do you think your father is going to say when he gets here?"

Max shrugged. "Where is he? Why couldn't he come pick me up?"

"Because he's building a fence," Harriett replied. "You know that as well as I do, and it seems to me you'd already thought of that before you managed to get into a fistfight with a girl nearly four years older than you."

"What?" Florence gasped. "Maxine! You're lucky they didn't expel you altogether. This is the third fight this year."

I looked down at Maxine, who was now on the floor cuddling with Happy. She didn't look like the kind of kid who fought all the time. She looked more like a kid who wore too much eyeliner and dyed her hair jet-black when she felt sad. I guess, in some small way, she reminded me of myself when I'd been her age.

Harriett opened her mouth to continue her scolding, but I cut in and said, "I need to take Happy out to do her business. Max, do you want to come with me?"

Max looked up at me, on her face surprise and distrust.

"You can stay inside if you want," I said to her, slipping Happy's harness over her head and hooking it up to the leash. "I'm sure Harriett and Florence have more to say."

"I'll go with you," Max replied, jumping up. "Thanks."

Once we got outside, I handed the leash over to Max and let Happy guide us around to a grassy spot across the street from the shop. The two of us watched her sniff at the ground, moving every so often to inspect a new smell.

Finally, after nearly ten minutes of silence, Max said, "I haven't gotten into three fights this year, you know. There have only been two. The other time I was just there when two *other* girls got into it."

"Two is still a lot," I replied. "I mean, it's only September."

Max shrugged and handed me back Happy's leash.

"What were they about?" I ventured. "The two fights?"

"Breanna Holland is a bitch," Max replied bitterly.

"I don't know her," I said. "But I'll take your word for it."

"She's the worst," Max continued. "She . . . she told everyone that she hooked up with my boyfriend last weekend at a party."

"Did she?"

Max's face clouded over and she looked down at her feet.

"Have you asked your boyfriend about it?"

She shook her head.

"Why not?"

Max looked up at me, and her eyes filled with tears. I led her over to a bench in front of the store. Happy settled herself down at our feet.

"Look," I said. "I'm literally the last person in the world who ought to be giving relationship advice, but I do know a thing or two about cheating boyfriends."

"You do?" Max sniffed.

I nodded and pulled my phone out of my pocket and opened the YouTube app. "I'm going to show you something, but you have to promise not to show anybody else, okay? I don't generally enjoy people knowing what an idiot I've been."

Max finally said, "Okay."

I found the clip, which was now one of the most watched videos in Seattle, and handed it to her. "That guy," I said, "was my boyfriend when this video was taken. That woman he's with? She's a reporter we both know."

Max watched the whole thing through and then started it over again, and I had to look away, at anything else, to keep myself from feeling ashamed and angry all over again.

When she was done with the video, Max said, "Wow."

"Yup," I replied. "I found out my boyfriend was cheating on me the same way everybody else found out—videographic evidence."

"What did you do?" Max asked. She handed the phone back to me. "I would have died of embarrassment."

"I considered it," I replied. "I also considered breaking into her apartment in the middle of the night and bleaching all of her clothes."

Max giggled. "I wish I'd thought of that."

"But you know," I continued. "At the end of the day, she wasn't who I should have blamed. She hadn't been the one to hurt me. She didn't owe me anything. The person I should have been upset with was my boyfriend. He'd been the one to break a promise."

"But she knew he was your boyfriend," Max replied. "Just like Breanna knows that August is my boyfriend."

"I'm not saying that what Breanna did was okay," I replied. "It's not okay."

Max sighed. "My dad is going to ground me for the rest of my life," she said.

"Probably not the rest of your life," I replied.

"You know what?" Max asked, looking up at me. "Breanna can have him. He's a terrible kisser. I can't believe she was even bragging about it."

I grinned. "That's the spirit."

Abel's Jeep rounded the corner, and even from where we were sitting, I could see his stern expression.

"Here we go," Max mumbled. "Let's go back inside."

We stood up, and I led a wiggling Happy toward the door. Her name sure did suit her. I couldn't help but smile at her genuine excitement over every little thing. It was quite the contrast to the somber expression Max was wearing, and I didn't expect it was going to be any better once we were inside.

Abel pulled into a parking space a few shops down, and I watched him get out of the Jeep. I couldn't help it. He was *so* good-looking. All that dark hair, his dark eyes, arms full of tattoos. It really was like I was watching a real-life Paul Bunyan, and I was just waiting for Babe the blue ox to appear.

Abel caught my gaze as I opened the door to the shop, and for a moment, his expression softened.

"Maeve?"

I tore my eyes away from Abel and looked over at Max. "Yeah?"

"Do you have a thing for my dad?"

"What?" I asked, startled. "No. There's no *thing*. I don't have a *thing*."

"Okay," Max said serenely, a small smile playing at her lips. "Whatever you say."

CHAPTER 24

B Y THE TIME I GOT HOME FROM THE KNITTING SHOP, I was exhausted. Florence had insisted on making me stay to have another lesson, and I'd learned casting on and the knit stitch, and surprisingly, I didn't have much trouble getting started this time around. Florence sent me home with yarn, even though I told her there was more than enough where I was going.

"This is *your* yarn," she'd said. "Keep it by your bed. Practice the stitch before you go to sleep."

So, instead of taking a shower or reading another chapter in Abel's book, I climbed into bed and tried to remember what I'd learned. It got easier each time I attempted a stitch. By the time my eyes started to burn, and I was ready to sleep, I'd finished nearly half the ball. I fell asleep sitting up with the knitting needles still clutched between my fingers.

I awoke the next morning to Happy's insistent barking. The dog sat at the foot of the bed, woofing up at me. I opened one eye and rolled over to stare down at the offending animal.

"What?"

Happy jumped up, putting two paws on the side of the bed. She licked my face, covering it in one swipe, and woofed again.

Next to me, Sherbet yawned and sat up. After a few moments of licking himself, Sherbet jumped up on my chest, knocking all the wind out of me, and then over Happy and onto the floor. The two trotted off into the living room, and I groaned, wondering if I could just roll off the bed rather than having to sit up. My head still felt as fuzzy as it had the night before.

From the living room, Happy's barking continued. It was so loud I almost didn't notice the impatient knocking on the front door. I shot up, remembering that my brother was supposed to be there that morning. I'd set an alarm, hadn't I? Surely I hadn't slept through it. I picked up my phone and looked at the display, cursing when I realized it was nearly ten a.m.

"I'm coming!" I yelled to the door, hopping out of bed and wrapping the comforter around me in the chilly morning air. I made a mental note to buy a space heater before the day was out. I'd turned up the heat the night before, but it hadn't seemed to make a dent. The bed had been so warm with Sherbet and Happy in it with me, I hadn't noticed the cold until someone was rudely pounding on the door.

I yanked open the door, and Holly was standing there, in one hand the largest energy drink I'd ever seen in my life.

"This is for you," she said. "I figure you're gonna need it. I've already had two."

"What are you doing here?" I asked, reaching out to hug her. My irritation vanished, and I pulled her inside. Eli followed on her heels. "Where's Dad?"

"Dad had some kind of retirement party for a buddy today that he forgot about," Eli said. "I called Holly last minute."

"And you know me," Holly said, plopping down on the couch. "I'm a sucker for this town, apparently." She looked around the living room. "Nice place."

Sherbet headed straight back for the bedroom with a hiss, but Happy wiggled her way in between us, immediately rolling over on her back in the hope of a few tummy rubs.

"What is this?" Holly asked, half-horrified and half-amused. "You have a *dog* now?"

"And a cat too," I said.

Eli and Holly shared a look and then burst out laughing. In less than two seconds flat, they were both on the floor giving Happy the attention she'd been begging for, and I left them there to take a shower. When I emerged from the bathroom half an hour later, Happy was sitting between them, and I could hear Sherbet meowing pitifully from the bedroom.

"Your cat doesn't like me," Holly said. "I tried to pet him, and he ran away."

"It's been a big week for him," I said, dabbing at my damp hair with a towel. "There's already one stranger living in his house, and now there are two more just hanging out."

"So the cat was . . ."

"Annabelle's," I finished. "Yep."

"What about the dog?" Eli asked.

"Some guy tied her to the front porch."

They both stared at me.

"I guess Annabelle used to take in a lot of strays," I said. "I told this guy I couldn't take her, and two days later, she was tied to the porch."

"Her neck looks like it hurts," Eli said, inspecting the wound on Happy's neck. "Is she all right?"

I nodded. "But that reminds me—I need to give her her medicine."

"Wanna give me the grand tour while you're at it?" Holly asked.

Eli stood up. "We brought doughnuts from Donut Dynasty," he said. "I'll run out and get them. Do you have coffee?"

"Yep," I said.

"Good," he said, and then glanced pointedly at the energy drink that was still sitting on the coffee table. "Because not all of us want to put that poison in our bodies."

I said, "Come on. Let me show you the place."

"It's really cute," Holly said, following me into the kitchen, where I made a big show of brewing the coffee. "It's got a lot of charm."

"It does," I said. "It really doesn't need much work either, from what I can tell. Maybe some new furniture."

"Are you going to be here long enough for new furniture?"

I shrugged. "I don't know. I kind of like it here."

"You sound surprised," Holly replied.

"Aren't you?" I asked. "I mean, I didn't even want to come here to begin with, and now I'm thinking about staying."

"Christine would say that this place has 'good vibes,'" Holly said. "I mean, you have a damn dog. It's like you've already got a life here or something."

"The dog was an accident," I said, but I grinned at her. "Speaking of Christine, how on earth did you get permission to be gone again?"

"She took the kids to visit her mom in Arizona," Holly replied. "For . . . an indeterminable amount of time."

"What?" I turned my attention away from the coffee machine to my best friend. "What do you mean?"

Holly let out a sigh. "You know we've been going to couples counseling, right?"

I nodded.

"Well, the therapist suggested we take some time apart."

"And she took the kids?"

"Just for three weeks," Holly replied. Her tone was light, but she sounded miserable. "My mom is flying in from Illinois to stay with me when they get back."

"Holls, I'm so sorry," I said, reaching out to hug her again. "I'm sorry I haven't been there for you like I should have been. I got so wrapped up in my own junk, I haven't been a very good friend."

"It's okay," Holly replied.

"Did you tell Eli?" I asked.

Holly nodded. "I think I'd spilled my guts before we even hit the interstate." She leaned in closer to me and continued, "Did you know he and Kate went to counseling after Rowan was born?"

"My mom told me," I said. "I think it was hard for Kate to give up her marketing career to stay home. At least, that's what I gathered from Eli."

"That's what he told me too," Holly replied. "I think that's true for Christine too, even though she still works part-time."

"Is that what the therapist thinks?" I asked.

"Yeah," Holly said. "I mean, Dr. Gillam diagnosed her with postpartum depression, even though the twins are nearly two years old. I feel like the worst wife in the world for not noticing it."

"Don't," I said. "It's not always obvious, and remember, you're doing something about it *now*, before it's too late."

"I think we're going to be able to work it out," Holly said. "But it's just so hard, you know? I didn't know it was going to be so hard."

"Raising kids?"

"Being an adult."

I grinned. "Yeah, I feel like we were really misled on that one."

We spent the rest of the morning and a good part of the afternoon carrying in boxes and unpacking them. Eli had been right—I did have a lot of stuff. My mother, true to her word, packed nearly everything I'd brought to her house from my apartment. She even bought me toiletry items and packed them in a separate box. I guess she figured I wouldn't have them, and with the exception of toothpaste and deodorant, she was right. I'd been using shampoo and hairspray that I'd found in Annabelle's bathroom. I meant to go out and buy my own, but I kept getting distracted.

I'd been heartened to see Holly and Eli, and I found myself wishing they would stay more than just the day. I knew they both had lives to get back to in Seattle, but it was comforting seeing their friendly faces. They were part of my life I could explain—part of a history I knew—and it hadn't occurred to me until recently how important that was. I had a lot of unanswered questions about a life I'd never lived and a mother I'd never met.

I was absently folding sweaters and putting them into the cedar chest in the spare bedroom when I heard raised voices coming from outside. One of them was Eli's. I wandered out into the living room, where Holly was sitting on the couch, pretending to be busy opening up a box full of my underwear.

"What's going on out there?" I asked. "Who is Eli talking to?"

Holly shrugged. "I don't know."

She stood up and followed me to the door. Eli was on the steps of Beryl's house, arms crossed over his chest, as Beryl pointed to where we stood.

"Who is that woman?" Holly asked. "She looks like a trucker.

I haven't seen a mullet like that since you and I went to watch an eighties cover band five years ago."

I didn't want to laugh at what Holly said, but I couldn't help it. Beryl *did* look like she and Axl Rose could be related. "What do you think Eli is saying to her?" I asked.

"I don't know," Holly replied. "But I doubt it's good."

I sighed and walked across the street.

"What's going on?" I asked. "Is everything all right?"

"Absolutely not," Beryl said to me. "I swear, child, this street was quiet before you moved in."

"Oh, good grief," Eli replied. "I don't know what you're going on about. Our truck hasn't done anything to your precious flowers."

"First it was that cat," Beryl continued. "Now it's that vehicle with those noxious fumes."

"Sherbet isn't hurting your garden," I said. "You haven't been able to catch him on camera, have you?"

"That doesn't mean he ain't destroyed them," Beryl said.

"Well, it does mean you don't have any proof," I replied.

"I know what I know," Beryl said.

Eli threw up his arms and glanced over at me. "I swear, I was just coming out here to get the last load of boxes, and she accosted me."

"Oh, big fancy words from your boyfriend here," Beryl said, rolling her eyes.

"He's my brother," I replied. "Are we done here?"

"I'll be sending you a bill," Beryl called after us. "Don't think this is over!"

"Are you sure you want to live here?" Eli asked, glancing back at Beryl, who was still glaring at us. "That woman is absolutely ridiculous."

"Oh, I think she's harmless," I said. "Her beef is mostly with Sherbet anyway."

"Your cat?"

"He's been a bone of contention since I got here."

"I hope all your neighbors aren't like that," he said.

"I haven't met them all," I confessed. "But I doubt there is anyone else in all of Washington like Beryl."

"I certainly hope not."

"What's left in the back of the truck?" I asked.

"Heavy lamps," Eli replied. "And a couple of boxes."

"I forgot about the lamps!" I exclaimed. "I love those things."

"Heavy lamps," Eli corrected me. "Where did you get wrought iron bases?"

"Remember I used to date that guy who dabbled in being a blacksmith and went to Renaissance fairs?"

"How could I forget?" Eli asked. "He offered to make me chain mail as a wedding present."

"He made them."

"Of course he did."

"Hey," I said. "It was the least he could do. Especially after he stole all my bedsheets."

"I remember that guy," Holly said. "He was a real winner."

"Let's just focus on the task at hand," I replied.

"You mean like Abel Abbott?" Holly asked, a sly grin on her face. "Is he the new task at hand?"

Eli stopped chewing and stared at the two of us. "Abel Abbott the writer?"

"I meant to tell you," I said. "He's basically my neighbor."

"Do you know him?" Eli asked.

"A little bit," I admitted.

"Can I meet him?"

"No," I said. "You can't meet him."

"Why not?"

"Because that would be weird," I replied. "I can't just walk you down to his house and knock on his door."

"Fine," Eli replied with a sigh. "But if we see him out and about, will you introduce me?"

"Sure," I replied. "If we happen to see Abel Abbott out and about, *in my house*, I will absolutely introduce you."

"I'm starving," Holly said, breaking in. "Those doughnuts didn't hold me at all. Can we go eat at that place . . . oh, what's it called? The one with the burgers?"

"Three Sheets?" I asked. "Sure, let's just get the lamps in and the last couple of boxes unpacked, okay?"

Holly sighed. "Fiiiiine."

"Where do you want the last of the boxes?" Eli asked.

"I guess just leave them here in the living room," I said. "I don't guess we have to unpack them now. I'm running out of room in the spare bedroom."

"What about the master?" Holly asked. "We can put the lamps and boxes in there until you find a place for them."

"That's Annabelle's room," I said without thinking.

Holly put her arm on mine and said, "I'm not trying to be uncaring, Mae, but it's not anymore."

"I know," I replied. "You're right. Go ahead—just set the stuff in there. Just don't mess with any of the knitting stuff."

Eli and I picked up one of the heaviest lamps and carried it up the porch steps and through the house into the back bedroom. Holly opened the door and directed us inside, and we set it down next to the bedside table.

"Wow," Holly said, looking around the room. "There's a lot of yarn in here."

"Yeah, I think Annabelle was some kind of master knitter or something," I replied. "She was in a club with a bunch of other women. They make *clothes for animals*."

"Christine is in a knitting club!" Holly said. "But she says all they do is drink wine and talk bad about their spouses."

"That sounds like my kind of club," I replied. "I'm trying to learn how to knit, but I'm not very good at it yet."

Holly sighed wistfully, and I knew she was thinking about Christine. I felt bad that I didn't have any relationship advice to offer her. I'd always thought of her and Christine like I did Eli and Kate or my parents—examples of what people did right in their lives. It wasn't that I necessarily wanted to be married and have a carload of kids, but I figured having that meant you were some special level of adult that I hadn't yet unlocked. More and more, I was realizing that really wasn't the case.

It was both scary and a relief to know that every person, every relationship, had cracks. Deep down, I'd thought maybe my cracks were too deep or, worse, I'd been born that way and the mother I'd been born to could see them even then and that's why she hadn't wanted me. The rational side of me knew this wasn't true, but I couldn't help longing for someone else with the same cracks so that at least I was part of a matching set. Now that Annabelle was gone, what if I never found that?

Lost in my thoughts, I let go of the lamp base without realizing that Eli and I had set it down on a rogue ball of yarn. The lamp wobbled, and before any of us could catch it, it fell backward onto the table by the bed, knocking everything off in the process, including the framed picture of Annabelle and her parents.

The picture tumbled to the floor and the glass in the frame shattered near my feet. Once we'd steadied the lamp, I bent down to pick up the pieces.

"I'm so sorry, Mae," Eli said.

"It's okay," I said, stacking the large chunks of glass on top of each other in my hand. "It's not your fault."

"I think I saw a broom behind the trash can in the kitchen," Holly said. "I'll run and get it."

Eli bent down to help me, picking up the frame and removing the shards of glass that were still stuck to it. "Hey," he said. "There's another picture behind the first one."

"What?" I took the frame from his outstretched hand.

Stuck to the back of the first picture was another. It was slightly sticky and a little faded, but it was clear enough that I could see Annabelle—older than she had been in the picture with her parents—standing hand in hand with a man, both of them smiling into the sun. I turned the picture over, but all that was written on the back was "June 1984."

"Do you know who they are?" Eli asked, peering over my shoulder.

"It's Annabelle," I said. "I don't know who the guy is."

Eli squinted at the picture. "And what does the back say?"

"June 1984."

"That's, what? Nearly nine months before you were born in 1985?"

I nodded. The man looked vaguely familiar, but I couldn't place him. I'd seen so many new faces over the last few days. I racked my brain trying to put his young, unlined face up to one of the older ones I'd seen at the funeral, but none of them matched. "I don't know him," I said.

"Do you think he could be—?"

"I don't know," I said quickly. I slid the pictures and frame back up on the table, careful to put the picture of Annabelle and the man underneath the one of her and her parents. "Don't say anything to Holly. She won't shut up about it if she knows."

Eli nodded. "Got it," he said.

Holly swept up the smaller shards of glass that were left on the floor, and then we carried in the other lamp, careful to set it down far away from anything that might break.

"I think that's everything," Holly said, dusting her hands off on her jeans. "I'm starving. Let's go eat."

"Where is this place?" Eli asked. "What's it called?"

"It's just down the road a ways," I replied. "It's called Three Sheets. I guess technically, it's a bar, but they've got great burgers."

"Works for me," Eli said. "You want to drive?"

"Well," I started, skipping ahead of them and into the hall-way bathroom to look in the mirror. "My car isn't exactly running right now."

"What?" Eli and Holly said in unison.

"I'm not sure what's wrong with it," I continued. "And that VW Beetle you saw has expired tags. So . . . maybe you should drive, Eli."

"I'm not going to mention this to Mom and Dad," Eli replied.

"I'll get it fixed," I said noncommittally.

"Like you fixed your last car?"

"That was different," I replied. I came out of the bathroom with my hair tied up in a loose ponytail. I looked a little worse for wear, but not so bad that I couldn't be seen out in public. "That car got towed by the city of Seattle for being a piece of junk."

"No," Eli said. "It got towed because it had hundreds of dollars' worth of fines and was parked in a tow zone."

"Same thing," I replied. "Anyway, can you drive?"

Annabelle

June 1984

Annabelle watched Billy stumble toward the door, his feet scarcely connecting with the ground long enough for him to walk.

"He must be out of his head coming here," Alice whispered. "When Dad sees him, he's going to flip."

"He's clearly out of his head," Annabelle replied, unlocking the door as quietly as she could and slipping outside.

"Anna!" Billy exclaimed, opening up his arms wide to embrace her. "I missed you. Come here."

"No," Annabelle said, stepping away from his outstretched arms. "Billy, you need to get out of here. When your dad sees you—"

"Fuck my dad," Billy said, his eyes rolling dangerously to the back of his head. "Come on, let's get out of here."

Annabelle backed up again, until her foot caught the edge of the step, and she came crashing down with a thud. Alice came outside. Anger filled her face, and she shoved Billy back from the both of them.

"What in the hell are you doing here?" Alice demanded. "Are you trying to get us all in trouble?"

Billy didn't respond. He just stood there, swaying back and forth, staring at Annabelle.

Finally, Annabelle couldn't take it any longer, and she stood up and went to him, taking his hand in hers. "Billy, you've got to get it together," she said.

"Come with me," Billy replied, his voice hoarse. "Please."

"And go where?" Annabelle asked. "You don't have anywhere to go. You don't have anywhere to *live*."

"We'll figure it out."

"No," Annabelle said. "You've got to get clean. You've got to get a job. You've got to find a place to live." She reached out and took his other hand and placed it firmly on her stomach.

Billy's eyes widened, and he opened his mouth to speak, but it was too late. William came rushing out of the house, pushing past Alice and finally Annabelle to grab Billy by the collar of his shirt and throw him back onto the gravel driveway. It was a surprising feat for a man who looked as withered and old as William, but his anger was stronger than anything Annabelle had ever seen before.

Billy scrambled up, his eyes wild. He doubled up his fists as if he might fight back, but when he looked over at Annabelle, it was clear all the fight had gone out of him. "Please," he mouthed to her.

Annabelle wanted to go to him. That was all she wanted. She loved him, and she wanted to pretend that everything was going to be okay as long as they were together, but deep down, she knew better. She couldn't leave. She was trapped, and she knew it. Billy needed rehab, and she needed a place to live until she could figure out what to do about the life growing inside her. What she'd managed to save working at the factory wouldn't be enough to get them a place, and it wouldn't be long before she would start to show. She knew she'd be fired from her job when that happened.

Beside her, Annabelle felt Alice slip her hand into hers, and together they watched Billy walk away, and Annabelle couldn't help but think that he was taking her whole world away from her as he went.

CHAPTER 25

THREE SHEETS WAS CROWDED, AND THE THREE OF US found a space at a cramped table toward the back.

"Is everybody in town here?" Holly asked. "It's packed."

"Looks like it," I replied. "You guys want a beer? There's a good local brewery here."

"None for me," Eli replied. "I've got to drive myself and Holly back, and I just got an alert on my phone there is a severe storm headed this way. In fact, we probably better eat and get out of here."

"Okay," I said. "You're both welcome to stay here."

"I need to get back," Eli said. "Mom and Dad will worry if I don't."

"We're finishing up a big project, and I know it's a Saturday, but I've got to get some shit done."

"Well, you two are a barrel of fun," I replied.

After we ordered our food, I scanned the room. There were a few familiar faces. Charlene was toward the back with a rowdy group of men who seemed to be spilling more beer than they drank. When she saw me, she waved, grabbed a pitcher, and headed over.

"Hey, Maeve!" she yelled over the noise. "What on God's green earth are you doing all the way back here? Who are your friends?"

"Hey, Charlene," I replied, scooting over to make room for her. "This is my brother, Eli, and my best friend, Holly. They drove up from Seattle to help me get settled."

"Nice to meet ya," Charlene said, extending her hand to each of them.

From the corner of my eye, I saw Abel come through the door, shaking off the rain that must have begun after we'd already come inside. He glanced around, but he didn't see me, and sat down with the rowdy group Charlene had just left. I poured myself a beer from Charlene's pitcher and tried to keep my glances in Abel's direction discreet.

The waitress reappeared and set a plate in front of each of us, including Charlene, and she dug in. We all began to eat, and Eli couldn't help but moan his approval.

"I don't get to eat like this at home," he said. "I might have to get a burger to go."

Charlene eyed him up and down and then said, "Your wife keep you on a tight leash?"

Eli grinned. "Something like that."

"You've got that kept-man look about ya," Charlene replied. "Those guys over there could use a good woman to keep 'em sober."

The men Charlene was talking about were laughing at something Abel had just said. Two of the men looked exactly alike, with blond hair and thin beards. They had to be twins. The other man was close to Abel's size, but he resembled a bear—both in weight and mannerism. As I watched, he spilled his beer twice and almost fell out of his chair.

"That big, drunk bastard over there is Scooter Marx," Charlene said, pointing with the stump of a half-eaten fry over to where Abel sat. "The other two are the Wasoon twins, Roland and Randall."

"The Wasoons," I said. "They own a brewery, right?"

Charlene nodded. "I prefer cheap beer like Natural Lite, but I would never say that here," she said. "Pretty sure the Wasoons own stock in this place."

Just then Scooter was successful in his latest attempt to fall out of his chair and landed hard on the floor. He managed to take his beer down with him as he fell, and the mug came crashing down beside him, shattering to pieces.

The bar fell silent for a few seconds until Scooter opened up his mouth and began to guffaw, and everybody else followed suit. Abel leaned over to help him up, steadying him on his chair, while an annoyed-looking waitress brought out a mop from the back and began to clean the mess.

I looked away from the scene and refilled my glass. I was

warm from the beer, and I felt myself relax. When Charlene offered to buy another pitcher, I didn't argue, despite the fact that I could feel Holly and Eli looking at me from their seats.

"I'm glad I ran into you tonight," Charlene said. "I was supposed to meet a guy here, but he bailed on me at the last second."

"Another married man?" I asked.

Charlene laughed. "No, not tonight. I met this guy a few months ago at work. He came in to buy a lottery ticket and won two hundred dollars right there in the store. Gave me fifty, then asked me for my number. I've seen him a few times, but he said he heard there were supposed to be some real bad storms and didn't want to take a chance that it might hail on his new Corolla."

"You're a fascinating person, Charlene," Holly said, finally, breaking her silence.

"Thanks," Charlene replied with a grin.

Eli was staring hard at Abel and it didn't take long before recognition dawned on his face, and he said, "Is that Abel Abbott over there?"

Charlene nodded. "In the flesh."

I thought for a minute that Eli was going to stand up and walk over to him, but he didn't. Instead he just stuck another french fry in his mouth and said, "Wow. It's really him."

"Oooooh," Charlene replied knowingly. "You're a fan."

"The biggest fan," I said, trying not to roll my eyes.

"Let me go get him," Charlene replied, standing up. "He's got to be tired of those assholes over there by now."

She sauntered over to the table, managing to avoid all the calls of her name, and stopped right in front of Abel. When she pointed at us, he craned his neck around her to look, and I found myself waving at him. He didn't wave back. Instead he just shook his head until Charlene walked away.

"He's in a mood tonight," Charlene said when she returned. "He said he came over here to have a beer."

I narrowed my eyes in Abel's direction, but he wasn't looking at me anymore. I could feel my face grow hot with anger and embarrassment, and before I could stop myself, I got up and walked over to the table where he was sitting.

"Well, hello," said one of the blond men. "To what do we owe this pleasure?"

He slurred the word *pleasure* so badly that it was hard for me not to laugh. I ignored him and said to Abel, "You couldn't even come over and meet my brother? He's one of your biggest fans, you know."

"That's your brother?"

I screwed up my face. "Yeah, who did you think he was?"

Abel shrugged. "I'm not in the mood tonight."

"I don't care," I replied. "It would have been the nice thing to do, and it would have taken you like five seconds."

"Sit down with us," the second blond man said. "Have a drink, pretty lady."

"No thank you."

The first blond man set down his beer so close to the edge of the table that I thought it might fall off, and I was too busy focusing on the glass to see his hand coming toward my thigh before it was too late.

The glass fell to the floor and shattered as Abel reached across his friend and grabbed his forearm inches before it made contact with my leg.

"You might want to rethink that, Roland."

Roland's watery eyes looked up at me, and he slumped back in his chair when Abel released him. "I was jus' tryin' to haves fun," he managed to get out, before his head hit the table and he passed out cold.

I stood there for a few seconds, my mouth open.

"I've got to get them out of here," Abel said. "Before they make even bigger idiots out of themselves."

"Well," I replied, turning to leave. "I guess you're in good company."

I could feel him watching me as I walked away, but I was too annoyed to turn around, because I knew if I did, he'd be smiling at me, and I wouldn't be able to resist smiling back. When I got over to my table, everyone was standing to leave.

"I haven't even finished eating yet," I protested.

"We've got to get on the road," Eli replied. "They're saying the storm is headed this way, and if we hurry up, we can beat it by an hour or so."

"Fine," I said, pulling on my coat and taking my burger with me. "I guess I'll see you around, Charlene."

"You bet!" she replied with a wink, and then disappeared into the swelling crowd once again.

I walked Holly and Eli to the truck and she climbed in. I turned to Eli.

"Thanks for coming today," I said to him, squeezing him a little tighter than I meant to. "I really needed to see you today."

"I miss you," Eli replied, squeezing me back. "But I'm glad you're staying here."

"Really?"

Eli pulled away from me and nodded. "It's good for you," he said. "Being here. I can tell."

"Rude writers notwithstanding," I replied.

Eli laughed. "I actually didn't expect much else," he said. "Abel Abbott has a history of being less than enthusiastic."

"Still," I said. "He's supposed to be my friend."

"Seems like he likes you just fine," Eli replied, his eyes twinkling. "He watched you walk all the way to his table and all the way away from it. I'd say you've made an impression."

"Shut up."

"I'm serious!" Eli said, turning around to wave at Holly, who was honking the horn at him. "Look, I've got to go, but will you let me know what you find out about that picture?"

My chest tightened. I'd almost forgotten. "I will," I said. "Please call me when you get home. Be careful."

I'd decided to walk home from Three Sheets, but the wind was really starting to pick up by the time I got back inside from letting Happy out, and I was glad to get out of the cold. I changed into my pajamas and sat down on the couch. I resisted the urge to go back to Annabelle's bedroom and look at the picture again. I kept going over it in my head, trying to figure out where I'd seen the man in the picture before, but I always came up with nothing.

Happy nestled herself against me, and I absently began to pet her. After a few minutes, I realized I hadn't seen Sherbet since I came inside. I got up and walked around the house, checking under all the beds. I called his name, but he didn't seem to be anywhere in the house.

I put Happy in the back bathroom and threw on my coat. There was a flashlight underneath the sink in the kitchen, and I grabbed it on my way out the door. I wasn't prepared for the amount of rain and wind. I expected Sherbet to be waiting on the porch, angrily meowing to be let back inside. When he didn't come, I set off across the yard, calling his name.

"Sherbet!"

I looked under cars and in ditches. My teeth were starting to chatter by the time I rounded the corner two blocks over, and my tennis shoes were completely soaked through. I didn't even know what street I was on, and I was beginning to panic that I wouldn't be able to find my way back home in the storm.

As I stood at the corner of the street, squinting to see the street sign, I noticed two people come out onto the porch of one of the houses. The porch light was the only light on for what seemed like miles—not even the streetlights seemed to be working. The people were yelling; rather, the man was yelling, and the woman was looking down at her feet. I stood there transfixed and watched.

When the man reached out to grab the woman, taking her by the shoulders and shaking her slightly, I realized that I was probably witnessing something I shouldn't have been. The woman tried to free herself, the man's grip tightened, and for a moment I thought he was going to hit her. Instead he whirled her around and gave her a little shove, forcing her down the steps and into the yard. She was wearing a T-shirt and panties. The woman didn't try to get back up onto the porch. Instead she stumbled out into the yard, hands over her arms and barefoot in the pouring rain. Her hair was plastered to her face, and she was shaking violently with each movement.

I was wondering whether I should call the police when the woman looked up and straight at me.

It was Yulina. I had to do a double take, but it was definitely her, which meant the man grabbing on to her and shoving her had to have been Gary. For a moment I didn't think she saw me, but when I made a move to get closer, she shook her head at me. It was an almost imperceptible movement, but her message was clear. Gary jumped off the porch and ran toward her, and I ducked down in between two parked cars so he wouldn't see me. He was right up close to Yulina's face, and what I could see through the rain told me that whatever he was saying wasn't an apology. After a few moments he left her standing there in the yard. She didn't attempt to move. She simply stayed there in the rain as if she were being punished for something.

I watched her for what felt like forever, and I could feel her eyes trained on me as well. I wasn't sure what to do, and so I advanced toward her again. This time she shook her head violently at me, desperately, and so I ran farther down the street, hoping there was some kind of explanation for what I'd just seen—some kind of reason for what I'd witnessed.

I stopped when my side began to hurt, and I bent over at the end of the street, gulping air and rain. In the distance I could hear sirens, and my phone began to make the same kind of noise—an alert that the severe thunderstorm warning had turned into an all-out tornado warning.

Behind me a horn honked, and I nearly jumped out of my skin. When I turned around, I was relieved to see a vehicle I recognized and a face I knew getting out of the driver's seat.

"Maeve? What are you doing out here?" Abel ran around to the front of the Jeep to where I stood, shivering. "Are you all right?"

I tried not to let the relief on my face show. "I'm fine," I tried to say, even though I wasn't sure my mouth was opening and closing the way it should be to form words.

"How long have you been out here?"

"I can't find Sherbet," I muttered. "He's out here in this mess, and I can't find him."

"Jesus, Maeve," Abel said. "Come on, get in." He led me around to the passenger's side and folded me into the seat.

"I have to find him," I said, still trying to get my mind off Yulina and Gary.

"He's a cat," Abel replied. "I'm sure he's hiding somewhere."

"It's so bad out here," I said.

"Yeah, and you were wandering around like a homeless person," Abel replied. "With tornado sirens going off."

I turned around to face him. "Well, what were you doing driving in this?"

"I had to take my buddies home," Abel replied.

"Where's Max?"

Abel raised an eyebrow. "She's with Harriett and Eva. She's working on a research project about the history of the old pillow factory, and they're helping her with it. They're fine. I already called. They're in the basement at Harriett's house."

We pulled into the driveway, and the sirens were still going off. The rain had let up for a few minutes, and it was eerily quiet. From the drain at the end of the street, I heard a strangled *meow*.

"I think I found him!" I yelled to Abel.

I ran to the drain and tried to reach Sherbet, but my arms were too short. Abel gently moved me out of the way and got down on his hands and knees and reached in. A few seconds later he pulled a very wet, very agitated Sherbet out of the drain.

"Let's get him inside," Abel said.

I found a dry towel in the laundry room and handed it to Abel and then went into the master bedroom to let Happy out of the bathroom. I could hear her whining and clawing at the door, but I wasn't prepared for what I saw when I got back there—the door, or what was left of it, had a giant hole chewed right through the center of it. Happy had her nose pushed through the hole in a desperate attempt to escape, and at that moment, I couldn't decide if I wanted to laugh or cry.

I opened the door and let her out, and she barked her appreciation at me before jumping up and placing her paws on my chest.

"What did you do?" I asked her.

"It looks like she chewed through the door," Abel replied. "Why did you lock her in the back bathroom?"

"I didn't know what else to do with her. I thought she'd be okay in there," I replied. "There's no basement, so this bathroom was the safest place for her."

"Well, now that all your animals are accounted for, do you think that you could maybe avoid going out into a dangerous storm?"

I shrugged. "I survived."

"I can see that."

"You look a little worse for wear, though."

"Well," Abel replied. "You're not the one who carried a soaking-wet cat into the house and dried him off. I'm pretty sure I'm bleeding."

"Oh my God," I said. "You are. And your shirt is ripped."

"I hope he's vaccinated."

I started to giggle. I couldn't help myself. "I have no idea," I said in between gasps.

"You find my bleeding torso funny?" Abel asked. His tone was serious, but there was a hint of a smile on his face.

"Let me see," I replied. "It can't be that bad, but if you'll remember, I was almost a nurse."

"Oh, I remember," Abel replied, and in one swift movement, his shirt was off and I was staring at his bare chest.

I think for a moment, I forgot to breathe. The large woodland tattoo that wound up his arm extended onto his shoulder and chest. Just below the two small cat scratches on his abs was the faintest trace of hair, leading down to the button of his jeans.

"I'll, uh, I'll get the alcohol," I managed to say, and backed myself up into the kitchen, nearly tumbling over a still angry Sherbet in my rush.

"It's your own fault," I whispered to him.

When I returned, Abel was sitting on the couch, his shirt in his hands. I sat down beside him and pressed an alcohol-soaked cotton ball onto his skin.

"Damn," Abel said, flinching. "That stings."

"Good," I replied. "That means it's working."

"Something tells me you're enjoying this," he said, grinning. "I guess I deserve it after the way I acted earlier."

My eyes flicked up to his. I'd nearly forgotten about that. "You weren't exactly nice," I replied.

"I'm sorry," Abel replied. "I don't like meeting fans. They generally want to talk about camping and roughing it, and that's just not something I've done for a long time. It's not who I am anymore."

"Who are you?"

Abel shrugged. "I'm not sure."

"That makes two of us," I replied, setting the bloodied cotton balls on the table beside the couch. "I think you'll live. Just try not to pick up any more cats for a few days."

"You know Annabelle found Sherbet as a kitten?" Abel asked. "It must've been a night a lot like this. I remember she came banging on my door about midnight, asking me if this sickly orange thing belonged to me. She had no idea what time it was." He chuckled. "That was just Annabelle. I was new to the neighborhood. I'd just lost my wife. I thought she was crazy."

"That sounds pretty crazy," I replied.

"So when I saw you out there tonight, looking for that damn cat, I had to stop."

"Because I reminded you of Annabelle?"

Abel looked down at me. "In some ways," he said.

"And in other ways?"

Abel brushed a damp strand of hair out of my face and said, "You're something else entirely."

I knew that I should scoot away from him. We'd agreed to be just friends. Still, knowing that, I couldn't stop myself from leaning over and brushing my lips up against his.

He didn't hesitate. He pulled me closer to him until our bodies were touching. I put my hands flush against his bare chest, feeling the heat of his skin. Abel groaned and shifted his weight so that I fell onto my back, and he came crashing down on top of me.

He kissed my forehead and then my nose and then my mouth. He kissed his way around my collarbone and then stopped, pulling himself away from me.

"What is it?" I asked, my heart pounding in my chest. Had he changed his mind? Had he realized we were probably making a giant mistake? "Do you want to stop?"

"I'm just admiring you," he said, his voice slightly hoarse. "It's been so long. It's just been so long."

My first instinct was to make a stupid joke to stop the flush that I was sure covered my entire body. But I didn't. I didn't feel exposed to him. Instead I felt open, comfortable in a way I didn't know I could ever be with a man, and when his mouth finally found mine, I didn't hesitate.

"You're beautiful," he whispered as I led him to the bedroom. "I've wanted . . . I've wanted this. I've wanted you."

I kissed him again, and he spread me out onto the blankets and hovered over me, his massive frame cloaking me in the darkness, and we didn't speak again.

ANNABELLE

July 1984

THE LOCAL NEWSPAPER CALLED IT AN ACCIDENTAL OVER-dose, but in Annabelle's darkest moments, she thought that maybe Billy had done it on purpose—died on purpose because she hadn't gone with him that night. There hadn't been a funeral, and there wasn't a grave to visit—Billy's parents had him cremated—and Annabelle felt sometimes as if she were wading in a vast sea of emptiness with no ties to anything but the small life growing inside of her.

She was starting to show—a fact Alice had mentioned more than once—and Annabelle thought, sitting in the waiting room at the Catholic Charities office in Seattle, that she'd been lucky nobody paid any attention to her. William, for his part, hadn't noticed anyone or anything unless he was in a drunken rage, worse now since Billy had died. She thought for a while that maybe she could keep it a secret, hide herself away and save enough to escape, but all of that hope vanished the week after Billy died. William burst into the bedroom she shared with Alice well after midnight, and when Alice had reached out and tripped him with her cane, he'd turned his rage to Annabelle, for the first time striking her across the cheek.

She knew then, knew it deep in her soul, that she couldn't keep her baby.

The woman on the phone had been nice when she'd called, and Alice drove her up one morning and stayed with her the whole time. Alice didn't ask any questions of her, didn't ask her if Billy was the father, because she knew just as well as Annabelle did that it didn't make any difference, not anymore. The only thing that mattered was keeping her baby safe, and that meant keeping it a secret from everyone else, especially Alice's parents. She knew how it worked; she'd seen it before, grandparents getting custody of a young mother's child. That was *never* going to happen while there was still breath in Annabelle's body.

The nuns would find a good family, a nice family, for the baby. She could stay in the dorms at the church with the other unwed mothers until it was time, and then she'd go back to Timber Creek as if nothing ever happened, because she had to.

Because she loved her baby more than she'd ever loved anything in her entire life, and she'd do whatever she had to do to make sure that, above all, her baby was safe in a way that she knew she never would be.

CHAPTER 26

I WOKE UP THE NEXT MORNING, SUNLIGHT STREAMING through the windows in the bedroom. It took me a few seconds to realize where I was and then another few seconds before I realized that I was alone.

I sat up and glanced around. Sherbet was at the end of the bed, looking much better, and Happy sat up from her position on the floor, tail thumping. I stood up and wandered around the house, feeling somewhat dazed from the previous evening. The last thing I remembered before drifting off to sleep was Abel draping one of his arms around me and pulling me close.

Abel wasn't in the bathroom taking a shower, and he wasn't anywhere else in the house either. On the table, next to my keys, there was a note scrawled on a piece of napkin from Three Sheets.

Had to go pick up Maxine. Didn't want to wake you. Thanks for last night. —A

I read the note a few more times before putting it back where I'd found it. Part of me was relieved that he was already gone. At least now we wouldn't have to have an awkward "morning after" conversation. We were, however, going to have to have it eventually, and the other part of me was irritated he'd clearly wanted to avoid it.

From the living room, Happy began to whine.

"Okay," I said to her. "Let's go out."

I pulled on a pair of sweatpants and a sweatshirt, stuffed my feet into a pair of shoes. Then I grabbed Happy's sweater and put it on before the harness. The house was warm by the time I woke up, but I knew it must be cold outside. I didn't want Happy to be cold in the yard. As weird as I'd thought it was for a bunch of women to be knitting sweaters for animals, I was thankful right now. I wondered how many other pets were trotting around their yards wearing St. Francis–style sweaters this morning.

I shivered in the front yard while Happy sniffed at the soggy ground. There were several small limbs down in the front yard, and my car, which I now considered to be a useless pile of metal, was also covered in limbs. Now that it was completely light outside, I could see that most of the houses on the street hadn't sustained much damage. In Beryl's front yard there were some bigger limbs down. She was out there throwing what she could pick up into the back of a truck. I watched her struggle with a few of the bigger branches before rolling my eyes. I had to go over there and help her, now that I'd seen her struggle. I led Happy inside, gave her a treat, and hurried back out and across the street.

"Can I help you?" I asked to Beryl's broad back. Today she wasn't wearing a muumuu at all, instead opting for a psychedelic pair of leggings.

"Huh?" Beryl dropped the limb she was pulling at and turned around. "You're trespassin'," she said.

I took a step back and onto the sidewalk. "Do you want my help or not? It's cold out here, and I could be inside drinking a cup of coffee and watching you from my window."

"Fine," Beryl replied, waving me over. "Grab that other end.

"I was not pleased at all with Annabelle when she hired some old boy to come in and cut down a few of the trees in her yard a few years back," Beryl said, huffing with her end of the limb. "She said she didn't want no trees fallin' onto her roof. Now I'm wishin' I'd done the same thing."

Together, we threw the limb into the back of the truck and moved on to the next one. "There aren't any limbs of this size in my yard," I replied. "That's for sure."

"She was a practical one, that Annabelle," Beryl said. "For the most part."

I smiled. "It's okay if you liked her," I said. "I won't tell anyone."

"She was a good neighbor," Beryl replied. "Except for that cat, we never had much trouble with each other."

"Well, I doubt Sherbet will be coming outside anytime soon," I said. "The storms last night scared him pretty bad."

"Maybe he'll stay out of my garden for a while, then," Beryl replied as we threw another limb up into the truck.

"I doubt it," I muttered.

Beryl laughed. "You're right. I don't think anything could keep that devil out of my yard."

Together, we loaded up about three more limbs. Beryl wiped her hands on her yoga pants, while I searched the yard for more limbs. "I think we've about got them all," I said. "I don't see any more big ones."

"There are a couple in the backyard," Beryl said. "But it's gonna take someone bigger'n me and you to pick them up."

"Okay," I said. "Is there anything else I can help you with?"

Beryl shook her head. "I'll call Abel," she replied. "Maybe in a couple of days once everything's settled down."

"Good plan," I said.

Beryl looked at me, squinting her eyes in the sunlight that peeked through one of the clouds in the sky. "I saw him leaving your house this morning, early," she said. "I didn't say nothin' to him, but I saw him."

I worked hard to keep my cheeks from reddening, although I'm not sure I was successful.

"He's a good man," Beryl replied, surprising me. "He's been more'n a little sad since Claire died. This mornin', he looked, well, he looked happy."

This time I couldn't stop the flush. I gave Beryl a wave and hurried back across the street to the house. I brewed a pot of coffee and sat on the couch with Happy, scanning the room for Sherbet. I knew he had to be hiding in the house somewhere. I found myself wishing I could explain to him that it was just a storm and that everything was fine now. Happy, for her part, no longer seemed to be fazed. I marveled at her ability to take the bad with the good and not hold a grudge. Less than a week ago, she'd been tied outside my house. She'd been hungry and thirsty, and she'd clearly never been treated like a beloved family pet.

Still, she didn't seem to hold any of that against people the way I probably would have. There were clearly some things that scared her—like car rides and storms—but after the offending event was over, she was back to her old self, and I thought that humans could probably learn a lot from dogs. I hoped Abel and I would be able to move past the things in our lives that made us afraid of each other. Last night, if anything, was a good start. I stroked one of Happy's ears, and she nuzzled into me, giving a little satisfied sigh.

After a few minutes, we were both snoring, completely exhausted from everything that had happened the night before, until there was a crash from the master bedroom that woke us. I stood up and Happy followed me to the bedroom, where Sherbet was crouched on top of one of the dressers, gazing down at a basket full of yarn.

"Really?" I asked him.

Happy jumped up onto the bed and the mattress shot forward, nearly sliding off the bed, taking Happy with it. I laughed and was moving to push the mattress back into place when I realized that there was a collection of papers nestled between the mattress and box springs. I grabbed the papers and righted the mattress.

Before I could look down at what was in my hands, my phone rang. I set the papers on the end table and fished my phone out of the pocket of my sweatpants and answered it.

"Hello?"

"Oh, Maeve, thank God."

"Florence?" I asked. "Florence, is that you? Is everything okay?"

"It's me," Florence said. "I'm sorry, I'm calling you from the shop's number. I just realized you don't have it."

"It's okay," I said. "What's wrong?"

"We've got some wind damage at the shop. Part of the roof's blown off."

"Oh my gosh, are you all right?" I asked.

"I'm fine," Florence replied. "But today is our annual sale of the summer knitting supplies, and I can't reschedule. It's been planned for months. I need some help keeping the shop open while I deal with the damage. Eva is coming too, but she can't do it alone."

"Uh . . . sure," I said. "Just give me a few minutes, okay? I need to shower."

"Of course," Florence replied. "Thank you so much. You have no idea how much I appreciate it."

I showered, fed Sherbet, took Happy out one more time, and

on a whim, placed the picture of Annabelle and the mystery man in my purse before I hurried out the door. I'd just pulled out of the driveway in the Volkswagen when I realized that the gas tank was on empty. In my old junker of a car, I could've gone at least twenty miles on empty before running out of gas. I knew, because I'd once tried to go twenty-one miles a couple of years ago, and my father had to bring me a can of gas. But in this vehicle, especially given its age, I wasn't sure.

Instead of taking a left at the end of the street, I coasted straight, just past Three Sheets, and to the little gas station right before the bypass. It was an older gas station, the kind with pumps I hadn't seen since the 1990s, where the gallons and price tick up with a rollover dial.

I got out and pulled at the pump. There was a sign that read, "Cash Only," and I hoped five dollars would at least get me to the shop and back, once I realized I'd left my wallet at home. All I had was five dollars in my pocket, and I wondered idly how it got there. On the other side of the pump was another car, a shiny black Lexus, and I recognized it as Gary's car. I poked my head around the side to see Yulina standing at the pump. I wasn't sure if I should speak to her, not after what I'd seen happening between her and Gary. Then I saw her peer around the pump at me.

"Yulina?" I asked. When she looked up and over at me, I continued, "Hey! It's good to see you."

At first I wasn't sure if she was going to speak. After a few halting seconds she said, "Hello, Maeve."

"How are you?" I asked. "Are you headed downtown to the sale?"

Yulina nodded. "Yes. It is nice today," she said. "We are taking Ani for a walk around."

"That sounds fun," I said.

"I believe it will be."

I put $4.96 in my tank and replaced the nozzle. I turned to pay and saw that Gary was inside at the register, and I hesitated. I turned back to Yulina and stepped over to her side of the pump.

"Are you okay?" I asked her.

Yulina looked at me, and something flashed in her eyes before she said, "Yes. I am fine."

I took her hand. "You don't seem okay," I said to her.

"I don't know what you mean."

She pulled her hand away from mine as Gary sauntered out of the station. He saw me and gave me a small wave. His mouth was smiling, but it didn't reach the rest of his face.

"Maeve," he said when he neared us. "How are you?"

"I'm great," I said, trying to sound chipper. "How are you?"

"Getting there," Gary replied. He turned his attention to Yulina. "Get on in the car, honey," he said. "We really shouldn't leave Ani alone in there."

Yulina did as she was told, and Gary and I were left alone. I moved to go back to my side of the pump when Gary's hand caught my shoulder.

I tried to keep smiling, but I just felt so angry. He was so fake. I wondered if anybody else knew what I knew, and the scene from the night before came rushing back to me. I felt sick.

"Is there something on your mind?" he asked.

I shrugged his hand off me. "I should get going."

"You know," Gary continued on as if he hadn't heard me, "I can tell you like Yulina, and I'm sure you're thinking she needs a friend. But trust me, she's got all the friends she needs."

"I saw you last night," I said. "I saw what you did to her."

Gary's smile vanished, and something behind his eyes flashed for a split second before he found his composure. "I noticed that those plates are expired," he said to me, pointing to the license plates on the Volkswagen. "You really should have that taken care of."

I glared at him.

"Just be careful," Gary said, his smile stretching across his face like a mask over a skeleton. "I'm sure the last thing you want while you're still new in town is to draw any kind of negative attention to yourself."

Gary tipped an imaginary hat to me and disappeared inside the sleek Lexus. He revved the engine twice and then peeled out of the parking lot. I watched him go, a sick feeling settling in the pit of my stomach.

There were dozens of people milling around when I finally got downtown, and the shop was full to the brim.

"Thank you," Florence said, breathless, when I got inside. "It's the Saturday walk around the square. We just have two of these a year, and most of the shops downtown make in one day what they make in three months. We can't cancel."

"It's fine," I said, trying to smile.

"You're an absolute doll," Florence said, giving me a quick hug. "You've saved my life today, kiddo. I mean it."

She hurried off, and I made my way over to Eva, who seemed to be sprouting yarn from every part of her body, and she didn't look happy about it—not one single bit.

"So, she conned you into helping today, did she?" Eva said to me when I stepped up beside her. "You're a sucker, Maeve."

"I would have helped anyway," I said. "But a few days ago, she told me she had enough help. I guess that changed this morning."

"Usually Alice and my mom and I all help out," Eva replied. "But it ended up just being me, and Alice was stuck having some kind of a misunderstanding with her neighbor."

"Mr. Rose?" I asked.

Eva nodded. "He and that vulgar daughter of his never give Alice a moment's rest."

"Oh, Charlene's all right," I said.

"Well, her father is about fifteen pounds of crazy in a five-pound bucket," Eva replied. "But it's good of you to come today. Really."

"I don't mind, Eva," I said. "Really, I don't."

Eva let out a long-suffering sigh. "I hate this day. It's always so crowded, and I see parents of my kids when it's not even parent-teacher conferences. They always want to talk about how their little darling is doing, and you know, I just don't have the energy to say that their child is smart and talented on a *Saturday*."

I laughed. "Do you have to say that?"

"No," Eva replied. "I suppose not."

"Oh, *hello*, Ms. Eva," a round woman wearing a polka-dot blouse said, laying several skeins of yarn on the counter. "How *are* you?"

Eva plastered on a smile and said, "Oh, I'm fine, Mrs. Wilkerson. How are you?"

"Good, good," Mrs. Wilkerson replied. "I just love the sale days, don't you? I've already been down to the frame shop to get a frame for Mackenzie's kindergarten diploma. Forty percent off! Isn't that a *steal*? I'm so hoping she'll have you next year for first grade just like her brother did."

"I hope so too," Eva replied. "Mackenzie is just so smart and so talented."

"You know," Mrs. Wilkerson said, handing Eva her credit card, "I hear that a lot, but I *never* get tired of hearing it!"

It was all I could do not to burst out laughing, but Eva jabbed me in the side with her bony elbow, and I cleared my throat instead.

"You have a good day, Mrs. Wilkerson," Eva chirped, handing her card back.

"Wow," I said once the woman walked away. "That was impressive."

"Now you see why I'm so insufferable after three p.m.," Eva replied.

We spent the rest of the afternoon helping people who didn't look like they'd ever used a knitting needle in their entire lives pick out discount yarn. By two p.m. we were both exhausted.

"Take a break," I said to Eva. "Go back to Florence's apartment and get something to eat like she told you to do three hours ago."

"Are you sure?" Eva asked. "It does look like things are slowing down a bit."

"I'll be all right," I said. "I can run the register myself, and I know enough about the yarn to pass for intelligent."

"You're a lifesaver," Eva replied, giving my arm a squeeze. "As soon as I splash some water on my face and grab a granola bar, I'll be out to relieve you."

"Take your time," I said.

Eva disappeared into the back, and I turned my attention to the handful of customers left in the store. We were nearly out of the summer stock, and I understood what Florence meant about making more money today than they would over a few months. The day I'd been at the store, we'd had no more than a dozen people the entire time I worked and had even fewer sales.

I was grateful when I heard the door jingle and two more people stepped inside. I looked up to see that it was Max and another girl about her age—a frail-looking blond girl wearing a dress about three sizes too small.

"Hey, Maeve," Max said.

"Hi," I said, surprised to see her. "How's it going?"

Max rolled her eyes. "Dad made me stay with Harriett and Eva last night to work on a research project. It's not even due for two more months."

"Well, it looks like you've managed to escape today," I replied.

"Not really," Max grumbled.

"Who is this you've got with you?" I asked.

"This is my friend Cassie."

"Hi, Cassie," I said.

Cassie gave me a shy smile and then looked down at her dirty fingernails.

"Cassie needs something," Max continued, leaning over the counter, her voice quiet. "She needs to get a starter kit to, you know, knit her father a scarf."

"Okay," I said. "Let me go back and get Florence. She said I was supposed to get her to distribute a kit. Something about instructions."

"No!" Max said, grabbing my arm. "Please, don't get Florence. She's in a hurry. Can't you get her a kit?"

"I'm really not supposed to," I said.

"Why not?"

"I don't know exactly," I replied. "It's just that Florence likes to do it herself."

"Please," Max persisted. "It's important."

I sighed. "Fine." I reached down below the counter and pulled out one of the starter kits. "Here."

Max took it and shoved it down inside Cassie's backpack.

"Thanks," she said. Together the girls hurried back out of the store, whispering to each other.

I shrugged. Teenage girls were weird.

Eva came to relieve me, and I ran home to let Happy out and then went right back to help close up for the night. By the time I got back, Alice was there, sweeping the floors with a big dust mop.

"Better than a cane," she said to me with a wink, holding out the broom.

"We had a good day," Florence said, reaching behind me to switch the shop sign to "Closed." "I think we did over three thousand dollars today."

"Wow!" I said. "That's amazing."

"It is," Florence replied. She stepped back behind the register and bent down. "Hey, we're missing a starter kit. Eva, did you give one away today?"

Eva shook her head. "No."

"I did," I said.

All three women turned to look at me.

"I meant to tell you, Eva," I said. "But we got busy after you got back and I forgot. Max and a friend stopped by. Max said her friend needed a starter kit for her father, and you and Florence were both busy. So I went ahead and gave her one."

"You did what?" Florence asked, her voice ticking up a notch. "I told you not to give out any starter packs. I told you to always come and get me."

"I couldn't come and get you," I replied. "You were outside

dealing with the storm damage, and Eva was gone. I couldn't leave the shop unattended."

"Then you should have told them no," Eva replied. "You can't give a starter pack to a kid."

"Why not?" I asked. "I've seen what's in them, Florence. You showed me yourself. It's just some yarn, a pair of knitting needles, and instructions about how to knit a scarf."

"That's not the point," Florence said.

"Then what is the point?"

"I told you not to give them out."

I was beginning to get frustrated. "I'm not a child," I said. "I don't understand what the big deal is about—"

"That's right," Eva said, cutting me off. "You don't understand."

"Look," I said. "I didn't ask for any of this. I didn't even know who any of you were two weeks ago. Now I'm standing here with my birth mother's friends, a birth mother who didn't even want to know me, I might add, and you're all acting like I'm some kind of horrible human being for giving out a stupid starter pack to a kid who probably didn't even have two nickels to rub together."

"That's not true," Alice said quietly.

"What's not true?"

"Annabelle did want you."

I felt like screaming. "I don't care," I said. "It doesn't matter now."

"You don't understand," Alice replied.

"Oh really?" I asked, aware that the other women were staring silently at me now. "Why don't you explain it to me?"

Alice hesitated, and I pushed past Eva and Florence and grabbed my purse out from behind the counter. Just before I slung it over my shoulder to leave, I pulled the picture out and handed it to Alice.

"You can start with explaining this," I said. "You know where to find me when you're ready."

I walked out the door, trying to keep them all from seeing the tears that were threatening to fall down my cheeks as I went.

CHAPTER 27

I PULLED UP IN FRONT OF ABEL'S HOUSE AND SAT THERE FOR a few minutes trying to decide if I wanted to go ahead and rip this Band-Aid off while I was at it, or if I wanted to go home and pull the covers over my head until January.

I'd honestly expected . . . *something*. If he regretted it, then I wanted to know. I wanted him to say it. I got out of the car.

Abel looked genuinely surprised to see me when he opened the door.

"Maeve," he said. "What, uh, what are you doing here?"

"Can I come in?" I asked.

He stepped aside so I could enter. "I was gonna call you," he said.

"No you weren't," I replied. "You don't have my number."

"Oh, right."

"Listen," I said. "I didn't come here to call you out. That's not my style, and honestly, I'm too tired to do that."

Abel reached up to scratch his beard. "Okay," he said finally.

"If you regret last night, that's okay," I continued. "I mean, it's not okay, but if you regret it, I'd rather know now. It'll be easier this way."

"Are you all right?" he asked, taking a step closer to me. "You look like you've been crying."

I stepped back. "Not over you," I replied.

There was a small hint of a smile on his face at that, but then his look turned serious, and he said, "Mae, I just . . . I didn't expect . . . there hasn't been anyone since Claire. I didn't think there would ever be, and then I met you. I wasn't thinking straight last night. Hell, I haven't been thinking straight since I saw you that first night in Three Sheets. You're all I can think about. . . ." He trailed off.

"But?" I asked, already knowing that would be the next word.

"But I have a daughter," Abel said. "I have a daughter, and I've worked really hard to make sure she doesn't forget her mom . . . to make sure *I* don't forget her mom."

I reached out and put my hand on his arm. It looked at that moment like I wasn't the only one close to tears, and despite the fact that it felt like my heart was being ripped out of my chest for a million different reasons, I felt nothing but sympathy for what he must be going through.

"Abel, I don't want to take her place," I said quietly. "I don't want to take her place, and I don't want to live with a ghost."

I removed my hand and put it down at my side to keep it from trembling. "I'm already living with one ghost, and I just don't think there's room for another."

A tear slid down his cheek, and he nodded.

"It's okay," I said. "I don't hate you, and if we just end it now, I won't have to."

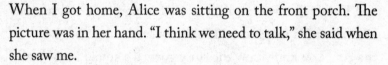

When I got home, Alice was sitting on the front porch. The picture was in her hand. "I think we need to talk," she said when she saw me.

I sighed. "I might be all talked out," I replied, sitting down next to her.

"Do you want to go inside?" I asked.

She handed me back the picture. "The man Annabelle is with is my brother," she said. "His name was Billy."

Suddenly I remembered where I'd seen him—in a picture at Alice's house. He was younger in the picture, but his eyes were the same.

"Is he my father?"

A strangled sob escaped Alice's throat, and then she said, "Yes. I think he was."

"You think?" I asked. "How can you not know if your own brother was my father?"

"Let's go inside," Alice replied. "This is going to take a little while to explain."

I got Alice settled on the couch, and I found some tea bags in the pantry. I poured us each a hot cup and asked her to start from the beginning.

"My father hated my brother," Alice said after a few sips of tea. "He hated me too, I know he did, even though it hurts like hell to admit it. I dealt with it by fighting at school and being tough. It was easy for people to underestimate me—the little crippled girl—but my brother, well, he was never much of a fighter. When Daddy drank, he usually took it out on Billy, and Daddy drank a lot. Billy started using drugs and running around with a rough crowd." Alice waved one of her hands in the air. "You know how the story goes. It's an old story, really. Billy was troubled, and eventually he got into trouble. He did some time in prison for drugs, and when he got out, he did really well for a while. By the time he got out, Annabelle was living with us, and Daddy wouldn't let him come home. He got a job at the factory, got his own place, and I was so proud of him. So proud. Annabelle and I used to go over to his place, and we had such a blast. Pretty soon they started to spend time together, just the two of them. I didn't mind so much. Annabelle was already like a sister to me. I always thought it would have been nice, you know, to have her in the family for real."

"So what happened?" I asked.

"Daddy loved Annabelle about as much as he hated Billy. He was fixated on her, I guess. I don't know. We never talked about it, but I'm not stupid. And when Daddy found out about Annabelle and Billy, well, when he suspected there was something going on, he did everything he could to break it up. Billy lost his job. His place. He lost everything, and he just couldn't handle it. He started using again, and then one night he came over to the house to try to get Annabelle to go with him, and she wouldn't—she couldn't. She was already pregnant with you. Billy didn't even have anywhere to live. Daddy lost his temper, and that was the last time we ever saw Billy. He was dead the next morning—drug overdose, they called it."

"Alice, I'm so sorry," I said. I reached out and took her hand.

Alice looked up at me. "You have to believe me, Maeve. Your mother *wanted* you. She loved you. That's *why* she did what she did. She didn't have any options, and she didn't want my father to know that you were his grandchild. She would have died protecting you from him. She was desperate, and she was scared. She did the only thing she could do."

I sat there for a minute, stunned. "I wrote her letters," I said finally. "When I was sixteen, I tried to know her, and she sent them all back. Every one of them back, unopened."

Alice nodded. "I know. They came to my house—to my parents' house. I sent them back. She never knew about them."

I scooted away from her. "You did what?"

"I'm so sorry," Alice wailed, putting her head in her hands. "I thought it would be better that way. God help me, I was just trying to protect you both."

I wanted to be angry, but the full picture of what Alice and Annabelle must have lived through was starting to develop, and it was terrifying. I couldn't imagine what they'd been through, and I realized that was exactly what Annabelle had hoped for—a life for me where I couldn't even fathom that kind of existence.

"So why did she leave everything to me?" I asked after a long moment.

"She hoped one day she could know you," Alice said. "And I think it was partly a way to make sure that you knew that she never forgot about you. Not for a second. Ever."

"You're my aunt," I said to Alice. "We're . . . related. I've never been able to say that to anybody before."

Alice looked over at me. "I've thought about you every single day for the last thirty-six years," she said. "I hope you've had a good life."

"I have," I said as she embraced me. "I have."

CHAPTER 28

I T MUST'VE BEEN THREE A.M. BEFORE ALICE LEFT MY HOUSE.
We sat up and talked about everything. She promised to bring
all the pictures she had at her house of Billy and Annabelle the
next day.

By six a.m., my phone was buzzing on the nightstand, and I
reached over and grabbed it, knocking it to the floor.

"Shit," I muttered, hanging halfway off my bed and running
my hands underneath the bedframe.

When the ringing stopped and then immediately started back
up again, I knew the person calling was my mother. I considered
not answering and going back to sleep for a few more hours,
but I knew that if I didn't answer, she'd just keep calling. Once,
in college, she'd called the campus police because she couldn't
get me on the dorm phone at six o'clock in the morning on a
Saturday.

"Hello?" I tried to pull myself back upright, but I lost my grip and slid off the bed and into a heap on the floor.

"Maeve?" My mother's voice was panicked. "MAEVE! Are you okay?"

"I'm fine," I mumbled, trying to untangle myself. "I fell off the bed."

"Are you drunk?"

"What?" I sat up. "Mom, no, I'm not drunk."

My mother clicked her tongue against her teeth and said, "Well, I don't know why else you'd be falling off your bed."

"Was there something you wanted, Mom?" I asked, already regretting my decision to answer the phone. "I'm really tired."

"I'm just calling to check on you," she said. "Your brother said he couldn't get you on the phone at all yesterday, and I was worried."

"I meant to call him back," I replied. "Yesterday was kind of intense."

"How do you mean?"

The events of the previous evening came spilling out, and I couldn't stop myself from telling her everything. She listened, silent on the other end of the phone until I was finished.

"I never really expected to find out who my father was," I said afterward. "And now that I know, now that I know everything, I don't know how to feel."

I expected my mother to have plenty to say about everything, but all she said was, "I'm so sorry that you lost them both without ever knowing them."

I couldn't say anything. I tried, but my words got caught in my throat, and I was afraid I might cry. I was sorry too. I was sorry about a lot of things.

"Mae?" My mother's voice came through the phone, slightly panicked. "Honey, are you there?"

"I'm okay," I sniffed, putting her on speaker and laying the phone down on the bed. "I'm just . . . sad."

"I think that's only natural."

"It hurts, Mom," I said, tearing up again. "I didn't realize how much until you called. But it just hurts."

"Do you want me to come up there?" my mother asked. "I can be there in just a few hours."

"I'm okay," I said. "I mean, I will be."

"Are you sure?"

"I think so," I replied.

"Maeve," my mother began. "I know that Annabelle was your mother."

"You're my mother," I said.

"Just listen." My mother let out a breath into the phone and then continued, "I know that Annabelle was your mother. She's part of you in a way that I'm not, and even now, all these years later, it's hard for me to admit. I never wanted for you to deny that part of yourself because you were afraid of hurting my feelings. I was supposed to set an example for you in that respect, and I know that I wasn't always good at it."

"You have always been a good mom," I replied. "Always, and I'm so glad that you chose me."

"I'm glad Annabelle chose us," my mother said. "I hope that you understand the courage it took for her to give you up, and I wish so much I'd been able to tell her that."

"I don't think I understood the kind of courage it took until yesterday," I said. "I don't think I understood a lot of things until yesterday."

"Life is full of things we don't understand," my mother replied. "You're lucky. Some of us never figure it out."

CHAPTER 29

I NAPPED ON AND OFF FOR A FEW HOURS, BUT I COULDN'T ever really get to sleep. I just had so much to think about, and when Alice called and asked me to meet her and Florence at the shop later that afternoon, I was glad for the distraction. I got up and, after getting dressed, found myself in Annabelle's bedroom, just staring at it as if I'd never seen it before.

I guessed in some ways, I hadn't. I'd been angry when I arrived in Timber Creek, and I'd felt guilty about feeling angry. In fact, this was the way I'd been feeling for a long time, and the way my life had been going lately, I was just used to feeling like nothing was ever going to be okay. For a long time, I'd believed that being an adult meant having my life together, and I'd convinced myself that since I didn't have my life together, I wasn't a real adult. I thought my life needed to be all smooth surfaces or I was doing it wrong. What I'd begun to realize, though, was that everyone, absolutely every-one, had cracks.

I sat down on the bed and began to look through a basket of knitting supplies. I knew that Annabelle had done the best she could with the life she was given, and I wished that I'd had the chance to tell her so. At the bottom of the basket was the beginning of what looked like a very small sweater. I knew that it must have been something she was working on with the ladies of St. Francis. I pulled it out and decided that when I got to the shop, I'd ask Alice for help.

I was a little nervous about what Alice and Florence wanted to talk about, but I figured it had something to do with the un-finished conversation the night before. At the very least, I could apologize for acting the way I had and for giving out a starter kit when I knew I shouldn't have. Still, I didn't understand why giving out yarn and some knitting needles was a problem.

The shop was dark when I pulled up outside, and the door was locked. For a minute I thought maybe I'd hallucinated the phone call. Then I heard the lock click, and Florence ushered me inside.

"What's going on?" I asked. "Why is it so dark in here?"

"Come to the back," Florence replied.

I followed her back into her apartment, and I was surprised when I got there to find not only Alice but also Yulina and Ani.

"Hi," I said to Yulina.

"Hello," Yulina replied. She shifted Ani from one hip to the other. She tried to smile, but faltered, and I noticed how tired she looked. There was another element there that I couldn't quite put my finger on. Fear?

"Is everything okay?" I asked.

"Have a seat," Alice said. "There's something we need to tell you."

Alice sat down beside me, and Florence sat down beside her. Yulina sat down on a blanket on the floor and released Ani to play. I stared at the three of them. Their faces were all so serious, and I felt for a moment like I couldn't breathe.

"Florence and I," Alice began, gesturing to her friend, "along with the rest of the women of St. Francis, have a secret, and given what you know now about Annabelle, we thought it was time for you to know about us too."

"What is it?" I asked, my heart pounding. "I don't think I can take much more right now. I've just about had my fill of secrets lately."

"This is a secret you'll have to help us keep, if we tell you," Florence said. "Lives depend on it. Lives in this room depend on it."

I looked down at Yulina and Ani. Ani had a small truck that she was raking across the carpet, making little truck noises. Yulina wasn't looking at me. She wasn't looking anywhere, really. She was sitting like a statue on the floor, her back rigid and her eyes unfocused.

"Okay," I said. "What is it?"

"Our knitting group," Alice said, "is also a network of women helping other women survive and escape domestic violence. The shop is a knitting shop, of course, but when a woman comes in and asks for a starter kit, it's because she's asking for help. That's why we didn't want you to give them out without knowing what they were for."

"Annabelle and Alice came to me just after I opened the shop with the idea," Florence cut in. "They didn't want anybody to have to go through what they'd been through—they didn't want another mother to be parted from a child because she had no resources and no one to help her."

"Annabelle tried to help me," Yulina said, finally looking up and over at me. "Before she . . . before she was gone. I was afraid."

"Are you okay now?" I asked her, moving to the floor to take her hands in mine. "Are you safe?"

"We're moving her and Ani to a safe house tonight," Florence replied. "Abel drives to the houses for us. He's the only one who ever knows where they go, because the fewer people who know, the better."

"I am sorry for putting you in the middle," Yulina said to me. "I should not have done that."

"How did you put me in the middle?" I asked.

"The knitting needles," she replied. "Annabelle gave them to me. She told me to give them to her when I was ready to leave."

"We knew what they were when you showed them to us," Alice said. "It was a signal."

"I am so sorry," Yulina repeated.

"No," I said, squeezing her hands again. "It's okay. I'm glad you gave them to me. I'm glad that you're going to be okay."

"Gary knows you saw us," Yulina continued.

Alice knitted her eyebrows together. "What are you talking about, Yulina?"

"I saw them the other night," I said. "During the storm. He made her stand in the front yard in the pouring rain. I was out looking for Sherbet, and I saw them."

"It was humiliating," Yulina said.

"And then I saw them at the gas station, and I said something to Gary about it," I said. "I was so angry and confused and I'm sorry. I shouldn't have said anything."

"No," Florence agreed. "You shouldn't have. You've put yourself in danger."

"He's going to think I had something to do with this?" I asked.

"He might," Florence replied. "I'm sure he's already looking for her. She's not answering his calls, and he knows something is wrong."

"It might be best if you went back to Seattle for a few days," Alice said. "Just until things calm down. Gary will be beside himself when he realizes what's going on."

"I'm not going back to Seattle," I said. "Not even for a few days. I'm here, and I'm staying, and I'm not going to let Gary intimidate me."

"Don't be stubborn," Alice replied. "This isn't about intimidation. It's about keeping you safe."

"I'm not leaving."

"She can stay with me," Abel said, appearing in the doorway.

"I don't want to stay with anyone," I said, exasperated.

"Please," Yulina said. "It will make me feel better if you do."

I sighed. "Okay," I said, and she reached out to hug me. "Fine, if it will make you feel better."

"We should get going," Abel said to Yulina. "Now that it's dark."

"You can stay here until Abel gets back," Alice said.

"I need to go get Happy and Sherbet. I can't leave Happy alone for too long. I think it makes her scared, and she eats things like doors," I replied. "And some clothes. I'm not going unless they can stay too."

"Of course," Abel said. "Get them, but don't go alone."

"You guys are acting like Gary might try to kill me or something," I said, half joking.

The four of them stared at me, and Yulina said, very quietly, "He might."

If I hadn't understood the severity of the situation before, I understood it now, looking into Yulina's frightened eyes. "Okay," I replied. "Alice, could you go with me? Then we can come back here and wait."

Alice nodded. "I'll follow you in my car," she said. "We can leave the Bug parked at the house. That way if Gary happens to drive by, he won't see it anywhere but at the house."

Abel caught my arm as we exited the shop. "I'm sorry," he said. "For the way I acted before. Can we talk tonight?"

"You don't owe me an apology," I replied.

"Please. There are some things I want to say."

"Me too," I said. "Okay. We'll talk tonight."

I watched him help Yulina strap Ani into her car seat, making funny faces at the little girl as he tightened the harness. I hoped with every single fiber of my being that wherever he was taking them, it would be the first stop on their way to a life where neither one of them ever had to be afraid again.

Chapter 30

ALICE PULLED UP TO THE CURB AND GOT OUT. "CAN I help with anything?" she asked.

"Do you know if Annabelle had a cat carrier?"

"I think she kept a couple in the garage," Alice said. "I can go check for you while you're getting your stuff together."

"That would be awesome," I said. "Thanks. It won't take me but a minute."

I busied myself packing and Happy came to sit beside me, her tail doing a *thump, thump, thump* while she waited for me.

"Don't worry," I said to her. "You're coming with me."

Sherbet peered out at me from under the bed. It was like he knew what I was about to do, and he had no interest in making it easy for me to catch him. Not even a tuna treat would lure him out, and I realized I'd probably have to close the bedroom door and crawl under the bed after him.

I waited for Alice in the living room, while Sherbet scratched at the bedroom door. When she wasn't back in ten minutes, I figured she was having trouble finding a crate and decided to go out and see if I could help. There wasn't a light on in the garage, and there was no answer when I called her name.

"Alice? Are you in there?"

From the back corner, I heard a soft moaning, and it took a second for my eyes to adjust once the lights came on. I saw her cane on the floor before I saw anything else, and then I saw her feet sticking out from behind a pile of boxes. I ran over to her and knelt on the ground.

"Oh my God. Alice, are you okay?"

There was blood pooling beneath her head, and her eyes couldn't focus on me. The cat carrier lay beside her. I looked above her to the shelf and wondered if the carrier had fallen on top of her and hit her head. The cat carrier had soft sides, though, and I didn't think that it could possibly have hit her hard enough to knock her to the ground.

"Maeve," Alice whispered, her voice barely audible. "M . . . M . . . Maeve."

"I'm going to call 911," I said to her. "Shhh. Don't talk. You're going to be okay."

"Maeve," Alice persisted. "Please . . ."

I pulled my phone from my pocket and unlocked it. "I promise, someone will be here as soon as they can."

I heard a crunching of leaves outside the shed, and I froze. It was getting late and it was dark outside. There wouldn't be any reason for someone to be walking outside around the shed, especially because it was in the backyard. Someone would have to be intentionally walking into the yard.

"Maeve," Alice whispered again, and I bent my head toward her so that I could hear her better. "Maeve, run."

"What?" I stood up and saw a shadow in the doorway. "Who's there?" I asked.

I didn't want to leave Alice on the ground, but I couldn't see who was standing there, so I moved forward and realized it was Gary. He was staring at me with a look on his face that made my blood go cold.

"Hey, Maeve," he said, his voice calm.

I took a step backward toward Alice. "Get off my property," I said. I tried and failed to keep my voice steady. "You're trespassing."

"Let's take a ride," Gary said, ignoring me.

"I'm not going anywhere with you."

"I thought you might say that," Gary replied. He moved toward me, and I saw the glint of steel in his right hand and realized he was carrying a gun. He held it up for me to see when he saw me staring at it. "You want to rethink your response?"

I shook my head. "No," I said. "I'm not going anywhere. Alice needs help."

Gary lunged forward and grabbed ahold of one of my arms and pulled me out of the garage and out into the alleyway to where his car was waiting. "Get in," he said. "Slide through to the driver's side."

I glanced around. There was nobody around, and I knew it wouldn't do any good if I tried to scream. "You want me to drive?" I asked.

"I can't drive and watch you at the same time," he said. "Get in."

I did as I was told, and he slid in right after me, keeping the gun trained on my head the whole time. "Where do you want me to go?" I asked.

"You tell me," he said.

"I don't know," I said. "I don't know what you want me to do."

"I want you to take me to her," Gary replied. "Take me to my wife."

"I don't know where she is," I said.

"Don't speed or do anything else that might get you pulled over," he said. "I'm only going to warn you once. Don't be stupid."

I licked my lips. They felt dry, and so did my mouth. I knew if I could keep driving for just a little while, keep him talking for just a little while, surely Abel would come looking for me if I didn't show up at his house, and he'd call someone. But I had to stay alive in the meantime.

I rolled to a stop at a traffic light two blocks from Maple Street and asked, "Which way do you want me to go?"

"Take me to her," he barked.

"Okay," I said. "Okay, I'll take you to her."

At that Gary seemed to relax, and he slumped down into the seat. I continued to drive, taking random turns and going down streets I didn't recognize, still trying not to get too far from my house.

"We've been down this street before," Gary said after a few minutes. "What are you doing?"

"I'm taking you to Yulina," I said.

"That's not how it looks to me." He pressed the metal so hard into my head that I let out a yelp and swerved onto the shoulder of the road.

I blinked back tears and kept driving. Gary sat beside me, mumbling to himself. It seemed like he was having some sort of a breakdown. He was becoming more and more agitated as the minutes ticked by.

"Gary," I said softly. "Yulina isn't going to leave you. Let's just pull over and talk about it. I'm sure we can come to a resolution about the whole thing."

Gary turned to look at me, and his eyes were wild. "She doesn't want to leave me, but you have her convinced. You have her convinced just like Annabelle had her convinced."

"I would never do that."

"Sure you wouldn't." Gary chuckled. "That's what Annabelle said too."

"Gary," I said. "I'm not Annabelle. I've just been here for a few days. How could I possibly have done this?"

"Where is she?"

In the distance I heard sirens, and I tried not to show my relief. Gary twisted himself around in the front seat to look behind us, and then he cursed under his breath. "Drive faster," he said.

"You told me not to," I said. "Remember? You said not to do anything stupid."

Gary cocked the gun. "I'll kill you right now," he said. "I'll kill you, and then I'll kill myself. I swear to God, I'll do it."

I couldn't see much except for what was in front of us, because it was completely dark outside. I could see that there was a roundabout coming up with a large culvert in the middle. I had to make a decision. The farther I drove, the more agitated Gary became, and the closer the sirens got to us. It wouldn't be long before he was going to pull the trigger, and once he made that decision, there wouldn't be anything I could do. I had to do something.

I took a deep breath and loosened my grip on the steering wheel. Finally I said, "You want me to drive faster?" I jammed my right foot down onto the gas pedal. "Fine. I'll drive faster."

The force of the acceleration slammed Gary back into the seat. When he regained his bearings, he reached over and tried to grab the steering wheel, but it was too late. I blew past the stop sign and hurtled through the roundabout, crashing right into the center of the culvert.

I heard the crunching of glass and metal just before I was thrown forward into the *pop* of the airbag and everything went black.

CHAPTER 31

WHEN I CAME TO, I WAS STILL INSIDE THE LEXUS WITH Gary. He was moaning beside me, and I turned my head to see his crumpled frame in the passenger's seat. Pain shot through me when I tried to move, but I managed to unbuckle my seat belt. The door was stuck, but the window was busted out, and I pulled myself up from the seat and through the window, landing on the ground with a sickening thud.

I could hear Gary yelling at me from inside the car. I didn't know if he still had the gun, and the sirens were pounding in my ears even though I couldn't see them. When I put my hands down onto the pavement, all I felt was glass. I forced myself to my feet and began to run, praying I wouldn't vomit. I ran toward the direction of the sirens, but it felt as though I was running through molasses, and I wasn't sure if I was really moving at all until a police car came to a screeching halt in front of me.

A uniformed officer jumped out of the front seat, followed by Abel from the passenger's seat, and I dropped to my knees.

Abel caught me just before I fell completely, and he held me there as I cried. "He's . . . he's . . . he's in the car," I stammered. "He's got a gun."

"Shhhh . . ." Abel said. "It's okay. You're safe. You're safe."

Abel released me when two EMTs with a stretcher appeared, as if out of nowhere, and loaded me onto it. "Don't leave me," I said.

"I won't," Abel replied. He took my hand.

All I wanted to do was close my eyes. My head was pounding. I could taste blood in my mouth and feel it running down my face. As the EMTs picked up the stretcher to put me into the ambulance, I tried to sit up. "Alice," I said. My voice sounded so far away from my body.

"She's okay," Abel said.

I let out a sigh of relief and closed my eyes.

ANNABELLE

February 1985

LABOR HAD NOT BEEN EASY. ANNABELLE HAD LAIN ON her back for nearly twenty-four hours before it had been time to push. The nuns took her to the hospital when her water broke, and two of them sat outside in the waiting room with the Stephens family, but Annabelle had labored alone. She'd delivered her baby girl alone.

The doctors and nurses were skilled when it came to delivering babies birthed by single mothers, but that didn't mean Annabelle had escaped their judgment in the big Catholic Seattle hospital. One of the nurses, a sweet-faced woman with sympathetic eyes, had told Annabelle that she was still a pretty girl and that there would be plenty of time to start a family in God's eyes once this whole, awful situation had been taken care of.

Annabelle tried not to think about the way it might have been if things had been different—if Billy or her parents were still alive—but it was hard. The maternity ward was filled with happy women and happy families, and Annabelle didn't know how to separate the incredible joy of giving birth with the excruciating pain of giving her daughter up to someone else, regardless of whether or not it was the best or right thing to do.

"You can change your mind," Alice said when she got there the next day to take Annabelle home. "You don't have to do this."

"They left with her this morning," Annabelle replied. "She's gone."

"Didn't you even get to say goodbye?"

Annabelle pulled her shirt on over her head and then sat down gingerly on the bed. It hurt so bad to sit. "I got three hours with her," she said.

Alice sat down on the bed beside her friend and took her hand. "You know I'm not good with all of this emotional stuff," she said. "But I love you, and we'll always have each other, okay? We'll always be there for each other."

Annabelle mustered a smile, even though smiling felt nearly as painful as sitting down. "I know," she replied. "I love you too."

Annabelle knew that she would have to go home to Alice and her parents. Right now there was no other choice until she could save up enough money to get her own place. What Annabelle hadn't told Alice was that she'd watched from her hospital room window as the Stephenses took their new daughter home. She'd watched them carry her outside and then watched the two of them fuss with a car seat, something Annabelle hadn't even considered a baby would need. There were lots of things, Annabelle knew, she hadn't considered, and for a brief moment there was almost a sense of relief to know that this baby's future was out of her hands. There was nothing she could do to mess it up.

Then June Stephens had looked up at the building, searching all the dark windows for Annabelle's until she found it. She'd smiled at Annabelle and waved, and Annabelle could see the older woman mouthing the words "Thank you" to her before sliding into the back seat with the baby.

Annabelle had murmured the same words back to her before closing the blinds and sliding back into bed, holding on to the blanket that smelled like the baby that was no longer hers, until the nurse came into the room to tell her it was time to dress and go home.

CHAPTER 32

THE NEXT TIME I WOKE UP, I WAS IN A HOSPITAL BED. THE pounding in my head was still there, but it was dull, and I was able to focus on the cream-colored ceiling. I could hear voices around me, and it took me a minute to figure out how to turn my head to see who was in the room with me.

I heard someone say, "She's awake!"

Then a doctor and several nurses descended upon me before my parents were there and calling my name.

"What," I said, my throat thick. "What happened?"

"You're in the hospital," my father said, stroking my forehead. "You're okay though."

"She's been out for three days," my mother said to him. "That's not okay in my book."

My father shot my mother a look and then he focused back on me and said, "You were in a car accident. You broke two ribs and fractured your left ankle. You had a pretty good concussion, and you've got cuts just about everywhere, but the doctors say you'll be okay, and that's all that matters."

"What hospital am I in?"

"Seattle Catholic," my father replied. "They had you airlifted after the accident."

"Can I have something to drink?" I asked. "My throat hurts."

"Of course." My mother handed me a Styrofoam cup with a straw sticking through the plastic lid. "Here you go."

I took several gulps. "Thank you," I said. "That feels better."

"Your brother and Kate are outside," my mother continued. "You've got a whole waiting room full of people. I don't think that big bearded man has left at all since we got here."

"Abel?"

"That's his name," my mother said. "He's been sitting with Eli."

I started to smile, but then I remembered why I was in the hospital. I remembered Gary and his gun and crashing into a roundabout, and I struggled to sit up as I said, "Where is Yulina? Ani? What about Gary? Is he in jail?"

"Slow down," my father said. "There's also a police detective waiting outside to speak to you too, but I do know that your friend and her daughter are okay."

"What about Gary?"

"He's dead," came a voice from the doorway. "Gary Johnson is dead, and he won't be taking anybody for a joyride anytime soon."

My parents stepped out of the way as a man wearing a suit stepped forward and into the room.

"Let's go tell everyone she's awake," my father said to my mother, taking her hand. "Let them have a few minutes to talk."

I reached out for my mother's hand. "Mom."

"What is it, sweetheart?"

"Alice, where is she? Is she okay?"

My mother nodded. "She's okay. She has something like fifteen stitches in her head, but she's okay. She's outside too."

I sighed. "Oh thank God."

My mother turned her steely gaze on the detective and said, "I don't know if she's ready to talk to you. Can't you come back later?"

The detective nodded. "I can, but I do have to speak with your daughter sometime."

"It's okay, Mom," I said. "You go on out with Dad. I'm all right."

"I'll be right outside," she replied. Then she pointed at the detective. "Don't you upset her. Do you understand me?"

The detective's lip nearly twitched into a smile, and he nodded. "Yes, ma'am."

"Is Gary really dead?" I asked once my mother was gone. "Did the police have to shoot him?"

"I'm Detective Carl Richardson," the man said, taking a step toward my bed. He had a kind face, and I began to feel myself relax. "Gary Johnson shot himself in the front seat of his Lexus. By the time the responding officers got to him, it was too late."

"I thought he was going to kill us both," I said.

"Can you tell me what happened that night?" Detective Richardson asked. "We've spoken with Alice, but she wasn't with you in the vehicle, and the only other person who knows what happened besides you is dead."

I took a breath and winced. My father hadn't been joking about those cracked ribs. "I was in the shed at my house on Maple Street," I said. "Alice had gone out to look for a cat carrier. I guess Gary came up behind her and knocked her out. When I went outside to check on her, she was on the floor of the shed. Then Gary showed up, and he forced me into his car and made me drive. He wanted me to take him to his wife, Yulina. He thought I knew where she was."

"Did you know where she was?" Detective Richardson asked.

"No," I answered honestly. "I saw her briefly at the knitting shop, and she was going someplace safe, but I didn't know where."

The detective made a note in his notepad and then looked back up at me. "Yulina Johnson maintains that he has hurt her or threatened to hurt her on several occasions."

"Yes," I replied. "I witnessed his abuse."

"Can you tell me about that?" the detective asked, flipping over to a fresh piece of paper in his notepad.

"Maeve?" I heard Abel's voice, and then he was standing right beside me, leaning over me and kissing my forehead. "I thought you were dead," he whispered. "I thought you were going to die."

"I'm sorry," the nurse said, following him into the room. "I couldn't stop him. I told him you were in here, Detective, but he wouldn't listen."

"It's okay," the detective replied, snapping his notepad closed. "I'm done for now. I'll come back later, Ms. Stephens, if that's all right."

"Of course," I said, my eyes still locked on Abel's.

"Give us just a minute," I said to the nurse once the detective was gone. "Then you can let everybody else in."

"How are you feeling?" Abel asked me. "You've been out for days."

"I feel about as good as I probably look," I said. "But I'm going to be okay."

"When you and Alice didn't show up at the house, I got worried and went to check on you. I knew something was wrong when I found Happy inside the house going crazy, chewing at her harness and barking."

"I didn't think," I said, swallowing. "I didn't think he'd really do anything."

Abel's jaw tightened. "I'm sorry you got dragged into this."

"It's not your fault," I said.

"Beryl saw his car pull into the alley. He didn't have his lights on, and she thought it was weird, so she called it in to the police. They showed up a couple of minutes after I did."

"I'm glad you caught up with us when you did," I said. "I don't know what would have happened otherwise. Where is Yulina? Are she and Ani safe?"

Abel nodded. "They are. They're safe."

"What about Happy? And Sherbet? They weren't left alone in the house, were they?" I tried to sit up. I was suddenly panicked at the thought of them alone and afraid in the house.

"I took them both to my house. Max has been having a blast taking care of them the past couple of days, although Sherbet is not at all happy with Max carrying him around all the time, and he's gone back to the house to look for you every day. Happy too, when I take her on walks," Abel said.

"Thank you," I said. "For taking care of them for me."

Abel leaned down and pressed his forehead into mine. "I'm sorry," he said. "For the way I acted. I don't have a good excuse. But when I thought you were gone, when I thought Gary was going to kill you, I almost lost my mind."

"I'm okay," I insisted.

"I can live with one ghost," he said, kissing me softly on the lips. "But I can't live with two."

I kissed him back.

CHAPTER 33

A LICE SAT IN ONE OF THE CHAIRS IN THE HOSPITAL ROOM, her cane leaning against the wall and a pair of knitting needles in her hands. "Okay," she said. "Try holding your needles like this." She held her handiwork up for me to see.

I sighed. "I'm never going to get the hang of this."

I'd been in the hospital for nearly two weeks, and I was going stir-crazy. Alice had finally gotten the stitches out of her head and been cleared to drive, and the first place she came was to Seattle to visit me.

"Sure you are," Alice said. "You're going to have eight weeks off your feet to get the hang of it."

"This is torture."

"Oh, hush," Alice replied. "I didn't like it either, and now I'm one of the best knitters in the tri-state area."

"Is Canada in the tri-state area?" I asked, grinning.

"Look," Alice said, pointing to me. "You did it, and you weren't even paying attention!"

I looked down at the sweater in my hands. "Hey! I did it!"

"I told you that you'd get the hang of it," Alice replied. "So, what time are you getting discharged tomorrow?"

I shrugged. "The nurses told me it would be in the morning, but they didn't give me a specific time."

"Are you sure it's okay for me to stay with your parents to-night?" Alice asked. "I hate to put them out."

"You're not putting them out," I said. "You're my ride back from Seattle."

"I about had to fight Abel for the honor," she replied. "He was bound and determined he was coming down with me, but Max has that science fair this weekend."

"I'm glad it's you bringing me home," I said. "He's got no business being on the road—he said he's been up past two a.m. every night working on an outline for his new book. Appar-ently his literary agent cried when he told her."

"I've never seen him so happy," Alice said. "And that's the truth."

"He and Eli have been talking quite a bit," I said. "Twice I've called, and Abel was on the phone with Eli, discussing his book plans. I guess they really hit it off after the accident."

"Your mother told me neither one of them left that waiting room," Alice replied. "You're lucky to have so many people who care about you."

"I know," I said. "It took me a long time to realize it."

"You know, it's odd," Alice said. "The last time I was here, I was bringing Annabelle home without you. Now I'm bringing you home without her."

I held my hand out to her, and she took it. I'd come to Timber Creek with a lot of ideas about the way things ought to be and no ideas about how to fix the mess I'd made of my life, because I thought for some reason that it was broken—that I was broken—and I blamed that brokenness on the cracks I assumed everyone else could see, the pieces of my life that I thought never fit together and all the years I thought I would never know what those pieces meant. For the first time in my life, the pieces meant more to me than it did to make them fit together.

I looked down at Alice's hand. I looked at the oval shape of her nails, the way her pinkie finger curled away just a little bit more than the rest of her fingers, and the way the delicate veins crossed over one another, pulsing beneath the skin. Her hands were eighteen years older than mine, but I would have known what those hands looked like, even if I hadn't bothered to look down.

I knew, because those hands were mine too.

"They would be so proud of you," Alice said, a single tear sliding down her cheek.

"Will you tell me about them?" I asked. "Will you tell me which parts of them I am?"

"Of course," Alice replied. "I'll tell you anything you want to know."

I smiled and leaned back into the bed, our hands still clasped together. "It would be nice," I said, "if you started at the beginning."

EPILOGUE

ANNABELLE WATCHED AS PARTYGOERS ARRIVED, WITH gifts wrapped in shiny paper carried by little boys wearing superhero shirts. Each of the boys, wide-eyed with excitement, shooed their parents away at the earliest possible moment.

At the hospital, June had come into Annabelle's room and sat with her for nearly an hour while Annabelle cried. Annabelle hadn't even understood why she was crying at the time, because it wasn't just the profound loss she felt. It wasn't just losing her baby—it was more than that in a way she couldn't explain, but June hadn't asked. She'd just sat herself down beside Annabelle on the bed and held her.

"I can't promise you I won't make mistakes," June had said to her. "But I can promise you I'll do my best every single day to be the kind of mother I know that you would want me to be."

"Thank you," Annabelle replied, trying to pull herself together enough to get ready to leave the hospital. She knew that Alice was waiting outside for her. "Have you decided on a name?"

June hesitated. "It's a family name," she said. "We've decided to call her Maeve, Mae for short."

"It's a beautiful name," Annabelle replied. "I love it."

Maeve emerged from the house with a little boy, maybe about six. He must be the birthday boy. He eyed the presents with interest before attempting to grab a hot dog. June scolded him, but there was no malice in her eyes. Not a hint of actual anger. The little boy grinned and ran away, and June called after him a warning about choking to death before it was his own turn to have presents. Maeve ran after him, laughing, and grabbed him around his middle, pulling him into a hug. Annabelle felt a sense of relief that she hadn't expected, now that she knew Maeve had a sibling. It was something that she, herself, had always wanted.

Both children were safe, happy, and loved, and Annabelle could see it written all over them, that sense of family she'd never really known. It made her heart ache, but not with envy or sadness, although she'd have been lying if she said she'd never felt either of those things at first, in those early days. What she felt now was a sense of pride at the daughter she'd helped to create with Billy, even though they couldn't be the ones to raise her. It was enough, in this moment, to know her child was thriving.

Annabelle watched the party for hours until it turned dark

and the guests went home, one by one, even the stragglers carrying sleepy children and paper plates full of leftover cake. Only Maeve remained in the yard. Ignoring calls to come inside, she lay on top of the picnic table and stared up at the sky, hands resting behind her head. Annabelle rubbed her eyes. She had a long drive ahead of her, and so she started her car. She hadn't realized she'd stayed so late. Hers was the only car left on the street. She pulled away from the curb and eased down the road, waiting to put on her headlights until she was at the stop sign, the house and the yard and the girl who looked so much like her, a beautiful memory, in the rearview mirror.

ACKNOWLEDGMENTS

I<small>T IS WITH SINCERE AFFECTION AND ADMIRATION THAT</small> I'D like to thank the following:

Priya Doraswamy—For never tiring of emails titled "I have this new idea for a book and I've written a 10,000-word synopsis instead of doing what I should be doing . . ."

Lucia Macro—For hearing the term "dog sweater patterns" and being just as excited about it as I was.

Asante Simons—For being very patient and also for totally understanding my love of early 2000s pop music.

Matt and Jude—For being my best friends and dreaming big right along with me.

My mom and dad—For literally always telling me it'll be okay.

Brittany—For listening to all my very long and complainy (yes, that's a word, sort of) voice memos and responding in kind. I love you.

About the Author

About the Book

Insights,
Interviews
& More . . .

Meet
Annie England Noblin

ANNIE ENGLAND NOBLIN lives with her son, husband, and four rescued bulldogs in the Missouri Ozarks. She graduated with an MA in creative writing from Missouri State University and currently teaches English at Arkansas State University. Her poetry has been featured in such publications as the *Red Booth Review* and the *Moon City Review*, and she co-edited and co-authored the coffee-table book *Gillioz: Theatre Beautiful*. ∾

Knitting Patterns

If you would like to knit your own cat scarf or dog sweater, look no further!

Sherbet's Knitted Cat Scarf Pattern

Materials:

- Size 6 needles
- Worsted weight yarn, two colors

Instructions:

BODY OF SCARF:

- With MC, CO 8 sts.
- Work garter stitch until you have 4 ridges.
- Change to CC, work garter stitch until you have 4 ridges.
- Work stripe sequence until you have 9 stripes. BO stitches and sew ends together. ▶

Knitting Patterns *(continued)*

TAIL 1:

- CO 8 stitches in MC.
  Work stripe sequence until
  you have four stripes. BO.

TAIL 2:

- CO 8 stitches in MC.
  Work stripe sequence until
  you have five stripes. BO.

TASSELS (OPTIONAL):

- Cut 8 four-inch pieces of MC and
  6 of CC. Each piece is one tassel.
- Line tail 1 up with tail 2, so that the
  top of tail 1 matches the last stripe
  of the same color, right sides facing.
  Center tails over the join in the main
  body of the scarf. Sew tail 1 to tail 2
  AND scarf at the same time.
  Sew top of tail 2 to edge of scarf.
- Put scarf on cat. Watch cat roll
  around as if being tortured.
  Take funny pictures. Remove scarf
  before cat plots your death.

NOTE: This scarf is NOT Sherbet approved.

Happy's Knitted Dog Sweater Pattern

Materials:

- Yarn required: 6.5 oz. sports weight yarn. You can break this up into two different colors if you want a contrasting neck and sleeves.
- Needles: Size 8 (5mm), Size 8 (5mm) circular needle/16"
- Stitch Holder
- Size: S (L) Chest size: 13 ¼" (25") Length: 9 ¼" (21 ¾")
- Gauge: 18 sts and 36 rows equals 4" in garter stitch
- (The garter stitch is knitting every row.)

Abbreviations:

- k—knit
- p—purl
- k2tog—knit 2 together
- Ssk—slip, slip, knit (slip next 2 sts as if to knit, one at a time, to right needle into fronts of these 2 sts and k them together.) ▶

Knitting Patterns *(continued)*

- M1—make 1 stitch. (An increase worked by lifting the horizontal thread lying between the needles and placing it onto the left needle. Work this new stitch through the back loop.)

Instructions:

BACK:

- Cast on 35 (51) sts with the straight needles.
- Knit in the garter stitch, increasing 1 stitch at both ends of the row, every 6th (4th) row, 3 (14) times.
- There are now 41 (79) stitches on the needle.
- Continue knitting in the garter stitch for 5 ¾" (14 ¼").

LEG OPENINGS:

- Place a marker at the end of the last row. This will mark the beginning of the leg openings.
- Decrease Row: k2, ssk, k to last 4 sts, k2tog, k2
- Repeat the decrease row every other row 3 more times—33 (71) sts.
- Knit 10 rows.

- Increase Row: k2, M1, k to last 2 sts, M1, k2.
- Repeat the increase row every other row 3 more times—41 (79) sts.
- Place a marker at each end of the last row to mark the end of the leg openings.
- Knit 4 rows.
- Work even in the garter stitch for 1" (5").
- Place 41 (79) sts on a holder.

FRONT:

- Using straight needles, cast on 19 (33) sts.
- Knit in the garter stitch for 1 ¼" (6 ¼").
- Shape the leg openings as you did for the back.
- Place 19 (33) sts on a holder.

COLLAR:

- Using the circular needle, knit across the Back stitches on the holder, then the Front stitches—60 (112) sts.
- Place a marker and join for working in the round. Size L only: *k2, k2tog, k3, k2tog; repeat from *, end with k4—88 sts. ▶

Knitting Patterns *(continued)*

- Both Sizes: Work even in rounds of k2, p2 until collar is 4" (7").
- Bind off loosely following the ribbing pattern.

SLEEVES:

- At each leg opening, with right side facing, pick up and knit—28 sts.
- Knit in k2, p2 until the sleeve measures 2 ½" (3 ½").
- Bind off loosely following ribbing pattern.

FINISHING:

- Sew the side seams on either side of the leg openings.
- Sew the sleeve seams and weave in the ends.
- Hope this knitted dog sweater keeps your pup warm all winter.
- Put the sweater on your grateful pup. He or she will love dressing up for you. Be sure to watch as your dog casts superior glances toward your cat, who is now most likely plotting your death for the scarf. ∽

Reading Group Guide

1. In what ways could Maeve's parents have handled telling her about her adoption differently? They waited until she was six, and she learned from a tattle-tale cousin. Could this have been avoided?

2. How did learning about Annabelle's backstory affect your enjoyment of the book? Was learning about her decision interesting to you?

3. Ultimately, did Annabelle do her best for Maeve? Why do you think she decided to leave her the property?

4. At what point in the novel did you suspect that things weren't right between Gary and Yulina? Why do you suppose Yulina suffered in silence for so long?

5. Small towns are generally supposed to be friendlier than big cities, but is this always the case? In what ways are small towns more welcoming? In what ways are they not? ▶

6. "Even cats can have broken hearts," says Yulina. Do you think this is true? Can animals really have broken hearts? Can they sense good and bad in people? (Remember, the cat knocks Gary over!)

7. At first Maeve is bitter toward Annabelle. Is this justified? Why or why not?

8. Annabelle was known as the animal lady, taking in strays. Was this a result of her having given up her child? Is this a trait that can be carried from generation to generation?

9. At one point Maeve thinks, "Wasn't it time my Real Life started?" Is Maeve's postponement of her Real Life a generational one? Has she put off facing Real Life because of her birth situation? Were her parents too easy on her, or was this something over which they had no control?

10. Did you suspect the secret behind the St. Francis Knitting Club? ᴄ⟋

No Annie England Noblin book would be complete without some photos of her dogs . . .

This is my Boston Terrier, Ruthie, who I lost in 2015. The first is a Halloween photo, the second is Ruthie in the prayer blanket knitted for her by an animal rescue group after she got sick.

Annie England Noblin's dogs... *(continued)*

This handsome fellow is Rufus in his Christmas sweater! ∿